WHY WE BREAK

HOLLIE LUCKIE

Book Cover by Dirty Girl Designs

Content Edited by Brittni Van | Overbooked Author Services LLC

Edited by Erica Rogers | Logophile Editing Service

Proofread by Caroline Palmier | Love and Edits

AUTHOR'S NOTE

Thank you so much for reading *Why We Break*. Hannah and Will's story has such a special place in my heart, and I'm so excited to share it with you. This book is full of farm chaos, sports, spice, and all the found family you could want. However, there are a number of heavier, more serious topics that are discussed throughout the book.

Why We Break contains mature content that may not be suitable for all audiences. For a full list of content warnings, flip to the content list at the back of the book. There is also also a note about the accuracy of the medical scenes at the end. Please note that both of these may contain spoilers.

PLAYLIST

Wanna Be Loved by The Red Clay Strays
Wild as Her by Corey Kent
Dirt Cheap by Cody Johnson
Straight and Narrow by Sam Barber
Strawberry Wine by Deana Carter
Greatest Love Story by LANCO
Wild as You by Cody Johnson
Always You by Trey Lewis
Over Now by Kameron Marlow
Hard to Leave by Riley Green
The Painter by Cody Johnson
Any Man of Mine by Shania Twain
All Again by Charles Wesley Godwin
She's Got Lovin' On Her Mind by Justin Moore
Look I Like by Alana Springsteen
Stronger by Cody Johnson
Pretty Heart by Parker McCollum
Dirty Looks by Lainey Wilson
Long Live Cowgirls by Ian Munsick and Cody Johnson
Something Like That by Tim McGraw
John Deere Green by Joe Diffie

Wide Open Spaces by The Chicks
Boot Scootin' Boogie by Brooks & Dunn
With You I Am by Cody Johnson
Your Heart or Mine by Jon Pardi
Girl on Fire by Kameron Marlowe
Nothin' on You by Cody Johnson
There's the Sun by Zach Top
A Cowboy Who Would by Chancey Williams
Worst Way by Riley Green
In The Kitchen by Reneé Raps
Last Night Lonely by Jon Pardi
Straight and Narrow by Sam Barber
Life With You by Kelsey Hart
On My Way to You by Cody Johnson
Different 'Round Here by Riley Green and Luke Combs
Get Your Shine On by Florida Georgia Line
Even Cowboys Cry by Dasha
I'm Yours by Alessia Cara
Sold by John Michael Montgomery
WAIT! by Kelsea Ballerini
Neon Moon by Brooks & Dunn
High Road by Joe Wetzel and Jessie Murph
Summertime by Kenny Chesney
Cowboys Cry Too by Kelsea Ballerini and Noah Kahan

Listen to the official playlist on Spotify here!

For anyone who needs the reminder: you're worthy of a full and beautiful life.

CHAPTER 1
HANNAH

Y ou know the people who say things can always get worse? It's usually thrown out by an elderly lady from town or that overly optimistic friend who doesn't know what to say after hearing an especially sad story. It's meant to remind you to be thankful for what you have. It seems like an answer for everything: Your boyfriend was cheating on you? It could always be worse—at least you had a boyfriend to begin with!

Well, I appreciate the sentiment, but as I stare down at the pile of bills in my hand stamped with the words "FINAL NOTICE" in glaring red letters, I would really like to punch every one of those well-meaning Betty's and Susan's in the face.

Don't cry, Hannah. Pull your shit together and figure it out. I close my eyes and repeat the mantra over and over in my head as though I can make the huge stack of invoices on the kitchen counter disappear if I just focus hard enough. Of course, that doesn't work, and when I open them again the proof of my failure is still staring back at me.

Blowing out a breath, I walk over to the sink to pour myself a cup of water from the filter on the faucet. As I turn the knob, my glass fills for a moment before the faucet goes haywire, and cold water sprays my face and chest.

Mother of Jesus, that is freaking FREEZING!

I fumble with the handle again, trying to stop the icy liquid only to accidentally turn it up higher, thoroughly soaking the Springside Cheerleading shirt I'm still wearing from coaching practice this afternoon. Once I finally get it to stop, I pull my tee over my head where it lands on the floor with a wet plop leaving me standing in my running shorts and sports bra.

Giving up on the sink and adding a plumber to the eventual list of expenses I'll need to figure out how to pay, I throw a towel on the ground to soak up the water before walking back to the stack of envelopes I feel certain will haunt my dreams for the foreseeable future. I glare at the offending pile of mail that's now a bit soggy, as if my withering stare will magically solve all my problems, and eventually, knowing they won't sort themselves, start to grab the three off the top. Laying them out to dry, I glance at the totals and struggle to remind myself, *it's going to be fine. You're going to make it work like you always do. There's literally no other option.*

I'd just gotten home from a long day of teaching and coaching cheer practice. All I'd wanted was to curl up with my Kindle and read the latest sports romance I have downloaded with the frozen pizza I'd picked up this past weekend. Clearly, my date with melty-cheese and a fictional six-foot-five football player is now as unlikely as me being able to cover all of these bills.

Every month it seems like the cost of the farm goes up a bit more, but I hadn't expected this big of a jump. I guess I should have expected it after all the repairs I've had to do around here, but I haven't let myself focus too much on it since I'm barely keeping my head above water as it is. It seems like every time I turn around, something else is falling apart, and no matter how hard I try, I can't seem to make everything work the way it's supposed to.

I've cut every corner I can think of, and I've watched every YouTube video on maintaining farm equipment that I can find to try to save when I can. Who knew single-handedly keeping the family ranch going required more than a can-do attitude and a good work ethic?

I never planned to be a twenty-eight-year-old high school science teacher with more farm animals and debt than I know what to do with, but what can I say? I guess this is what happens when your parents run off on you while you're in middle school, and the only family member who ever gave a damn about you is slowly slipping away in a nursing home down the road.

Before my parents decided to ditch me, I'd always looked forward to weekends and summers spent out here. There was just something magical about Falling Oaks Farm. I used to look forward to coming to visit Gramps and my MiMi, his late wife, and they always made sure I was happy and well taken care of, despite the lack of interest my parents had in actually being parents. When I was younger, Gramps would show me the different parts of the farm, making up stories and giving me little jobs as we went. And now, Falling Oaks is the only home I've ever known.

After spending a few minutes prioritizing the most important bills, I separate them into piles of "pay this now" and "it can probably wait until next month" before picking up my phone and calling my best friend, Caroline. She's been my rock for as long as I can remember, and I know if anyone can help me figure out what the hell I'm going to do, it's her. Over the last decade, Caroline's become the closest thing I have to family outside of my gramps, and I love her to death. You'd think that between working and coaching together, in addition to our weekly Monday margarita dates, we'd get tired of each other, but it sure hasn't happened yet.

"Hey, Han. What's up?" Caroline says after she answers on the second ring.

"If I decide to rob the Piggly Wiggly, will you be my getaway driver?" I ask, skipping over any platitudes and getting straight to the point.

She lets out a quick burst of laughter before saying, "Babe, you know I love you but I'm not risking a lifetime in orange for the four hundred dollars you might get from the Pig. You know Melvin ordered those new heavy-duty cash registers after Miss Mabel pitched a fit and whacked the old one with her cane when they quit stocking the sugar last year anyway. We'd never get the stupid thing open."

I blow out a sigh before agreeing, "Yeah, you're right. I'm definitely thinking too small. Maybe we should try the Walmart in Crestview. I bet we could make bank there!"

"Han, what's going on? You know I'm always down to help you, but I think we can find a less extreme way to solve whatever issues you have right now," my best friend reminds me gently.

"Damn it, I know you're right," I say. "I'm just trying to figure out what the hell I'm doing," I tell her while putting my phone on speaker and walking into the kitchen to grab my favorite three-dollar bottle of Moscato out of the fridge.

I'm reaching for a glass by the window as Caroline asks, "Is it your grandfather? Whatever it is, we can figure it out."

I open my mouth to respond to her before something out the window catches my eye across the field. "Mother fucker!" I mutter, startling Caroline on the other end of the line.

"Okay, enough. What the hell is going on over there?" she asks, sounding increasingly alarmed.

"One of the cows is trying to give birth and I see her straining from here. I noticed she looked like she was ready yesterday, but I'm worried the calf is stuck. And it looks like a tree also fell on the fence again at some point today while I was at work, so some of the others are making a run for it. It's on the other side of the field, so I didn't notice when I pulled in," I yell, grabbing my phone and throwing my shoes back on my feet.

"Damn it," my best friend says. "Theo is out in the fields

right now, but I'm going to get him now. We'll be there ASAP. But I'll send a text to the group too, because Margaret, Will, and Seth can probably be there quicker than we can."

"God, don't call them. Just bring the grumpy fire chief," I say, referring to Theo, Caroline's new fiancé. They met a few months ago and fell fast for each other. They are perfect together, and I couldn't be happier for her.

His arrival also brought his sister Margaret into our lives, and she quickly turned Caroline and my friendship into a trio.

As for Seth, I wouldn't mind putting his muscles to work with the situation in front of me. But it's the remaining member of our friend group that causes me to feel the frustration rising in my veins just thinking about him witnessing my current predicament.

Here's the thing—Coach Will Thompson is the bane of my existence. The two of us have been endlessly joined together thanks to our small town and our friendship with Caroline, but we haven't been able to get through more than a few minutes together without arguing in years. Inwardly I know he's not as selfish as I like to pretend he is. But we both have too much pride to ever let the other get the last word in.

It hasn't always been that way. There was a time when he was —*God, Hannah, we are SO not going there right now. We hate him, remember?* I think to myself, not believing I even let my brain veer down that path.

I hear Caroline shuffling around which pulls me from my internal thoughts. "Han, I love you, and I know you think you're Superwoman. And normally I'd agree with you, but even you can't help deliver a calf, get the other cows back in, and fix the fence by yourself. Plus, it'll take us a bit to get there, and it'll be getting dark soon."

I withhold the frustrated scream I want to let out, but knowing she's right, I finally say, "Fine."

My best friend knows that's as much enthusiasm as she'll get on the topic and she hangs up as I run to the old, beaten-up

Polaris I use to get around the farm. After jumping in, I turn the key and pray the engine turns over and works without a fight for once. Thankfully, it purrs to life, and I take off toward the chaos in the fields only stopping to open the gate.

It's not until I'm halfway across the pasture that I realize I didn't bother to grab a new shirt in my haste to get here. I feel a shiver run through my veins as the wet clothes cling to me in the breeze of the October afternoon. As soon as I pull up to the heifer, I see I was right. The poor thing looks completely exhausted, and she doesn't seem like she can even hold her head up. I see the nose and feet and know I don't have long considering she hasn't moved since I noticed her from the window. I give her a minute to see if she makes any more progress on her own, not wanting to startle her while I call the emergency vet line. Dr. Ava Bozeman's assistant answers and tells me she's out on another call across the county, but she will be there as soon as she can.

Realizing I'm going to have to help her, I reach out my hand and nuzzle her wet nose. "It's gonna be okay, Momma. You're doing so good." She blows a weak, tired breath on my hand, and I continue to comfort her for another moment until she's ready.

I start to pull the calf the way my grandfather taught me when I first moved in with him as I see Seth's truck pull down the dirt driveway. Knowing I don't have time to wait on them, I continue pulling the calf until it finally comes free just as Seth, Margaret, and Will pull up beside me.

"Oh my gosh, Hannah, this is wild!" Margaret yells as she gets out of the back seat. "Are they going to be okay?"

Knowing Margaret is pretty new to the whole farm life, I give her a weak nod before answering, "I hope so," before turning back to the red heifer laying at my feet and her new calf and saying, "it looks like the hard part is over now, Momma. You did so good," while giving her a reassuring pat.

"You want us to work on getting them back in while you take care of them?" Seth asks, pointing to where I had momentarily forgotten half my herd was attempting the great getaway of the season.

"That would be great. Thanks for coming. I told Caroline not to call you, but we all know she doesn't listen for shit," I say begrudgingly.

"Yeah, great idea, Scott. Patch a fence, deliver a calf, and get all your runaways in after dark by yourself. That's real fucking smart," Will says sarcastically with an eye roll. "Go on up man, I'll be there soon."

Have I mentioned I can't stand this man? The fucking audacity he has sometimes will never cease to amaze me.

I glare at him and am preparing one of my usual snarky retorts when we hear a loud crash back in the direction of the house. Startled, I look up just in time to see my pet pig Leroy break loose from his pen and take off in the opposite direction toward his favorite mud puddle.

Things could always be worse though right?

CHAPTER 2
WILL

O ne thing about Hannah Scott—her life is anything but boring.

Seth, my roommate and best friend, and I had been debating walking over to Maracas, the local Mexican restaurant, for dinner when Caroline called us to come help. Seth teaches construction and coaches baseball at Springside High, where I'm the head football coach, and he's been my closest friend since I moved back to Springside after college.

As soon as we got the call, we jumped in Seth's truck, bringing Margaret along for the ride since she lives in the apartment next door. It only took us about ten minutes to make the drive to Falling Oaks Farm from downtown, but it looks like we're here just in time.

As I take in the roaming cattle, the broken fence, the heifer and calf still lying at her feet, the setting sun, and the apparent runaway pig—not to mention the fact that Hannah's in a sports bra, soaking wet from head to toe, and dirty from pulling the calf —all I can do is shake my head at her antics.

"Damn, Han, what's got you all wet and bothered?" I tease with a smirk, offering her a hand while Seth takes his old Ford off toward the break in the fence, and Margaret jumps on Hannah's ancient Polaris toward Leroy.

"Hmm, I know it's unusual for you to have a woman dripping at your feet, so I wouldn't expect you to know what to do about it anyway," she snaps, refusing to take my hand and pushing herself up to her full almost six-foot height.

I roll my eyes at her and try to ignore how tanned her long legs still look, despite the fact that it's fall, and we've been back to work for months. *I wonder if they would feel as good wrapped around me as they did the time we—damn it, Will—you cannot be thinking about that right now,* my subconscious screams.

Shaking my head to get rid of the thought I turn my attention back to the heifer lying at our feet. "You know you're gonna need to keep an eye on these two throughout the night to make sure they're okay, right?

"Really? I had no idea, Doctor Will. Pretty sure you're forgetting that I'm the one who taught you all of this farm shit. Not to mention, I've lived on this freaking farm for more than ten years. But by all means, please continue to mansplain how to take care of my animals, though."

Hannah turns and twists the water spigot on the fence line beside us, before leaning down to clean her hands and arms as she continues to glare at me in contempt.

I'm getting ready to snap back with an equally sarcastic response when Theo's black truck races down Hannah's driveway. Theo's one of my closest friends, but it definitely hasn't always been that way. I'd been ready to beat his ass when he insulted Caroline and the previous fire chief Huey on his first day of work. Huey's always been a bit of a stand-in father for me after I caught mine having an affair with a woman named Sandy during my sophomore year of high school. If it wasn't for Mayor Brian coming to me as soon as it happened and asking me to bring Theo on as an assistant football coach to help get the town back on his good side, I'd probably still hate him. But he's long since apologized for his misstep, and outside of becoming a part of our group, I have to admit he's a hell of a coach.

I chuckle when I see Caroline's entire chest hanging out the window waving at us while Theo gestures for her to sit her ass down and wait for him to stop. She and Theo couldn't be more opposite, but somehow they work.

Caroline and I have been friends since high school. When I walked into the locker room and heard the Austin brothers talking about sneaking up to her place while her parents were out of town to force her into going out with them, I'd come unglued. I knew her parents were always leaving her home alone—Caroline called them free spirits, but I just called them assholes. Either way, I instantly felt like she needed someone to protect her.

While Caroline is a beautiful girl, I've never been the slightest bit attracted to her. *Her best friend on the other hand...*my subconscious chimes. *Shut the hell up*, I remind myself again.

Before Theo even puts the truck in park, Caroline is throwing herself out the window and catapulting herself over to Hannah's side. "Goddamn it, woman," Theo yells at her from the open window. "I swear to Jesus you are going to give me a damn heart attack one of these days."

Caroline just turns and blows him a quick kiss which seems to shut him up before turning back to her best friend and me. "God, I should have known you two would already be at each other's throats. And wait, Hannah, where's your shirt? And why are you wet?"

"It's a long story. I'll explain later, but right now we have a farm to put back together," Hannah retorts, pointing across the pasture where Seth is gesturing wildly at the runaways, trying to get them back through the opening in the fence.

Caroline lets out a chuckle before replying, "Right. Will and Theo, why don't you help Seth get the cows back in? I'll stay here with Han."

"Yeah, you boys run along, and we'll bring up the materials

to fix the damn fence in a few minutes," Hannah says, leaning down and patting the heifer at her feet. "We've gotta go check on Margaret anyway."

"Where is my sister?" Theo asks, looking around the field where it's quickly growing too dark to see without the glow of the headlights.

"My asshole little piggy broke his pen again and was headed toward his favorite mud puddle. She tried to stop him while I pulled the calf, and I'm sure she's still running after him knowing how fast Leroy is. In the meantime, Seth started rounding up the other runaways," Hannah replies without taking her eyes off the calf. "If you can't tell, it's been a freaking disaster of an afternoon. But thankfully these two look like they're gonna make it, and Doctor Bozeman will be here as soon as she can to check them over."

Caroline lets out a snort of laughter before shouting, "We're coming Margaret! Come on boys, we'll drop you at the fence before we check on her."

"Babe, I love you, but do you really think I'm gonna let you drive my truck through this bumpy ass field after dark?" Theo asks with a smirk.

"Excuse me, what?" Hannah asks, getting ready to come to Caroline's defense. "What is it, the 1800's? I'm pretty sure we don't have to have a dick to drive a truck!"

I hold in my burst of laughter, not wanting Hannah to have the satisfaction of knowing I think her desire to defend everyone around her can be amusing at times.

"I'm well aware of that, Hannah," Theo says calmly. "You don't understand. Sunshine, do you want to tell her or should I?"

Caroline's face grows pink before she sighs. "Ugh, it was just the one time…"

"No, it was just the one time that you got us stuck in the pond because you didn't believe me when I told you we were close enough to sit on the tailgate and see the fish. If I hadn't had the tractor, I would have had to call a tow truck out there. And there was the time last week you insisted that we needed to go to the top of the property to see the sunset and hit fucking sixty in the driveway. I just think we have enough chaos around here tonight. We don't need to pop an axel too."

Hannah and I both try to hide our grins at Caroline's shrug. "You're such a grandpa. Fine, you can drop us off. But you'll hear about this later, Cowboy!"

"Never doubted it," Theo says with a smile before wrapping an arm around her shoulder and dropping a kiss to the top of her head, making eye contact with me over her head and rolling his eyes at his fiancée's antics.

They lead the way to his truck, and he pulls her into the front seat, leaving Hannah and me with no choice but to slide into the backseat together. Normally this wouldn't be an issue, but since Theo has bags of feed piled in the seat behind the driver's side, there isn't much room for us both. After a moment of staring each other down and waiting for the other to move, Hannah groans out. "God, I so do not have time for this today," before sliding in and scooting as far from me as possible in the cramped space.

It only takes us a few minutes to make our way down the pasture toward Hannah's farmhouse, but it feels like it takes forever. Every time Theo hits a bump in the field, Hannah's tanned leg bumps mine and her exposed shoulder taps my arm. I pretend not to notice, but I most definitely do. On top of that, her vanilla perfume seems to fill every inch of the space, and I fight thinking too much about the times I drank in that scent like it was the air I needed to breathe... *Not again, stop thinking about that*, my subconscious reminds me again.

After what feels like an eternity, we pull up to Leroy's pen, and Theo throws his truck in park. The girls scramble toward Margaret who seems to still be in an epic stare down with the wiggly pig.

Throwing her hands in the air, Hannah bellows toward her

mischievous critter, "Leroy! We have more than enough runaways without your help right now! Come on!" before taking off, running full speed toward the mud, her feet sliding out from under her when she makes contact with the wet dirt and landing flat on her ass.

The rest of us fight to keep from laughing as she sputters and screams before we all lose the battle, Caroline and Margaret doubling over in giggles.

Have I mentioned, life with Hannah is always a damn adventure?

CHAPTER 3
HANNAH

God, this night is a disaster.

After spending thirty minutes wrestling my muddy pig and trying to get him back in his pen, I turn to my best friends who look just as exhausted as I feel. All three of us are completely covered in the red Alabama mud Leroy is so fond of from our ponytails to the shoes on our feet. As I click the lock into place and turn back to my friends, we stare at each other for a moment before bursting into laughter.

"Damn, ladies, when I told Theo I wanted to be dirty tonight, this wasn't at all what I had in mind," Caroline says, reaching out to steady herself with the gate beside us.

Margaret shoots Caroline a disgruntled look before saying, "Babe, you know I love you and I think you two are perfect together, but I really can't deal with hearing any more about my brother's sex life. After I almost walked in on y'all last week when I came to grab my backup mixer from the house, I think I've hit my quota for the month."

I look at my best friend who has the decency to look slightly embarrassed before we burst into laughter again. "Sorry, Marg, I'd say I'll try to tone it down, but I don't think I mean it."

Margaret joins in our laughter before looking down again. "So, Han, what's next? Put us to work."

"I can take it from here. You two have done enough," I say as I make my way to grab an old towel to throw across the seat of the Polaris.

"Bullshit, Hannah. We aren't leaving you with all this. So we can spend the next hour standing around and arguing about it, or you can just tell us what you need," Caroline calls out over her shoulder as she walks to my back porch and grabs us all a bottle of water. "Let's run these to the boys and see how the fence is coming."

I roll my eyes at her, secretly grateful they didn't take me up on my offer for them to leave as much as I hate having to ask for help. The girls pile in beside me on the old seat and we take off into the darkness toward the boys.

"I need to check on the calf and her momma on the way up, but it shouldn't take more than a second once we find them," I call out over the rattling of the ancient side-by-side.

Both of my friends nod at me and Caroline leans forward to search the compartment for the spotlight I keep handy. After pulling it out and turning it on, we search the area where we'd last seen the pair before looking further up the hill.

One thing I love about living this far out in the county is the fact that you can always see the stars thanks to the complete darkness that blankets the hills, but tonight I wish there was a bit more light. The moon is just a sliver in the sky, and aside from the yellow headlights in the distance where the boys are getting the other cattle situated, it's almost impossible to see more than a few feet in front of us.

After about ten minutes of riding, I finally see the small red calf and her mother lying on the edge of the woods. As we ride over, I smile at the calf feeding and happily nudging at her mother. I'm about to pull away, when I see a glimpse of blood out of the corner of my eye. Pulling closer, I realize immediately that once again something isn't right. The large heifer is barely breathing, and after further examination, I realize she's prolapsing. Over the years I spent on the farm with Gramps, he taught me how to recognize most of the problems I might run into, but this is the first time I've had to handle it by myself.

Taking a deep breath, I pull out my phone and redial the emergency vet line. "South Springs County Emergency Vet line, how may I help you?" the same assistant I spoke to earlier answers.

"Hey, this is Hannah Scott from Falling Oaks Farm. I called earlier, but Dr. Bozeman hasn't made it yet. I delivered the calf, and she seems to be doing great. But it looks like Momma is prolapsing. She's barely breathing," I say in a rush.

I give her a few more details, and the girl on the other end of the line sighs. "Oh dear. Dr. Bozeman just left the other side of the county. She's heading your way now, but from what you just told me, I don't think she'll make it in time. Just try to keep her calm until she gets there."

After thanking the woman, I hang up and take another deep breath. I'm certain Caroline and Margaret's heartbroken expressions mirror mine, but I can't dwell on that for long given the current circumstances. I grab the towel we've been sitting on from the side-by-side and lay it on the ground before sitting down next to the large animal.

Sometimes, it's easy to forget how brutal life on the farm can be, but today is a bleak reminder that farming isn't all cowboy hats and cute animals like I used to think it was before I moved to Falling Oaks. The curious calf starts to realize something isn't right and lets out a little *moo* of anguish. I sit and pet the large heifer on the nose for a moment before I realize it's too late and there's nothing else I can do. I look up to see headlights coming down the driveway and blink back tears.

Caroline grabs the spotlight and signals to Dr. Bozeman who pulls her large farm truck up beside us. She is relatively new to town, after moving here last year from what she claimed was a nasty divorce. She relocated to Springside from a small city in

Mississippi, and I've had several chats with her as I've worked to find my footing as the head of the farm. She's a beautiful and witty woman, and while her kind smile usually manages to calm whatever anxiety I'm feeling, tonight she just looks at me with sadness.

I've lost my share of animals since I moved to Falling Oaks in middle school, but it never gets any easier. I feel hot tears welling up and threatening to spill down my face but I try to tune out my own emotions as I fill her in on the events of the last few hours. As defeated as I feel, I don't have time to fall apart right now.

"Dr. Bozeman, thank you so much for coming! We lost the momma, but I think the little one's okay," I explain.

"Hannah, I've told you that you can call me Ava. Obviously this isn't the outcome we wanted, but it sounds like you've done everything right," she says with a comforting smile. "Let me check on the calf and make sure the little one seems okay."

Moving slowly to make sure she doesn't startle the little ball of fur at our feet, she checks over the newborn. "It looks like she got some of the colostrum, so she has a pretty decent chance at making it. But you're gonna have to bottle feed her for the next few months. I think I might have some mix in the truck to tide you over for the night. Why don't you go get your cattle trailer and we'll load her in there? That'll make it easy to feed her, and it'll keep her safe for the next few weeks until you can get her somewhere more permanent."

I nod my head before replying, "Yeah, let me go grab it. Caroline, will you sit here with the little one while Margaret runs me down to get the truck?"

They quickly agree, and thirty minutes later, Dr. Ava is headed back down the driveway after helping us load the calf and talking me through how to feed her.

"Well, ladies, looks like I have another little love to take care of. She needs a name. Y'all have any suggestions?" I ask as I push down the lock on the cattle trailer.

"She looks like a little Ruby," Margaret suggests.

"Ruby it is then. Let me take the trailer down, and we'll go see if the boys are finishing up. I don't know about y'all, but I'm about dead on my feet. Come pick me up again by the house?" I say as I settle back into the seat of the old farm truck.

The girls nod, and after making sure Ruby has plenty of hay to keep her comfy, I jump back in the Polaris with my friends and make the trek back across the pasture where the boys are trying to finish up their job of patching the fence.

We spread out to try to help them patch it, working quietly.

"Hey, Han, are you okay?" Will asks, coming over and inspecting where I'm working.

For the first time in a long time, we're alone, and I feel a small smile cross my face at his sincerity. "Yeah, I guess. This farm just keeps falling to pieces."

"I know it's a lot, but you've gotta do something about this fence. Pretty sure a wall of construction paper would do a better job of keeping the cows in," Will says, looking over to where I'm struggling to make the strand of wire stay on the old, worn post the way I want it to.

"Fuck you, Will. I am not sure when you last priced fencing companies, but unless you've got the twenty thousand I'd need to redo it, I don't want to hear it. No one made you come," I say, the moment I thought we had, clearly over. *God, I know it's mostly my fault, but I hate how things are between us now.* Scowling at him, I turn away from him, working on the fence and trying to ignore the way I feel my throat tightening.

Usually, I have a pretty good grasp on my emotions, but between already feeling like a complete failure at keeping the farm going, losing the sweet heifer earlier, and coming to terms with the fact that I now have the responsibility of taking care of a calf on my own, I'm at my wit's end. *I swear to God, if I cry in front of this man, I will never hear the end of it. Nope, not gonna happen. Pull it together.*

Will opens his mouth, probably to snark back at me, but Seth walks over, interrupting him. "First of all, shut it Will. I can't deal with y'all's bullshit tonight. We've known this fence needs some serious attention for a few months, but that price is outrageous. Why don't you let me price out some materials this week, and see if I can't get that way down. If so, Will and I will do the labor free of charge."

Will looks like he's about to argue, but before he can get a word out, Theo chimes in. "Yeah, I'll come help too when I can. It'll be a lot of work, but we should be able to knock it out in a week or two if we work in the evenings and on the weekends."

Caroline must see that I am about to tell them not to bother because she hastily agrees. "That sounds perfect. I can help you with Ruby and some of the other farm chores while the boys work, and Margaret can cook us some of those yummy snacks she's always trying out," she offers, smiling at me.

The boys jump back to work while Margaret and Caroline grab the bottles of water we brought for them out of the cooler on the tailgate. Meanwhile, I take a moment to stare into space, feeling both thankful for their friendship and longing for the days when I didn't have the weight of the world on my shoulders before focusing back on the farm.

CHAPTER 4
HANNAH

SEVEN SUMMERS AGO

"God, Caroline, are you sure you don't want to come home with me for the summer?" I ask for the millionth time, making sure to school my expression into the most miserable one I can manage.

She lets out a laugh before nodding. "You know, as fun as that sounds, if I leave Tuscaloosa, I won't have my job in the fall. Plus, my parents sold the house when they moved to Brazil, so I don't even have a place to stay in Springside right now."

"I told you that you could stay with me!" I remind her pitifully.

"I love you, Han, but your grandfather has enough on his plate. You both just lost your grandmother, and we've already paid for the lease through the end of the summer. Plus, you'll be back here soon! In two months, we'll be together so much you'll be sick of me again." Caroline reminds me while I make a final lap around my bedroom ensuring I have everything packed.

"Okay, fine," I tell her begrudgingly. "I just can't believe you're sending me home to rot this summer. What the heck am I going to do? I know Gramps needs me, but I'm gonna be bored to death."

"I highly doubt that. You and I both know there's more than enough trouble for you to get into at home. But really, just focus on making sure the farm is back in order. And remember our rule—this is a boy free summer. We both need a break from the frat boys who are only looking for a one-night-stand, and if we're gonna make the most of junior year, we can't have a boy keeping us from partying it up," Caroline says with a little shimmy of her shoulders.

"God, like you even have to remind me," I retort with an eye roll. "Besides, who the hell am I going to date in Springside? You'll be the one with all the hotties!"

"I promise I won't have a bit of fun without you. But next semester, we're going to have the best time!" my best friend exclaims.

"I can't wait!" I say, giving her a squeeze. "August can't come fast enough!"

CHAPTER 5
WILL

"Come on, guys, let's run it again! We're never going to beat Mills Corner tomorrow night looking like this!" I yell as I blow my whistle and shake my head at the other coaches beside me.

The team lines back up and runs the new trick play again, but the ball whizzes past the receiver's head before he's in position just like it has the last four times we've practiced.

"Blake, you've got to make sure you're hitting those outside passes! That's an interception waiting to happen. And, Drew, why aren't you getting there in time?" Marcus, one of my assistant coaches, yells above the groans of the other boys.

I blow out a frustrated breath at the scene in front of me. Marcus isn't wrong. Mills Corner is currently undefeated, and several of their players are being recruited by teams in the SEC. Plus, they have one of the loudest student sections in the state along with home field advantage tomorrow, so we have no room for error if we want to come away with a win.

"Okay guys, grab some water and hustle back! We're gonna keep running this until it's right." I groan with a frustrated breath before turning my attention to the four assistant coaches beside me. Once the rest of the team is on the opposite side of the field, I ask, "Anyone have any ideas? Because if we play like this tomorrow, we'll get our asses beat."

The men beside me start offering suggestions, and after talking through a few options, I feel myself starting to relax. "Okay, Jason, I like your suggestion of shortening the route, and Theo's right that Wesley's a bit faster than Drew. Why don't we swap them out and show them the new route so he isn't getting held up and see what happens?"

Everyone nods at my suggestion, and after calling the team over to implement the suggestions, they set up again to run the play. As soon as the ball is snapped, I know they're going to hit it this time. Sure enough, Blake gets set and throws the ball right into Wesley's waiting hands before he runs it into the end zone. A few of the boys on the team let out a loud whoop while Marcus throws his hands in the air like he just won the Super Bowl.

"Okay, guys, good job. Now let's run it about a hundred more times," I yell before blowing my whistle again.

After another hour of running through our plays and working with special teams to be sure we're prepared for anything Mills Corner could throw our way, I signal for the team to gather around before we end practice.

The team jogs over to where I'm standing beside my coaching team before taking a knee and waiting for me to wrap up practice. I gesture for the other coaches to go first, and Marcus does his usual job of hyping the boys up while Theo, Kent, Jason, and I watch on with amusement. Marcus is in his late thirties, but I'm pretty sure he'd put on a jersey and take the field tomorrow if he could. His love of the game makes him a great coach, and his enthusiasm always gets everyone ready for game day.

Once he's finished, I look at my team seriously before saying, "Good practice today, Saints. You have all worked hard, and I'm proud of what I saw out there. We're gonna need every bit of that hustle tomorrow if we want a chance at beating Mills

Corner. Y'all know this is a region game, and this is a pretty big stop on our road to state. And you know those boys have a reputation for having some short tempers, but I expect y'all to keep your head on straight and make sure we don't give the refs anything to call us on. We've got a long day tomorrow, so get some rest and be on the bus after school ready to dominate. See you then."

The team turns and makes their way to the locker room with the other coaches while Theo and I pick up the little bit of equipment left over from practice. We work in silence getting everything put away before he finally starts. "So, I talked to Seth and we're going to get started on the fence on Saturday. Are you going to be able to help around Hannah's farm without the two of you ripping each other's heads off?"

"Aww, you big softy. I didn't think you'd care if we tore each other to shreds," I say with a chuckle.

"Oh, I don't, but my woman would, so that makes your shit my problem. You two can barely stand to be in the same room with each other. Has it always been like this? I asked Caroline, and she said she just remembers it getting really bad when you both started working here a few years ago," Theo asks skeptically, not making eye contact but clearly still curious as to what I'm going to say.

I think back to the younger version of Hannah from high school and the girl I once shared so much with all those summers ago. And while I can't tell Theo about it, all I can think is—no, we definitely weren't always like this.

CHAPTER 6
WILL

SEVEN SUMMERS AGO

When Huey called me to tell me he'd found me a summer job at Falling Oaks Farm, I wasn't sure what to expect. But given the fact that I need to be in Springside this summer to help my mom with my siblings and the fact that there never seems to be enough money to cover all their expenses, I was pretty desperate for a job. Ollie has senior fees coming up this year, and I know Mom will struggle to cover them without my help. I accepted the job immediately, hoping I'd be able to save a little extra to help her around the house once I go back to school.

Mr. Scott has always been kind to me when I see him around town, but I don't know anything about him other than he took Hannah in when her parents ran off a few years ago. Hannah and I have never been close, but I know she and Caroline have gotten to be pretty tight over the last few years.

Pulling my old beat-up truck into his drive, I'm met with the sight of one of the largest farm properties I've ever seen. The pastures seem to stretch for miles and there are hundreds of cows grazing on the grass.

Noticing me pulling in the drive, Mr. Scott waves and pulls the Polaris from the side of the garden where he was checking the corn. After throwing my truck in park and grabbing my beat-up Saints hat, I step out into the sweltering Alabama heat.

"Will, good morning," the older gentleman says with a smile. "You sure you want to spend the summer helping an old bastard like me?"

Chuckling, I extend my hand to shake his before replying. "Heck, I don't see why not. Huey told me that you need a hand around the farm. Anything in particular?"

"Damn, son, what doesn't this place need? I've spent the last few years trying to do it by myself, and I'll be damned if every time I fix something, something else doesn't break. I should have sold this place years ago, but it's my home and I just can't imagine looking out of my window and only having a patch of grass to my name. But that's neither here nor there. We've got quite the workload ahead of us. We need to add in a fence line halfway between the house and the edge of the property so I can get another bull or two and keep some of the cows split up. We also need to bale at least a thousand bales of hay over the next two months to be sure we've got enough to get us through the winter and sell to the farms that buy from us every year. You can't see it from here but there are about two thousand acres behind the woods of the house we'll cut. We've also got the garden to tend to as well so we can keep up our business at the Summer Farmers' Market. And there's the horses too, which are in that old barn back down there on top of all the broken shit I can't keep up with anymore," he finishes with a sigh.

Damn. I had no idea this farm was this big. He wasn't lying that we had our work cut out for us. I had no idea how he'd been managing a farm this big by himself. "Sounds good, Mr. Scott. Is it just the two of us?"

The words are barely out of my mouth when the front door to the house opens and Hannah bounds out in denim shorts and a hot pink tank top. Her blonde hair is tied into braids, and she's tucked them into a gray Springside Feed trucker hat to keep the sun out of her eyes.

Shit. This is definitely not the Hannah Scott I remember. I haven't seen her much over the last few years since I moved away, and all my weekends at home have been consumed by taking care of my mom and my siblings. The girl I remember had been pretty, but she had braces and hadn't quite grown into her nearly six-foot frame so she hunched awkwardly as if she was scared to take up too much space. But now? She's a fucking bombshell.

Mr. Scott smiles at his granddaughter and gestures to her. "My Hannah Banana's home for the summer, and she loves the farm almost as much as I do. So she's offered to help out too."

"Gramps," Hannah groans and rolls her eyes. "I'm twenty years old, you have got to quit calling me that in public."

"Hush, hush," Mr. Scott says with a laugh. "We've got work to do. Why don't you and Will head over to the garden and take some inventory of what we might have ready for the market this weekend? I've got some cows to check on."

She nods before murmuring, "Oh wait, Gramps. Leroy tried to dig through his pen again." I look around in confusion as Hannah walks over to a chain link pen.

"Yeah, I noticed he's been doing that every once in a while, but I think he'll grow out of it," Mr. Scott says with a laugh.

"Uh, is Leroy your dog?" I ask Mr. Scott while Hannah leans down and reaches into the huge dog house, talking softly to the creature.

"Actually, he's my Hannah Banana's pet pig," Mr. Scott replies, laughing at my shocked expression as Hannah stands with a huge pink pig in her arms. Leroy squeals in excitement when he notices me standing there, wiggling in Hannah's arms until she puts him down and he makes his way over to me.

"You have a pet pig," I observe, not knowing how to respond.

"Yeah, and he's the best boy. He's still a baby, though.

Gramps gave him to me two years ago, but since there aren't too many apartment complexes in Tuscaloosa that are pig friendly, he stays here with Gramps while I'm in school," Hannah says, leaning down to pat him again. "Go on and pet him. He's really sweet."

"Oh, uh, okay," I say skeptically, bending down to pat the pig's head. He's softer than I expected, and after my shock wears off, I smile as he wiggles his butt in excitement. "Never met a pig before, but he's pretty cute."

"Yeah, he is," Hannah agrees, standing and looking back at her gramps. "You think he's okay to go back in his pen? I don't want him to get out and wander."

"I think he'll be fine. Like I said, I'm sure he'll grow out of his digging phase and even then, he won't go far," Mr. Scott reassures his granddaughter, and she nods.

Hannah leads the pig back to his pen, while Mr. Scott turns back to me. "Okay, you ready to get started? My Hannah Banana can teach you pretty much anything you need to know, but I'll give you my cell number just in case you need it."

"Gramps, if you're gonna give people your cell number and tell them to call you for help, you've gotta remember to charge the dang thing," Hannah teases, causing both her grandfather and I to laugh.

"Hush, granddaughter. Leave this old man alone. But, I guess I do need to try to remember to do that," he says with a shrug. "But, like I said, I'm sure Hannah will take good care of you. I'll be in the cattle pasture if you need me. I'll see y'all around dark."

"Sounds good. Thank you again, Mr. Scott," I call as he walks toward a red ATV parked beside the house.

He pulls off, leaving Hannah and I alone. I glance at her, and she gives me a friendly smile before asking, "Are you ready to get this day started?"

I nod and follow her to an old farm truck. She jumps inside

and fiddles with the radio until "Summertime" by Kenny Chesney blasts through the speakers.

As she cranks the truck, I can't help but smile. Getting paid to spend the summer with an incredibly gorgeous girl? Don't mind if I do.

CHAPTER 7
HANNAH

By the time I step into the assisted living facility on Thursday night, I'm dead on my feet. It was close to midnight by the time my friends left last night and all the cows were back in their rightful place. After they were gone, I'd gone to check on Ruby, just intending to make sure she had enough hay to rest on for the night. But when I got there, she looked so pitiful in the large cattle trailer by herself, whining for her mother who definitely wasn't coming back to comfort her. And as different as our situations were and as much as I liked to pretend I didn't care, I was all too familiar with that feeling. So instead, I sat down in the hay and let her lay her small head in my lap while she finally went to sleep.

It had been almost two in the morning before I'd stumbled into the house, taken a shower, and collapsed into bed. But since the farm requires some attention in the mornings before I head off to school, I'd been back up at five to refill the water troughs, check on the horses, and feed Ruby and Leroy.

I try to hide my exhaustion as I step into my gramp's room, but the concern that flashes across his face is enough to let me know I've failed.

"Hey, old man! How are you feeling?" I say, much more cheerfully than I feel.

"Well, my Hannah Banana, I'd be a lot better if you'd get me out of this damn place and let me come home to help you with the farm. You look like you could fall over dead any minute now," he says with a snarl of frustration.

"Gramps, don't do this to me tonight. You know I'd give anything to have you home with me. But you've had four major surgeries in the last year, and you're recovering from a heart attack. The house isn't accessible for your walker, and you fell down the stairs the last time you tried to get in the tractor," I say sadly, and he must hear the defeat in my voice because he just nods sadly.

"You're right, my sweet girl. I'm sorry. You know I'm just an old grumpy bastard. And I feel horrible I've left you to take care of that huge farm by yourself on top of taking care of me. This place is expensive. Just get me out of here and leave me on the side of the road to rot," he says with a wink.

I roll my eyes at him before saying sarcastically, "Great idea, Gramps. I'll get right on that. But, you hush. This is one of the nicest facilities in the area, and don't think the nurses haven't told me about your girlfriend, Gladis, down the hall. What would she do if you didn't show up to your Friday night bingo date tomorrow?"

He lets out a chuckle before he relents. "Okay, fine, you're right. I don't mind this place, but I just wish I could help you, Han."

I feel moisture gathering in my eyes, but I blink it away quickly, knowing if I start crying he'll start asking questions about the finances and state of the farm which I definitely can't answer right now. As I look at the elderly man sitting across from me, all I can feel is frustration with myself for letting it get this bad. Gramps never hesitated to take me in when my parents decided they didn't want to be parents anymore and left me with him while they went on a vacation they'd never intended to come home from. This man has done everything he could for me to make sure I was always taken care of, and here I am letting the only other thing he ever cared about waste away.

I paste on a fake smile before I respond. "Don't worry, Gramps. I've got it all under control. Will and some of the boys are going to redo the fence for me, and I'm working on some plans for the spring to get the garden going again. That way when the Farmers' Market comes around I'll have some extra income there. It's all going to be fine."

He gives me a content smile before nodding. "Oh, that would be nice. And tell Will thank you for me. He's such a good man. When are you two going to finally admit that you're in love?"

I almost choke on the sip of water I had just taken before responding. "Gramps, what kind of meds do they have you on in here. Clearly, it has to be some of the good stuff because you're delusional."

Gramps lets out a laugh before holding up his hands in a sign of surrender. "Okay, fine, fine. Say what you want, but I'm convinced you two will end up together. He looks at you the same way I used to look at your MiMi."

I snort because I'm pretty sure the only way Will Thompson has looked at me in the last seven years is in annoyance, but I just nod since I don't have the energy to argue with my gramps tonight. We spend the next hour chatting about the farm and the activities he's enjoyed here since I came to see him on Sunday. By the time I hug him and stand to leave, I'm feeling a bit more like myself and like maybe there's a way to figure all of this out.

"Okay, Gramps, I'll be back on Sunday. I love you," I say as I go to leave his room.

"Love you too, my Hannah Banana. I'll see you then," he calls after me, right before I close the door.

I make my way back to the front lobby and am just about to exit through the double doors in the front when one of the receptionists calls after me. "Miss Scott, could I talk to you for a moment?"

I turn to see it's Mia, the young girl who usually handles my monthly payments, who called for me.

"Oh, hi, Mia. How are you tonight?" I say with a smile, hoping it isn't obvious I'm about to fall over in exhaustion if I don't get home soon.

"Oh, I'm okay. I just wanted to talk to you because of the issue we're having with your grandfather's Medicaid. As you know, you've been paying for his room and board while Medicaid has covered some of the medical expenses through a waiver due to his most recent surgery. But I got a notification today that they're unwilling to continue paying their part since he's several months out of recovery."

It feels like all of the blood drains out of my body as I stare at her. "Okay, so how much will the cost increase?" I ask.

"Probably around an extra thousand to fifteen hundred dollars a month," she says sadly. "We're going to do what we can on our end, but I did want to give you a warning."

I just nod at her and mumble, "Thanks, Mia. Have a good night."

And without another word, I scramble to my car where I finally bust into a fit of sad, hot tears.

"Blue!! Black!! Let's go, Saints!" I cheer along with Caroline and our squad as they finish their halftime performance. It's Friday night, and after what felt like the longest two-hour bus ride of my life, we arrived in Mills Corner. The first half was a brutal mashup between the boys, and it seems like the next hour or two would be the same.

We spend the next few minutes passing out water to the girls before collapsing back into our seats on the front row of the bleachers while the girls build up their stunts for kickoff.

"Let's GOOOOOO, Saints!" the squad cheers when Wesley catches the ball and sprints toward the end zone. We all groan as he's taken down on the five-yard line, just shy of a touchdown, but the crowd goes wild as the team gets set to push the ball across the end zone.

The Mills Corner sideline boos loudly, and I can tell a few of their players are mouthing off at our boys, but thankfully our team seems unbothered.

"Are they seriously booing a bunch of teenagers?" I ask, my eyes wide as a few of their fans throw trash toward the field. I can hear their sideline start yelling and cursing at their team until the referee blows his whistle and throws a flag for unsportsmanlike conduct.

Trying to ignore it, Caroline grabs my hand, and we cheer like the duo of crazed fans that we are. I feel the smile I've been missing all day creep up on my cheeks. Despite how shitty everything is right now, I think there must be just a little bit of magic in these small town stadiums because as I cheer for my alma mater and the kids I spend almost all of my day with, I feel just a little bit of the weight I've been carrying the last few days lift off my shoulders just as the Saints' player scores a touchdown.

The stands erupt in a chorus of excitement while the squad dances along to "Oh When the Saints Go Marching In." After the kick goes through the goalposts, Caroline and I collapse back into our seats, both wearing happy expressions.

My best friend looks at me for a moment before saying, "There's my bestie. What's been going on, Han? You've looked like someone kicked your puppy all week. I'm worried about you."

I blow out a breath before giving her a small smile. "Oh, I'm fine. There's just been a lot going on lately, but I've got everything under control."

I feel Caroline's gaze on me, looking for any sign I'm not telling the truth. I can't tell if I pass her inspection, or if she just knows there's no use in arguing with me. "Fine, but I would really hope that if that wasn't true, you'd know you could come to me. We're in this together, Han."

I try not to let the myriad of emotions I'm feeling show on my face, and since I don't trust myself to speak I just nod at her and give her a quick hug. Thankfully, both of our phones ping a second later, drawing the attention off my current issues.

> MARGARET: Ladies, I need an update!

Caroline and I both smile at our phones before she says, "I'll respond for us."

Margaret and Theo may have only been in Springside for a few months, but they've fit themselves so easily into our lives I don't know what we ever did without them. She decided not to make the two-hour trip since all of us were riding the bus, but because she understood how important tonight's game was to our chances at the playoffs, I'm sure she's desperate to hear how it's going.

> CAROLINE: We're up right now 27-21 going into the fourth quarter. But it's been a tough game. Hoping we can hold out a little longer
>
> MARGARET: OMG me too. Literally biting my nails here. Keep me updated.

After liking the text, Caroline stands and motions for the girls to get set for their quarter cheer. We cheer along with the girls and holler when all of their stunts hit cleanly at the top. As soon as they dismount, Maggie, the captain of the squad, runs over to us.

"Oh my gosh, you were right about those rippled lib stunts with the signs! The crowd was so loud! Do you think we could work that into our competition routine? I know regionals are coming up, but if we advance, it could be great for state!" she asks with a huge smile on her face.

Caroline and I nod at her before she runs back to the squad to build back up for kickoff. "You were right about the new stunts, Han. I know it's only our second year competing, but I think we really have a chance of making it past regionals this year!" Caroline says excitedly.

"I hope so! I want to work through a few more tweaks to the —" I start before I look at the field and see one of the Springside defensive players reach out and snag the ball as it hurdles through the air for an interception. "Oh my gosh, run!"

The stadium erupts once again, all of us screaming and yelling as the player runs the ball the remaining thirty yards for a touchdown. We cheer along before Caroline remembers to grab her phone and update Margaret. All the while, the atmosphere in the stadium feels more and more hostile as the players line up for the field goal attempt. Just as the center goes to snap the ball, one of the Mills Corner players charges from the line and tackles one of the Springside offensive guards, hitting him hard enough that his helmet flies across the grass before the play starts. Once he's down, the Mills Corner player kneels above our guard and punches him hard across the face.

And with that, the stadium dissolves into absolute chaos.

CHAPTER 8
WILL

Y *ou have to be fucking kidding me.* I know it's not the most profound thought, but it's all I can think as I watch the Mills Corner defensive lineman punch my player in the face.

I'm on my feet before I can think, grabbing the boys on the sideline who are ready to charge the field and pointing them back towards Theo, gesturing for him and the other coaches to get the rest of the team the hell out of there.

"Get your asses to the locker room, or you'll spend the next week doing as many conditioning drills as I can think of, understand?" I bellow.

I know they want to defend their teammates, but shit's gonna get a lot fucking worse if half our starters are benched a couple weeks before the playoffs.

The Mills Corner sideline is completely empty now except for the coaches, who are just standing around doing jack shit to stop their players from beating the hell out of my team. I shouldn't be surprised since their head coach is an asshole and has always been known to play dirty, but this is another level.

I sprint across the field and manage to grab my kicker and two of my linemen who are attempting to avoid the Mills Corner players and gently shove them toward Jason, who followed me into the chaos. The other eight are trying to defend themselves the best they can, but I can already tell that there's at least fifty guys coming at them. *Fuck, this is gonna be a damn mess.*

Jason and I divide ourselves between the two biggest fights while the refs take on some of the smaller scuffles. After a few minutes, I start to feel like we're making progress, and I am pretty sure we finally get the worst of it under control when one of the Mills Corner players comes out of nowhere and lands a punch straight to my right eye.

"Fuck," I mutter before whirling around and gesturing to the opposing coaches. "Are you gonna get your asses over here and stop this or not?"

The bastards roll their eyes at me, but finally start moving to get their players off the field. I can feel my eye starting to swell, but I try to ignore it as I search the sea of players in front of me to make sure all of mine have made it to the safety of the locker room. On the sidelines, I notice that the Mills Corner fans are standing, only being held back by a few police officers who happened to be in the crowd.

"Refs, we're done, right? I need to get my boys the hell out of here before this turns any uglier," I yell at them over the growing noise.

"Yeah, Mills Corner will be disqualified. I'm sure you'll be hearing from the AHSAA this weekend. Get your fans and your team out," one of the refs calls back.

I nod and turn back to the stands, grateful when I see that Hannah and Caroline already have the cheerleaders and the band on the buses. I yell to the parents that we'll all be on the bus and to meet us back in Springside before finally walking toward the guest locker room.

Before I get there, Hannah comes running over from the direction of the bus, the concern obvious on her face. "Oh my God, Will, that was freaking wild! Are you okay?"

I can barely see out of my right eye at this point, but I can still hear the Mills Corner fans yelling behind us as Hannah continues talking.

"I mean, your eye looks pretty bad. Why the hell didn't you duck?" she asks, and I feel my temper snap.

"Hannah, I don't have time to fucking chit-chat with you right now. You need to get on the bus so we can all get the hell out of here. You can make whatever smartass comment you want about my reflexes when we're back in Springside," I tell her, stepping around her and rushing toward the locker room.

Damn it, I didn't mean to snap at her, but the idea of some of those crazy ass fans starting another brawl with her in the middle of it has my temper even shorter than usual.

Finally making it inside, I find the team sitting quietly, waiting for me. "Okay, boys, you all okay?"

I hear a chorus of "Yeah, Coach," before looking around and taking inventory of their injuries. The boys that were on the field when the fight broke out have a few scrapes and bruises, and Blake's eye looks about like mine but other than that, everyone looks okay. I blow out a relieved breath before nodding my head at my assistants.

"Great. We're going straight to the bus. You can take your shoulder pads and other equipment off when we get on the road. We don't have time to kill. Grab your stuff and let's go. It's gonna be a long ride," I say before grabbing my backpack and heading toward the door.

"Yes, sir, I understand. Thank you," I say into my phone. "Thank you for your help, Principal Hale. I will let them know."

It's Sunday afternoon, and even though the week hasn't started yet, I'm already exhausted. I've spent the last two days handling the fall out from Friday's fiasco. Thankfully, the parents weren't an issue—they'd seen everything play out and knew that there wasn't much we could do, but the questions from the state athletic organization, the media, and the district have seemed endless over the last two days. I know there will be an official discussion with AHSAA later, but from what I've just been told, we shouldn't have to worry about any official blowback.

The other coaches are spread out across my living room, waiting for me to press play on the film we're supposed to be watching. It's become a tradition for us to get together on Sunday afternoon and get our game plan together for the following week. The four of them look at me expectantly, waiting for me to tell them what Principal Hale just said.

"He talked to his guy at the state, and they think we're in the clear."

As soon as the words are out of my mouth, Marcus, Kent, and Jason let out whoops of excitement while Theo just nods his head at me.

"Anyway, he said it was clear as day that we didn't do anything. The state is pushing for Mills Corner to be out for the season. But even though we didn't do anything, those fuckers put a bit of a target on our backs. He asked me to talk to the team and make sure we don't do anything to increase the chances of this happening again," I say before blowing out a breath.

"Hell yeah! So we're on to the next one, huh?" Marcus asks, standing and grabbing a beer out of my fridge.

"Yep, we've got the Brookside Bulldogs this week, and it's also Homecoming. So we all know what that means," I say with an eye roll.

The other coaches nod at me except for Theo who sits up a little bit straighter. "Wait, I don't know what that means. What's special about Homecoming?"

We all chuckle before I respond. "Well, it means that all week our players will be out all hours of the nights rolling our yards for the unofficial Homecoming war. We pray no one rolls an ankle and try to keep them focused with all the bullshit events the school tries to cram in. And on Friday, we'll have a bunch of alumni coming in and talking shit about how we don't know what we're doing since we're all under forty, despite the fact that we're sitting at six and oh for the year."

Theo gets a look of horror on his face. "What do you mean they'll be rolling our yards? Why the hell would they do that?"

"It's a tradition for the juniors and seniors to roll each other's houses with toilet paper during the week of Homecoming, but they also like to team up and go after the teachers and coaches too. Officially, the school doesn't condone it, but as long as they behave and keep it to just toilet paper, we let them have at it. Between both you and Caroline, I feel like they'll get you pretty good," Kent explains while Theo's face becomes more and more concerned.

"God, this fucking town," Theo says with a groan, causing us all to grin before turning our attention back to the film.

We settle in, turning our attention to the television. We've been watching the footage from Brookside's last game and taking notes for at least thirty minutes before Marcus asks, "So, Theo, have you and Caroline set a date yet?"

"Not yet. She wants to get married in the spring, so it'll be sometime next year," Theo replies, and it's hard not to notice the way his scowl lifts for a moment when thinking about his fiancée.

"Gotcha. Well, I'm happy for you. I keep thinking it might be time for me to settle down. I've been thinking about asking Hannah out," Kent says.

I'd been halfway through a sip of my beer, but after hearing that announcement, I choke and sputter on the liquid. I wait for him to laugh or give us a hint that he's not serious, but it never comes. "What, why would you do that?"

"Um, man, I know y'all hate each other, but in case you haven't noticed she's a damn bombshell. Plus, all the kids love her, and I think we'd have fun together," he says with a shrug.

"I think it's a terrible idea. She's insufferable. Plus, you can't date her even if you wanted to because of the rule at the school," I say with a frustration I don't understand at all.

Why do I care if he wants to take her out? It's none of my damn business anyway.

"Well, technically, I'm not employed by the school district anyway," Kent reminds me, and I try to ignore the way the pit in my stomach sinks a bit lower. But he's right. Since Kent owns his family business and only comes in to coach during the season, he isn't really a South Springs County employee.

"Well, she's still insufferable. You'd be miserable with her," I insist anyway, unable to let the topic go. Kent is a nice guy, and I've known him for years, but all of a sudden, at this moment, I can't stand him. I've heard the girls in town calling him one of Springside's most eligible bachelors, but I still can't picture him and Hannah together.

"Actually, she only acts that way with you, Will. I think she's a lot of fun," Marcus interjects, and Jason nods in agreement.

Theo just listens, but I practically see the thoughts running through his head from here. If I'm not careful, I'll have Caroline calling me before the day's over wanting to know why I care about who Hannah goes out with. And to be honest, I wish I had an answer to that question myself.

"Okay, do what you want, but don't say I didn't warn you. Anyway, what's our game plan for this week?" I ask, thoroughly frustrated with myself and the way this afternoon went.

CHAPTER 9
HANNAH

"Oh my gosh, I don't think I've ever needed a margarita more than I do right now," I groan as I slide into our usual booth at Maracas on Monday night.

As usual, Caroline and Margaret are waiting for me to begin our weekly tradition of Monday night margaritas. Caroline and I started this tradition years ago when we were first year teachers as something to look forward to at the start of each week, and I don't think we've missed a week since.

"I saw you pull in the parking lot and ordered you a peach one. It'll be here in a second," Margaret informs me. "I want to hear about your day in a minute but first I am dying for the tea. What the hell happened on Friday night?"

"God, it was a disaster," I groan. "I've never seen anything like it. One minute we were watching the game, and the next Caroline and I were sprinting toward the squad and trying to get them to the bus in case anything got even more out of control. To be honest, I didn't see much more than the first punch. But from everything I've heard, Will, Theo, and the other coaches did a great job keeping the situation from escalating any further."

"That is wild! I still can't believe that happened," Margaret says, while Caroline and I just nod. "But anyway, I'm so glad you're both okay. How was school today?"

"My day was okay," Caroline responds while the waitress hands me my drink, and I take a long tequila-filled sip. "Between the fight last week and Homecoming this week, it was like herding cats trying to get anything done, but I guess it's all in good fun. I can't wait to see Theo's face when he looks out to our yard this week and sees all of Springside High throwing toilet paper around his trees. He said he's sleeping in his jeans so they don't catch him off guard and he can run out at them as soon as he knows they're there."

Margaret and I both burst into a fit of giggles at the thought. "Yeah, I'm going to need a video of that one," Margaret says with a smile.

"Yeah, I agree," I interject. "I'm not looking forward to the cleanup of my yard, but as long as they stay out of the fields I don't mind it too much. This was one of my favorite weeks in high school. But I agree with Caroline, the combination of Homecoming and last week made today tough. I'm exhausted. Anyway, it's nothing a little tequila and a girls' night can't fix!"

We clink our glasses full of peach margaritas and spend a moment sipping our drinks before Margaret asks, "Caroline, how is Michael doing?" referring to one of Caroline's students who had become a problem at the beginning of school, but has quickly turned into someone who comes to her for advice and help.

Immediately, her face softens and she replies, "He's actually doing so much better. We've been working with the social worker, and I think we've gotten him on a good path to getting caught up in school. He's actually with Theo now, helping him out around the farm. I never imagined the way those two would hit it off, but I think they're really good for each other."

Margaret smiles at that, and I can't help but feel incredibly happy for my best friend. She and Theo might have had some ups and downs early in their relationship, but I can't imagine anyone making her any happier.

Too bad you won't ever have anything like it... My inner voice snarks at me but I try to tune it out as I listen to Caroline and Margaret talk about wedding planning.

"Yeah, we want to keep it as small as possible. Obviously, I want the two of you to be standing with me, and Theo will probably ask Will and Seth to be his groomsmen," Caroline says before taking another sip of her drink.

"You know we wouldn't want to be anywhere else. I just cannot believe how good this move has been for both of us. A year ago the idea of my brother not only having a fiancée but also a group of friends that want to celebrate with him would have seemed impossible, but here we are. I just really can't thank you enough for bringing him back," Margaret whispers, and I can hear the emotion clogging her throat.

Caroline's eyes water a bit too, and they share a quick hug while I distract myself from their emotional moment with the basket of chips in front of me. When they moved to town, Theo was battling with a good bit of PTSD over the loss of his parents and brother, but Caroline had given him the push he needed to work through some of his trauma with a support group, and even I could see the changes in him over the last few months.

"You know I'll do anything I can to make sure you have the most perfect day," I tell her honestly before adding, "please tell me Theo has a hot cousin or something for me to walk down the aisle with."

Caroline laughs and grabs a handful of chips before answering, "Well, actually, the only people we plan to have in the wedding are you two and then Will and Seth."

"Oh, well, that's fine. Just don't pair me up with Will," I say, causing the other girls to share a look of amusement.

"We'll see. I mean, I would prefer that the church is left standing when we're done with it, and I'm pretty sure the two of you would find a way to bring the place to the ground with the way y'all fight," Caroline teases before adding, "but we can figure all that out later."

"So I know I'm the newbie here, but I still can't quite figure you and Will out. Sometimes you act like you hate each other, and others I'm pretty sure you're about to rip each other's clothes off," Margaret adds while dipping her chip in the queso in front of her and waiting for an explanation.

Caroline chuckles while I roll my eyes at Margaret, hoping that it hides the fact that I don't hate that idea at all. "Oh my gosh, can we give that a rest already? Even if I didn't find him absolutely repulsive, he probably couldn't handle me in the bedroom anyway. I bet he's as boring and selfish there as he is outside it," I say, hoping that they don't hear the lie in my voice.

"Whatever. Anyone with as much sexual tension as the two of you have is just like a can of gasoline waiting on someone to throw a match on it. And when it happens, you'll end up taking down everything around you," Margaret teases playfully.

"Stop, Caroline, tell her she doesn't know what she's talking about," I argue, turning to my best friend sitting next to me.

I expect her to jump to my defense immediately, but instead, she hesitates for a moment. "Welllll, I don't know."

I look at her incredulously before bursting into a bout of uncontrollable laughter. "Gosh, how many margaritas did you two have before I got here? 'Cause clearly neither of you are thinking clearly."

And with that, while my friends continue to giggle about the possibility of my supposed nemesis and I dating, I try to ignore the twinge of sadness over what almost was.

CHAPTER 10
HANNAH

SEVEN SUMMERS AGO

"So, are you ready for this?" I ask Will as I pull the tractor up next to where he's standing, waiting for me.

"Sure, let's get to it," he says as he makes his way toward me.

I wasn't sure what to think when Gramps told me that Will would be helping us around the farm this summer, but I have to admit that it's nice having some extra hands around here. Add in the fact that he looks like he belongs in a GQ magazine, and I have no complaints.

"Uh, where am I supposed to sit?" he asks, looking up at the cab of the John Deere tractor where I'm sitting.

"Well, unless you're ready to drive this thing by yourself, you're gonna have to ride the buddy seat here for a while," I tell him, gesturing to the small buddy seat I pulled down before heading this way. "It was either this or the open cab where you'd be sitting on the wheel well, and trust me, that's not a fun experience."

"No problem," he says, pulling himself up and folding himself into the small seat beside me.

I try to fight the urge to laugh at the sight of his knees nearly touching his chin, but when he leans over to close the door and almost falls off the small seat, neither of us can hold it in anymore.

"Sorry 'bout this," I tell him, trying to keep a straight face, starting up the tractor and watching him try to get settled in the small space. "After today, you'll be able to take this on by yourself. So you ready to get started?"

"Yes, ma'am," he says with a grin.

"All right, let's get right to it then. First things first, when you go to start, you're gonna press the clutch," I explain, before pushing the pedal down with my foot while I continue. "Then, you're gonna grab this gear shift and put it in drive. There are a bunch of different gears that we can worry about later, but just to cut hay, you don't have to worry about that too much."

"Got it," Will says, watching me intently as I move the gear shifter beside the wheel.

"And then you're gonna slowly let off the clutch with your foot. But if you do it too fast you're gonna choke the damn thing down and you'll have to restart.

"Okay, so press the clutch, shift gears, and then let off slow?" Will asks, and I feel hyper-aware of how close we are in the little cab of this tractor while I try to focus on pulling us into the hay field we'll be spending the day cutting together.

"Yep. Then you take it easy to get through the gate, and once you're ready to start cutting you're gonna stop, press the clutch, and shift this lever to engage the PTO," I explain, ignoring the way his breath feels on my bare shoulder while he looks at the switch I'm pointing to.

"PTO? Pretty sure those are the meetings my mom keeps getting messages about attending for my siblings," he teases with a laugh.

"Not this time," I say with a giggle. "This is the power take off, and when it clicks on, you'll hear a hum. It's what cuts the hay. That noise means you're ready to go. After that, you just drive around in squares until everything's cut."

"Simple enough," he replies, leaning back in his small buddy seat as I start to drive. "So have you and your grandfather really run this farm completely by yourselves?"

"Yeah, pretty much," I tell him, feeling the weight of his gaze burning through me as I try to focus on the field outside instead of meeting his gaze. I've never been super confident talking about myself, and combined with our proximity and how freaking hot he looks, I need something else to focus on.

We make small talk for a few more minutes before I ask, "You ready to try your hand at this thing?"

"Heck yeah. Let's swap," he agrees, rising from the buddy seat and waiting for me to slide over.

I look at the small space and stand, having to press my front to his as I try to maneuver myself into the small space. I'm pretty tall, and I've grown used to towering over all my friends, but Will is well over six feet, so he still towers over me. I imagine how it would feel to curl up in his lap as he drives, before shaking my head at the ridiculous turn my thoughts just took.

I settle into the seat and feel myself blush as he grazes against me, taking his place in the main cab seat. "Okay, let's see if I've got this… We're gonna push the clutch, shift gears, and let off— shit that wasn't right," he says as the tractor groans and shuts off. "What the hell did I do wrong?"

"Remember what I said about letting off the clutch slowly? That was still a little quick. Just try again," I tell him.

After a few moments, he gets it going and re-engages the PTO to start cutting again. "So, this hay we're cutting. What do we do next?" he asks, looking between me and the field.

"Well, we let it dry out for the next day or two, then we'll come back through with the tetter and fluff it, then we'll get the baler after it," I explain, relieved we're talking about something other than me.

"Damn, I don't think I realized how many steps were

involved in this whole process. I guess we have our work cut out for us this summer, huh?"

"Yeah, there's a ton of shit we need to cross off the list before I leave Gramps alone again," I say, already dreading how much work lies ahead of us over the next eight weeks.

"Good thing I don't mind the company," Will says, looking over at me with a wink.

Damn, I guess the next few weeks might be more eventful than I planned.

CHAPTER 11
HANNAH

"One, three, five, seven. One, three, five, seven. One!" I count as the squad hits the final stunt formation the next day at practice. The girls cheer as they dismount from their stunts, and Caroline and I smile at each other as we watch their excitement.

"Great job, girls! That's what we need to see!" Caroline calls out.

"Yes! That was great! But since we all know there will be tons of alumni on campus this Friday for the Homecoming game, we want to be sure we show them our best. Let's run it a few more times to make sure everyone's ready to go," I say, feeling a rush of pride at the girls in front of me. Coaching isn't something I ever thought I'd do, but this rush of pride never seems to go away as I watch the squad work toward a new routine or stunt.

The girls start to line up to run it again, and I step over to grab my phone and cue up the music again. After making sure they're set, I hit play and grin as "Thunder" by Imagine Dragons starts to blare through the speakers. Caroline and I continue counting as the squad flips, dances, and moves to the final stunt formation. I fight the urge to jump up and down as Maggie, our captain and center flyer, executes a perfect full down and reloads back to a lib to end the routine.

"Gosh, that's gonna look so good when we add it to our competition routine," Caroline says as we clap for the girls again.

"Right? Especially when we add in the pyramid sequence too," I say, my excitement evident as the squad gets set to run it again.

"Okay, girls! One more run! Make sure we're hitting those motions hard," Caroline yells out.

"And big smiles too!" I add before hitting play on Caroline's phone one more time.

The girls execute everything perfectly again, and I smile as I watch their confidence grow each time they run the routine.

As soon as they dismount, the girls move to sit at our feet, and Caroline starts going through our announcements for the day. "Great practice today, girls. We'll run this and the rest of the pep rally line up again at practice on Thursday, but as long as you all bring it again, we won't be here too long. Don't forget that we also have the parade Friday morning, so we need to put the finishing touches on our float by then too. I've talked to Coach Will, and he's agreed to let us park the trailer at the field for the next few days so we can work on it there after school. Hannah, do you want to go over the items we're still missing?"

I check my phone for the list of items I made during my planning before saying, "Well, we have the majority of it done, but we have a few holes in the background we pomped last week at practice, and we need to make a few signs for us to hold. Maggie, you signed up to bring blue and white tissue paper, and Suzie, you said you have some posters, right?"

Both girls nod in agreement, and Caroline smiles. "Great. Plan to meet me at the field tomorrow then. Make sure you check the group text this week too, because I'll be posting all the info on uniforms and everything else. Mrs. Smith from the

Homecoming committee also mentioned they may need our help with some other duties over the next few days."

She's met with a chorus of "yes ma'am's" and "sounds good" before we nod to Maggie to signal the end of practice. The squad gathers around her and she calls out "One, two, three, Saints on me! One, two, three…"

The girls and I yell back "Saints" before everyone moves to grab their things and leave.

As the rest of the girls make their way to the door, Maggie hangs back before asking, "Hey, do the two of you have a second to talk to me?"

Both Caroline and I smile at her encouragingly before responding, "Of course, what's going on?"

"Well, you know it's my senior year, and I'm really hoping to cheer in college. I'd originally planned on Crestview University, but my dad and I toured a few schools last month, and I'm just not sure. But some programs are like really competitive. So I was wondering if you're still willing to help me train? We talked about it earlier in the season, but I'm just making sure you both still have time. I just want to make sure I'm ready for tryouts in the spring. I know y'all both have like a ton on your plate, but my dad doesn't really know anything about the sport, and I can't drive to a gym in Crestview and make practices too," she explains in a rush.

Caroline and I both smile at the girl in front of us, before she says, "Of course, Maggie. You know we'll both do anything we can to help you."

"That's right," I add. "Your tumbling has come a long way already, and I'm sure that with a few more training sessions, you'll be able to out-flip and out-full anyone out there."

Maggie smiles and moves to hug us both, and I have to choke down the wave of emotion that threatens to overtake me. Maggie lost her mom to breast cancer a few years ago when she was a freshman on the squad, and Caroline and I have done everything we can to support her and her dad in the aftermath.

"Thank you so much. I know we're about to be gearing up for comp season, but just whenever either of you have time. Seriously, I'm so grateful," Maggie says, before grabbing her things and heading out the side door.

"Gosh, I hope she makes it, wherever she ends up," Caroline says as we both start to head toward the parking lot.

"Me too. But she's super talented. I think she'll be fine," I say, checking my phone as we walk out to our cars and trying to ignore the sinking feeling in my gut when I see I've missed calls from the bank and the local farm supply company I use. When I'm teaching and coaching, it's hard to focus on all the problems I have at home since my day consists of putting out a million little fires in my classroom. But as soon as I walk away, it's like all the other problems rush in, determined to see how fast they can ramp up my anxiety.

I put my phone back in my bag, and try to put the calls out of my mind as I listen to Caroline talk about ideas she has for the wedding. It's after five now, so there's no point in worrying about it today, but it doesn't help my nerves any as I think about the pile of bills that arrived earlier this week.

"Earth to Hannah. You good?" Caroline asks, and I pause to realize she stopped a few steps back and is waiting on me to answer.

"Oh, uh, sorry. Yeah, I'm fine," I say, but even I know I don't sound convincing.

"Come on, Han. You've gotta talk to me. What's going on? Is it your gramps?" she asks, concern obvious on her face.

I open my mouth to insist that I really am okay, but I can't get any words to come out. Instead, I feel a lump rise in my throat and suddenly I'm fighting tears. "I promise I'm fi—" I start, but before I can force the lie from my lips, my control over my emotions fades and I start to sob.

Caroline's face morphs into a mask of concern and she stops as we make it to the staff parking lot. Without a word, she immediately drops her bags to pull me into her arms and traces her hand soothingly down my back.

After a minute, she says, "Come on, Han, you know you can talk to me. Whatever it is, we can figure it out together."

"I—I—I just can't do it." I sob, trying to choke down the tears that are flowing down my cheeks. I despise crying, but now that I've started, I don't seem to be able to stop. I take a moment to be grateful that the parking lot is deserted, as Caroline continues to wait for me to continue.

"Did something happen with your gramps?" she finally asks after a few minutes, and I gulp in a deep breath of air, trying to regain my composure to answer her question.

"Everything's just falling apart, Caro," I whisper, wiping my tears with the arm of my sweatshirt. "I thought if I tried hard enough, I could hold everything together, but I just can't. And every time I think I have one thing put back together, something else seems determined to break down."

My best friend continues to rub her hand down my arm and nods at me to continue. It's like I can't stop the words from spilling out of me now that I've started, and I let it all out. "We're so behind on the farm, I don't know what I'm gonna do. Even when Gramps was at home, we were barely staying afloat, but now that I'm trying to do it all by myself... Plus, the damn place is falling apart, and everything costs a fortune. And on top of all that, the nursing home told me last night that I'm gonna have to come up with another thousand dollars a month because insurance is refusing to continue paying for his services. So unless I win the lottery, it's looking like we could end up losing the farm."

I haven't allowed myself to say those words out loud, but hearing the reality of the situation causes me to dissolve into a fresh fit of tears. Caroline doesn't say anything for a few moments, just stands beside me as I grapple with my emotions before she says, "Han, I'm so sorry. I hate that you've been trying to deal with all of this on your own, but you know we're here for you. And I don't care what you say, but you aren't losing the farm. We'll come up with something to make this all work. I don't know what it is yet, but there has to be a way. But we can't help you if we don't know what's going on. You've always been the one that holds us together, but you have to let us help you, Han."

I know she's right but the idea of burdening our friends with my predicament made me feel sick to my stomach. "I know you're right, but I just feel like the biggest failure ever. Five generations of my family have found a way to keep the farm going and after a year of me taking it over, I've driven the damn thing into the ground."

"Bullshit," my best friend says, and I blink at her in confusion.

"What?" I ask. "You and I both know it's true."

"Hannah, you can't be serious. Yes, your family has kept the farm going for generations, and that's definitely an accomplishment, but we both know that your gramps was struggling with a lot of this before his heart attack. And I'm sure if he heard you talking like this, it would break his heart. I know it looks pretty bleak right now, but this isn't all your fault. Let's talk to the guys and Margaret this weekend and I'm sure they can help us come up with some ideas."

"Fuck," I groan. "There's no way I can talk about this with Will. He'll find something smart to say about how I can't help but ruin everything I touch or some other stupid shit like that."

"Now Hannah Scott, you can't be serious. I know you and Will have this weird thing between you two, and you stay at each other's throats, but you and I both know that he would want to help. He cares about you, and he loves that farm too."

I blow out a frustrated breath, knowing she's right, but not wanting to acknowledge the truth in her words as she continues, "Listen, I'm not going to force you to share anything if you don't want to, but I think you should. I bet the men could have some ideas on how to do some of the upkeep without spending too much, and Margaret might have some thoughts about other ways to bring in some revenue too. Just think about it, okay? I know you think you're Superwoman, but you don't have to hold it all together by yourself."

I feel my throat tighten again, and I nod in agreement. "Okay, okay, I will. I promise."

"Plus, it's like we always say, brighter days ahead, right?" Caroline adds, referring to a phrase we've used for most of our friendship to remind ourselves that the hard times don't last forever. "There's nothing we can't figure out."

"Yeah, you're right," I tell her with a smile, pulling her into a hug. "Thanks for always being my hype woman."

"You couldn't get rid of me if you tried," she teases. After a minute, she looks around the quickly darkening parking lot. "Well, we both better head home. You and I both know that the kids probably have both of us on their hit list tonight, and Theo's been talking for weeks about his plan of attack."

I can't stop the laugh that bubbles out of me at the thought of her grumpy soon-to-be husband devising a plan for a group of teenagers rolling his house as part of the Homecoming traditions. "Oh yeah, and what all does this plan entail?" I ask, unable to keep my curiosity at bay.

"Well, I haven't gotten the full extent of the details yet, but I do know there've been about fifty water balloons sitting in a bucket by the back door since I got home from Maracas last night," she says with a laugh.

"Oh my gosh, that man," I reply, giggling along with her at her fiancé's antics. "Well, I need a full play by play."

"Don't you worry, I'll send you and Margaret all the details," she responds before turning to get in her car. Once she settles in the seat, she studies me again before saying, "You know I'm always here for you, right Han?"

I smile, feeling some of the weight I was feeling earlier start to lift off my shoulders before nodding. "I know. And I couldn't love you more for it."

"Love you back, babes," she says with a wink before pulling out of the parking lot, and for a moment I allow myself to relax and trust that everything really will be okay.

"Guys, she's totally gonna hear us if you keep that shit up."

I'm finally curling up with my Kindle and a glass of wine after taking care of all the farm chores and getting Ruby situated for the night, when I hear the sound of giggling outside followed by the deep voice of who I'm pretty sure is Ralph from my second period class. I shake my head and fight the urge to laugh at their failed attempt to be quiet before standing and sneaking toward the window.

From my new position, I can see a group of about twenty students moving stealthily through the yard and throwing rolls of toilet paper at my trees. I pull out my phone, firing off a text to our group chat as I continue watching their antics.

> HANNAH: They're here. Did they come for y'all yet Caroline?

> CAROLINE: Yep. A group just left here about ten minutes ago. I thought Theo was gonna have a fit when he walked outside and saw the winter wonderland that they left for us.

> HANNAH: What happened? I thought he had big plans and lots of water balloons.

CAROLINE: Bless his heart, man was trying to
move the bucket to hide by the bushes, and he
managed to knock the whole damn thing over.
The kids obviously saw him, stole the water
balloons, and turned on him. And then they
rolled the house.

MARGARET: NO WAY. Please tell me you got a
video…

CAROLINE: Unfortunately no…but don't worry.
The kids will make sure everyone knows how
clumsy the fire chief is.

I can't hold back the laugh that titters out of me as I read her message, before turning my attention back out the window where my students are stringing rolls of toilet paper through my trees and bushes. I've just decided to make my way outside when I hear a few girls screaming. Alarmed, I rush outside, regardless of the fact that I'm in my pajamas and barefoot to see what's wrong. I swear to fuck if Leroy slipped his cage again, I'm gonna come unglued.

But by the time I've made it outside, I have to fight my racing heart, only to realize that the girls are squealing as they look into the cattle trailer I have parked beside the house. As they notice my arrival, a few of the boys start to sprint down the driveway, but the girls are obviously too enamored by my calf to make a run for it.

"Um, Miss Hannah, why didn't you tell us that you have the cutest little calf in the world?" Riley, one of the girls from the squad, asks.

"Yeah, can you bring it to school and make it a class pet?" Jenny, another of my cheerleaders, asks.

I let out another laugh at the absurdity of the evening before responding, "Well, I'm not sure that's the best idea. This is Ruby and she's only a few days old."

The girls continue to coo and call to the calf through the bars of the cattle trailer, and I make my way over to them. "Don't crowd her too much, okay, girls? She's really sweet, but I don't want to stress her too much."

They immediately take a few steps back, and I unlatch the door to pet my newest calf. "I just finished feeding her a few minutes before y'all got here, so she's probably pretty sleepy."

"We love her," Jenny says, her eyes full of adoration as she looks at the small animal. "When will she—" she starts but stops when we hear a loud sploosh sound on the other side of the trailer.

"What was that?" one of the other girls asks, but I'm already moving to lock the door of the trailer, and blowing out a groan of frustration.

"LEROY! You better get your butt back in your pen and stop trying to show off for our guests!" I bellow, as my students look at me in confusion.

"Umm, Miss Hannah, who's Leroy?" Riley asks as a few of the boys pull their trucks into the drive, presumably to pick up the girls they left behind when they made a run for it to wherever they parked. As the truck pulls in, the headlights illuminate the side of my drive where my pig is happily rolling in a puddle of mud.

"Leroy! I swear, the digging has to stop! You've slipped your gate three times this month!" I say in exasperation, pausing when I notice that a piece of toilet paper is trailing from his hoof. "God, you're such a mess," I tell him with a laugh.

"Miss Hannah, that's a pig," one of the boys says as he makes his way over.

"Great observation, Trent," one of the other boys teases, while the girls walk over to the puddle.

"Oh my gosh, he's huge!" Jenny says with a laugh. "But he's also really cute."

"Yeah, I didn't know you had so many animals," Riley adds.

"Yeah, I have more than I know what to do with," I tell them with a laugh. "So, since you're here, who wants to help me get him back in his pen?"

CHAPTER 12
WILL

"Hey, I'm here to see Arthur Scott," I tell the front desk at the nursing home.

I've come every Wednesday evening to visit Mr. Scott since he was admitted last year. I'm pretty sure neither of us has ever mentioned it to anyone else, but I don't think we've missed a week yet. Outside of Huey, Mr. Scott has been the most positive male role model I've ever had, and I look forward to our weekly meetings.

"He's waiting on you in his room; you can go on in," the receptionist tells me with a wide smile.

Making the familiar journey down the halls, I wave at a few of the other residents I recognize before knocking on his door.

"Come on in, son," Mr. Scott says as I open the door and find him pulling out the box of checkers he keeps stashed away for our visits. "You ready to lose again?"

"Oh, old man, I think you're forgetting that I happen to be the reigning checkers champion around here," I say with a laugh before pulling out the chair across from him. After settling in, I help him place the pieces on the board as we sit in comfortable silence.

We make our first few moves before he asks, "So is this

week's game looking like it's gonna be any less dramatic than last weeks?"

I let out a groan and run my hand over my face before responding. "Damn, I hope so. I don't know how many more of those I have in me."

"Yeah I heard it was a bit of a mess," he says, jumping two of my pieces and claiming them to start his stack. "But really, Han mentioned it was Homecoming when she came by earlier this week. Who are y'all playing?"

"Brookside," I tell him, looking at the board and trying to decide which move will be best. "I can't believe we only have two more home games left in the regular season. This year is flying by."

"That happens when you start getting old," Mr. Scott teases, and I roll my eyes in his direction.

"Hmm, tell me about it, old man," I quip, jumping one of his pieces.

"So, what else is new? Come on, you know I need some entertainment in this place," he asks, and I have to fight the urge to laugh.

"Now, Mr. Scott, you can act however you like, but you and I both know you love being close to Gladis," I tease, and he lets out a laugh at that.

"Damn, you and Hannah both have thrown that at me this week. But you're right. I don't mind it here. But I'd like it a lot more if I didn't feel so guilty for leaving Hannah with that damn farm. I know how much work it was for me. And I had help from the two of you if I needed it. Not to mention that I didn't have a full-time job," he tells me, and I don't miss the guilt on his face.

"Oh, don't start all that," I tell him, knowing Hannah would break at hearing his guilt. "You and I both know Hannah's one of the toughest people in the world, and she'd beat both of our asses for talking like she couldn't do something."

"I know, you're right. But I do have a favor to ask of you," he says, suddenly looking way more serious than normal."

"Uhh, sure, whatever you need," I tell him, shifting in my seat.

"Can you just do me a favor and promise me you'll keep an eye on her? When she came to visit me earlier this week, she just looked so defeated. I've tried to get her to let me come home so I can take care of some of that shit, but we both know I'm not nearly enough help, even if I was healthy. And I know we usually just talk about football or town drama when you come, but to be honest, I can't stand the thought of her fighting all of this by herself. I know it's not a fair ask, but please just promise you'll make sure she's not taking on too much."

I think about earlier this week, and all of the chaos that was ongoing when we pulled up to Falling Oaks Farm, and I try to hide my expression of guilt. It's clear Hannah's doing everything she can to keep everything afloat but it doesn't seem to be working.

"You know, that ask would probably be a hell of a lot easier if your granddaughter wasn't so damn stubborn," I joke, not sure what else to say. "Plus, I'm pretty far down her list of favorite people, so I'm not sure she'll even take my help. She kinda hates me."

Mr. Scott smiles and shakes his head at me. "Listen, son, I don't know what happened to you two after that summer and to tell you the truth, I don't want to know. And while I know that my granddaughter can be a real pain in the ass if she wants to be, I know for a fact that she doesn't hate you. She just needs someone that she can't push away. She'll try, Lord knows she tried with me for years after her momma left, but eventually, she let me in. Just don't let her fight whatever this is by herself."

I blow out a breath as I take in his words. I've been visiting for years, but he's never asked me anything about Hannah, and I don't miss the guilt in his voice. "Sure, Mr. Scott, I promise."

Now to just figure out how in the hell I'm gonna keep my word on that one.

I'M STILL THINKING about Mr. Scott's request the next night, as Seth and I work on the fence at Hannah's farm.

"Will, did you hear me, man?" Seth asks while I hold the wire of the fence line straight for him to replace the post.

I blink at him, trying to figure out what he just said. Shaking my head, I reply, "Sorry. I don't know what that was. What'd you say?"

"I asked if you could hand me the hammer that's by your foot. I need it to drive in this staple to hold the wire up."

I grab the hammer and hand it to him without saying anything. We work in silence for a few more minutes, before he says, "So, you wanna talk about whatever's got you distracted as fuck today or not?"

I rub my free hand over my face, resisting the urge to let out a groan. "Nah, it's all good. I just have a lot on my mind right now."

"Yeah, you worried about the game tomorrow?" my room-mate asks.

"Uhh, sure, something like that," I say noncommittally.

"Well, I'm sure y'all will beat the breaks off Brookside," he says, nailing in the tie to connect the new post. "So snap out of whatever this is."

I just grunt, allowing him to think I'm agreeing with him, but honestly, I wish it was that easy. But I haven't been able to get Hannah Scott out of my mind in years, so I shouldn't expect today to be any different.

CHAPTER 13
WILL

SEVEN SUMMERS AGO

"Okay, so our job for today is to check on all the animals, and then focus on the garden later this afternoon. Gramps is tettering the hay, so it'll probably be on us to get it baled tomorrow. Sound good?" Hannah asks as soon as I pull up at the farm this morning.

"Sounds great," I tell her honestly, looking forward to spending the day with her again. She's wearing jean shorts, and I try not to stare at her long, tanned legs while she walks ahead of me.

"Well, come on then, we don't have all day," she teases over her shoulder, and I hurry to catch up with her.

I hadn't been looking forward to this job when Huey helped me set it up, but over the last week, I've enjoyed settling into a routine with Hannah. She has a way of making me laugh, and she's also hot as hell which makes the day go by faster. Plus, the farm seems to bring me an unexpected sense of peace that I'm not quite used to.

"We're gonna take the Polaris around to check the fence line after that wind we had last night first, so let's get that over with," she suggests, already getting ready to jump in the driver's seat of the ATV.

"Sounds good. Did the weather get too bad here?" I ask, taking the seat next to her and looking out at all the land in front of us.

"Uhh, not too bad. But let me tell you, Leroy was not happy about all the racket the storm caused. I didn't think we'd ever get him to settle down," she says with a laugh.

"He certainly keeps things interesting around here, huh? I've never seen a pig with such an attitude."

"Yeah, he's a mess but I love him. Anyway, like I was saying we had a lot of wind, but that was about it. What about you?" she asks, taking off toward the cattle field.

"It got a little bumpy in town," I tell her, thinking about the hour and a half I spent trying to get my little sister Kit to calm down after a limb fell in the yard. Mom was at work, and Kit's always been terrified of bad weather. It's on the tip of my tongue to tell Hannah about it, but I stop myself, unsure why she'd care that my little sister doesn't like bad weather.

"Well, I didn't want it to get bad but God, we need some rain. I can't believe we didn't get a drop with all the thunder and wind we had last night. But also, I guess it's kinda a good thing since we just cut hay. Gramps always says that the best way to get rain is to cut hay, since that's the only time you need it to stay dry. But apparently, that didn't even work this time," she says with a laugh.

I hum in approval, as Hannah nears the fence line toward the back of the property. "So we're basically just looking for any limbs that might have fallen, but we just want to make sure there isn't any way for the animals to get loose. These little shits love causing chaos."

We ride in comfortable silence for a few minutes, both of us looking out at the fence line in front of us before something hits me. "Wait, where are the cows?"

Hannah bites her lip, and I have to focus to keep from getting distracted at the question. "Umm, I'm hoping they're just in the front of the field over the hill where we can't see them. If not, we're about to have a much bigger headache on our hands."

"Oh, well, hopefully you're right," I say, squinting to look ahead and see if I can see the animals in the distance.

"Damn it," Hannah groans, and I look at her in confusion.

"What's wrong?"

She gestures to a spot in the distance ahead of us, and I can barely make out a huge tree limb down on the fence by the road and several of the cows are already trying to butt the slack in the wire.

"Great. Well, the good news is it doesn't look like any of them have gotten out yet." She sighs.

"And the bad news?" I tease.

"It looks like there's a chainsaw or two in our future," she replies, causing me to laugh.

But an hour later, as I'm dripping in sweat and wood shavings, I can't say I can still see the humor in the situation. *God, it's barely even eight in the morning, and it's already hot as hell.* Despite the heat, we're able to clear the limb and fix the fence without too much work. I grab a bottle of water out of the cooler in the back end of the ATV and gulp it down while Hannah inspects the area.

"Okay, I think that's good enough here, but now we're behind on fields so finish that up so we can get going," she tells me, wiping her brow with the bottom of her T-shirt and drawing my attention to her bare stomach.

I watch her for a moment, before needing something else to focus on. "This farm thing's pretty fun, but damn if it isn't a shit ton of work," I tease.

"Tell me about it," she says, rolling her eyes. "I love this place with my whole heart, but damn it wears me out sometimes."

"Yeah, I knew I'd have my work cut out for me when I started, but I don't think I realized how much went into all of this," I admit.

"Well, don't go quitting on me now," she says with a laugh. "We've still gotta pick corn and the rest of the veggies for the farmers market this weekend, and then somebody has to check the horses this afternoon."

"No problem. You wanna take it all on together today?" I ask, suddenly desperate for her to say yes. The idea of spending the day with her even if we're working sounds like the perfect way to make the day pass.

"You not tired of me yet?" she asks with a laugh.

"Not even close," I tell her, and I don't miss the way she smiles at that.

"Okay. Well, I was going to offer for us to split once we got to the fields, but if you insist," she says. "But don't you come complaining to me when I start to get on your nerves."

"Oh, I'm not worried about that one bit, Hannah," I tell her truthfully.

CHAPTER 14
HANNAH

"Ugh, I swear I just went to bed," I groan to myself the next morning, rolling over and turning off the alarm on my phone.

I soak in my last few minutes of peace, before forcing myself to get up and get ready for the day, knowing that since it's Homecoming, I'll be running around until late tonight, trying to make sure everything's perfect. Blowing out a sigh, I pull myself out of bed and immediately tap my phone to bring up Spotify and hit Riley Green's newest album, smiling when "Worst Way" starts to blare through my speakers.

I set to work, making Ruby's bottle out of the powder I keep by the sink, and I take in the view of the sun rising over the farm. Damn, this place is a real headache sometimes, but I love it to death.

Once I have everything ready, I throw on my farm boots I keep by the door and make my way outside to the trailer while still in my pajamas. By the time I open the door, Ruby is already awake, doing what I'm pretty sure is the calf version of the zoomies. It makes me smile to see her up and moving, and I blow out a sigh of relief that she already seems to be gaining weight and strength the way she's supposed to.

"Good morning sweet girl," I coo at her, reaching out and rubbing the coarse hair on her sweet little head. "You hungry, huh? You want some breakfast"

In response, she twirls herself in a circle and lets out a soft *moo* that makes me giggle. "I know it, girl. Here you go," I tell her, gripping the bottle with both hands and tilting it down to her.

The little calf immediately grabs it with her teeth, and I have to grip the plastic a little harder as she starts to pull on it. I let out a little laugh at her antics and continue talking to her while she eats until the bottle is empty.

Once she's done, I pull the bottle away and pet the top of her head again as she curls up in a little ball. "You sleepy now, huh?" I ask, as she sticks out her sandpaper tongue and licks my palm. "Oh I know it. You're so sweet. And you're getting so strong. I know it may not feel like it right now, but you're gonna be okay. And I'm gonna work on building you a pen this weekend so we can get you out of this trailer. What do ya think about that, huh?"

Once again, she lets out a little *moo* before laying her head down beside where I'm standing, her eyes closing almost immediately.

"All right, sweet girl, you take you a nap, and I'll see you later," I tell her, relocking the trailer door and turning to check on Leroy.

When I make my way over, I can't help but laugh at the sight of him in his little piggy bed. It took us a while to get him back in the pen and fill back in the hole he'd managed to dig with his snoot after his escape, but now that he's lying in his bed with his food bowl flipped over his face, blocking the rising sun, I feel any last bits of frustration with the animal fade.

When I first got him, I had no idea how notorious pigs were for being great escape artists, and I completely panicked the first time he left his pen. But over the last few years, I've gotten used to his antics. He never goes far, and he just loves to roll in the mud. I've considered bringing him inside to see if it would help since he pretty much thinks he's a dog anyway, but the idea of adding anything else to my plate right now makes me want to lose my mind, so I've just decided to let him do what he wants.

"Morning, my little precious piggy," I tell him, and I laugh when he wakes with a start and flings his head, moving the metal bowl off his face with a clang.

He jumps up fast and wiggles his little butt while he waits on me to open the pen and pet him. After getting the gate open, I go in and spend a few minutes giving him some attention and rolling his favorite ball for him to chase. I don't know if it's normal that my pig likes to play fetch, but it makes me smile so I'm going with it anyway.

My Apple Watch pings, letting me know it's time to start getting ready, so I reach down and rub his stomach for a moment, laughing as he snorts and rolls in excitement.

"Okay, big guy, I've gotta get ready to go to work, and I need you to promise me you're gonna be a good boy today and stay where you're supposed to be. No big escape plans today, m'kay?" I tell him, patting his head as I stand from where I was crouched over, and grabbing his overturned food bowl.

"You want some breakfast too?" I ask him, already reaching down and grabbing the scoop I keep in the plastic bucket of his feed. Leroy lets out a squeal of approval, and I roll my head at his excitement.

"Yeah, yeah. I know. Here you go," I say, dropping the bowl and patting him one more time before letting myself out and making sure that both latches are locked before making my way back inside to shower and get dressed.

"Let's get this day started then I guess," I say to myself, trying to ignore the loneliness I feel when I look at the empty house.

"OKAY, girls, get set. We're gonna be between the band and the football team, and we're bringing up the end of the parade, so we're gonna have to be ready once they start moving," Caroline tells the squad later that afternoon as we wait for the police to signal the start of the parade.

The band starts playing the fight song, and the girls get ready to walk, grabbing their poms from the ground and straightening their new navy uniforms.

"Big smiles, girls, let's go," I remind them as we start making our way toward the middle of town. The float we've spent the last week working on is in front of us, and I can't help but smile at how good the banner designs look.

Caroline and I wave to people along the parade route as we walk behind the girls, and it never ceases to amaze me how many people pile into the streets of our little town for this. Springside might be small, but I love seeing how the community makes sure to support our kids.

Before we know it, we're back at the school, and we make our way to the football stadium where we'll have a small pep rally before the boys get ready for the game. Behind us, the team is piling off the flatbed trailer that one of the parents let the team borrow for the parade, and I see Will and Theo talking to one of the other coaches.

"Okay, girls, you have ten minutes to run to the gym and freshen up before the fans start getting here. Go on and meet us back at the field," Caroline tells the team, dismissing them before turning back to me. "Come on, Han," she says, grabbing my arm and pulling me toward the boys.

"Ugh, I can't deal with him today, Caroline. I'm in a good mood, and I don't feel like ruining it," I complain with a groan.

"Oh my gosh, stop being such a baby." She laughs, ignoring

my reluctance. "Hey, Cowboy," she says as we reach her fiancé standing with the man who knows how to push all my buttons.

Theo immediately reaches out for her and pulls her to him without stopping the conversation he and Will are having and presses a kiss to her forehead. After a moment, he smiles down at her. "Hey, Sunshine. Morning, Hannah. You two ready for whatever this is about to be?"

Despite my annoyance at having to put up with Will, I laugh at his question as Caroline tells him yes, immediately launching into the plans for the pep rally.

I can tell Will's about to say something when one of the assistant coaches makes his way over to us. I know his name is Kent, but I don't know him that well since he isn't a teacher, although I think he's pretty close to our age.

"Hey, ladies," he says, smiling kindly at both of us. "You ready to rock this pep rally?"

"Yep, we sure are," Caroline says excitedly, "What about you? Are y'all ready for tonight?"

Will starts talking about their strategy, and I try to look bored, despite the fact that I've always loved football. Unfortunately for me, Will is actually a really good coach, and the new play he's talking about actually sounds really damn cool. Oh well, he doesn't need to know that.

I check my phone for the time just as Caroline asks, "So, Kent, are you coming to the bonfire at our house tomorrow night? It won't be anything fancy, but we're celebrating our engagement and we'd love to have you."

"Yeah, Theo mentioned it at practice earlier this week. You'll be there too, right Hannah?" he asks, looking up at me and it takes me a moment to realize he's talking to me.

"Oh, yep, I'll be there," I tell him with a smile.

"Hmm, good. I was thinking we could chat? If so, I'll come find you?" he asks, and I don't miss the hopeful expression on his face as he asks.

"Sure, I'd like that. I'll be the one with the margaritas," I tease, already looking forward to the peach mix and tequila I grabbed last week at the liquor store.

"Margaritas? At a bonfire?" Will interjects. "Really, Hannah? Can't you just drink a beer like a normal fucking human?"

I glare at him, ignoring Caroline elbowing him in the ribs at his outburst. "Yes, Will. We both know I like beer too. But what the hell's wrong with finding some of the little joys in life? Clearly, it's something you should start doing, since you're boring as hell."

We glare at each other for a minute, before Kent breaks the silence with a tight laugh. "I've gotta grab something out of my office before this thing gets started, but I'll see you tomorrow, Hannah."

"See you then," I tell him, admiring how attractive he is. He towers over my six-foot frame, and his tan and tattoos should be just my type. I try to feel a jolt of excitement that he seems interested in me, but it never comes. Instead, I compare him to Will in my head, despite the fact that he's still sneering at me in disgust.

"You got something to say?" I ask, knowing I'm provoking him. But the air feels electric, and I'm desperate to see him snap.

He opens his mouth to fire back at me before Caroline interrupts him. "Okay, enough of that. We've gotta go get ready, and I can't listen to the two of you bicker anymore today. We'll see y'all later."

I roll my eyes at her, letting her grab my arm but just as we start to walk away, Theo pulls her back and drops a kiss on her lips before whispering, "See you after all this hoopla, Sunshine."

She smiles and pulls away from him, grabbing my arm again for us to start walking through the crowd starting to pile into the stadium. I'm about to tease her about how adorably nauseating she and her fiancé are, but she just says, "I already know, we're too much and I don't care."

We both laugh at that, and she changes the subject. "Oh don't think you're getting away with us not talking about you. What was that with the coach? He's totally into you, Han! And he's *cuuute*," she sings, stretching out the word as far as she can.

"Yeah, yeah, he's not terrible looking or anything like that. But he's probably just being nice. I'm not reading much into it," I tell her seriously.

Caroline groans at that, but thankfully lets it go since we're walking through the gates of the field where most of the girls are waiting for us to give them instructions.

"All right, ladies, let's warm up that stunt sequence and be ready to hit it full out," I call out, desperate to get lost in something other than this conversation with my best friend. "Let's get it, ladies."

CHAPTER 15
WILL

"All right, guys. I know it's been a busy week, but it's time to get focused," I tell the team after we finish warm-ups for the game. "There's already a packed house tonight, and we need to go out there and prove that we have what it takes to make the playoffs this season."

A few of the players cheer in agreement when I mention what's at stake with this game, and I wait for them to calm down before continuing.

"Like I was saying, I don't think I need to tell you that we need this win. Brookside's in our region, and if we get this win we're guaranteed a spot," I tell them, motioning for them to quiet down as they start to cheer again. "But I've told you all week we're gonna have a lot of eyes on us after what happened last week. So when we go out there, keep your heads down and your mouths shut. Do you understand?"

The boys respond with a chorus of "Yes, Coach," and I nod.

"Okay. Remember your routes and leave it all on the field. Take a minute, get your head on straight, and let's win this dang thing."

The team and the other coaches hoop and holler, and after a few minutes I gesture for Blake to lead the pregame ritual. He nods before standing and gesturing for the team to crowd around him. The other coaches and I watch as he yells, "Who are we?" and the boys respond with "Springside" over and over, getting louder, jumping and yelling until it feels like the concrete walls of the locker room are shaking with the volume. After a few minutes, they break the huddle and the locker room goes silent as they start to line up, waiting for us to lead the Saint Spirit Stroll.

There's still almost thirty minutes until kickoff, but I can hear the energy outside already ramping up as the fans line up and wait for us to make our way outside. As the team gets set, Theo leans over and looks out the small window before whispering, "Okay, I knew tonight would be intense, but I've never seen this many people at a high school game in my life. Where the hell did everyone come from?"

"I told you this place takes Homecoming pretty seriously," I tell him, straightening my headset.

"Yeah, no shit," he responds, shaking his head as Jason, Kent, and the other coaches join us.

"Let's go make playoffs, huh, gentlemen?" Kent says, just as I open the door to the chaos outside.

I ignore him, letting the other coaches lead the way and trying to push aside the tug of annoyance I'm still feeling at him from the way he flirted with Hannah earlier today.

Seriously… you have a game to coach. You do not have time to be worried about Hannah's love life. And you certainly can't ignore your defensive coordinator during the game. My subconscious reminds me, and I shake myself, trying to get my head right as I step out of the locker room where hundreds of fans are lined up chanting along with the cheerleaders. "Black, blue, white… Fight, Saints, fight."

I try to tune out the lines of people as we make our way to the field and nod along as the band starts to play the fight song. Eventually, Theo opens the gate that leads to the field, and I take my position on the sidelines as the band gets reset for the national anthem.

As soon as they finish, the captains step on the field, shaking hands with the players from Brookside, before the refs step up to toss the coin. I pump my fist when we win the toss, deferring to receive after the first half, and wait for the team to bust out of the run-through sign that the cheerleaders painted.

"You're still good with us trying the new play on our first possession, right," Marcus asks, and I just grunt in agreement, mentally sizing up the players on the Brookside sideline. They have a couple of boys that I know from watching films who are fast as shit, but if we can keep them contained, we should be okay. I turn to remind Kent to tell the boys to make sure they keep their eyes on number seven for the bulldogs one more time, but when I turn to my left, Theo's the only one still standing beside me.

"Where the hell'd the rest of 'em go?" I ask, searching the sideline as the team runs through the sign and heads toward us.

"Those two went to make sure the special teams are ready to go," Theo replies, gesturing to where Marcus and Jason have pulled the kickoff team to give them their last few reminders.

"Right, but where's Kent?" I question, "He was just right here."

"Looks like he's talking to Hannah," Theo answers, gesturing to where Hannah is standing with the cheerleaders, talking to my defensive coordinator like we're not less than a minute from kickoff.

I feel my anger rise because what the fuck are they thinking. Without responding to Theo, I turn and barrel toward them, feeling my temper get stronger and stronger the closer I get. Just as I step beside them, Hannah lets out a laugh at something Kent said, and I snap.

"Sorry to interrupt the party, but since it's clear both of you forgot, we have a fucking game to win. And it just so happens, I need my defensive coordinator to do that," I growl, thankful there aren't any students around to hear me.

"Sorry, man. She said she needed to talk to one of us," Kent says, already turning and heading back toward the team.

I turn back to Hannah and cross my arms as I scowl at her. Her blonde hair's blowing in the breeze, and I catch a whiff of the damn vanilla perfume she always wears, which only makes me angrier for some reason.

"I know this is hard for you to understand, but the world doesn't revolve around you. Some of us actually need to focus on this damn game, Hannah, so if you could leave my staff alone, that'd be great."

"Screw you, Will. I came over to bring this," she says, holding out one of the armbands with our plays on it. "One of the players left it at the spirit line and I thought you might want it. But since I clearly think the world revolves around me, just forget it."

"I don't have time for this," I growl, taking the damned band from her hand. "Get to your seat and stop distracting my staff."

She opens her mouth to respond, but I'm already walking away, throwing the band at Kent. "Find out which one of your players can't keep up with their shit."

He just nods, before saying, "Listen, man, I didn't—"

Before he can finish, I cut him off, "It's fine. Let's win this thing." It's really not, but I can't afford to lose this game because we can't communicate.

He smiles tightly and nods, before turning to the field as we watch Bobby kick the ball off to the waiting Brookside receiver's hands. He catches it, but only makes it a few yards before one of our players takes him down.

I clap once, trying to focus on the game, but after that encounter, I feel off-kilter. I spend the next few plays telling myself to focus, but it's clear when Theo and Marcus both ask me a question through the headset multiple times before I register what they're saying that my head isn't where it's supposed to be.

I blow out a frustrated breath, willing myself to forget about whatever the fuck has my head in such a mess, but I know I'm just going through the motions. Thankfully, the team is executing all our plays pretty well, so there isn't a ton for me to correct. Before I know it, the refs are signaling for halftime, and I motion for my assistant coaches to lead the speech. Theo gives me a look that clearly asks what the hell is wrong with me, but I ignore him.

This game can't be over soon enough.

THANKFULLY, by the time the fourth quarter starts, I've managed to shake off whatever the hell had a hold of me, and I hold my breath as the offense lines up on the Brookside thirty-yard line. It's third and two, and we need this one to make sure the drives we've made in the last few plays aren't wasted.

Marcus looks at the sideline to check the play we're running, and I pull in a tight breath, waiting to see if we can put this one away. We're up by ten, and if we can score again, we'll have a big enough lead that Brookside won't have a chance of coming back in the last few minutes.

The ref blows his whistle signaling the start of the play, and the center snaps the ball into Blake's waiting hands. I know it's just in my head given the crowd we have tonight, but everything goes silent for a moment in anticipation while Blake takes a step back and pumps twice while looking for the receiver downfield. One of the Brookside players rushes him, and he throws the ball just as he's tackled from behind.

The ball soars through the air and I'm pretty sure it'll be incomplete when Stephen, one of the sophomores on the team, snatches it and runs toward the end zone. I start running down the sideline, desperate to see if he makes it until he scores. I pump my fist and let out a whoop of excitement as the stadium erupts in cheers and the band starts playing "Oh When the Saints Go Marching In."

As special teams lines up for the extra point, I turn to say something to Theo when my eyes fall on the sideline where Hannah's jumping up and down with Caroline in excitement. The smile on her face hits me like a punch to the gut, thinking about all the times she used to smile at me like that.

What the fuck's wrong with you, man? my subconscious screams, and I struggle to figure out where that thought came from. I don't know what's gotten into me these last few weeks, but I need this shit to end.

Frustrated with myself, I turn back to the field just as the ball soars through the field goal, and Marcus jumps up beside me, slapping me on the back. "Looks like we're playoff bound, huh, Coach?" he asks, and I try to match his enthusiasm, before just nodding as we get ready to kick off again.

After that, the last few minutes of the game pass quickly. Brookside fumbles during their next possession, and we send in some of the younger players to kill time off the clock until the buzzer sounds. The stadium erupts again, as the announcers declare that the Saints are officially playoff bound.

"Good game," the Bulldog coach says, making his way over to shake my hand. "You have quite a team here."

"You too," I tell him honestly, before adding, "good luck this season," as I turn back to the sideline. Mayor Brian and Huey are making their way over, and I feel the corners of my mouth tip up in a grin as they reach me.

"Hell of a game, son," Huey says, wrapping his arm around my shoulder and patting my back hard.

"Yeah, great game, Will," Mayor Brian says, reaching his hand out to shake mine.

We make small talk for a few minutes before Theo walks up beside us and shakes hands with both men.

"Well, Theo, I heard you had quite the experience with your first Homecoming this week," Huey says with a wink, and Theo lets out a growl of frustration, causing Brian and I to chuckle.

"How in the hell do you assholes know about that?" he groans, rubbing his hand over his face.

"Well, one of the boys that took the video is Miss Ethel's grandson," Huey explains, referring to one of the town's nosiest residents. "Pretty sure she put the video in an STS blast, so the whole town's seen you bust your ass by now."

At the mention of the STS, or Small Talk of Springside, Theo rolls his eyes. The email chain started as a place for one of the Sunday School groups to send prayer requests, but it quickly evolved into a town-wide gossip chain. Thanks to the controversy around Theo's arrival into town earlier this year, he's made quite a few appearances, and each time, he becomes a little more annoyed.

"Yeah, not sure that's the strategy I would have used, but whatever works for you, man," Brian adds with a laugh.

"Yeah, yeah. Enough of this shit. I'm going to find Caroline," he says.

"See you and Caroline for dinner Sunday afternoon?" Huey asks, ignoring Theo's usual grumpy demeanor.

He nods before responding, "You know we wouldn't miss it. See you then, old man," and turns to find Caroline in the crowd and pulling her into his arms.

I'm about to say something else to the men beside me when I see one of my least favorite people making a beeline for me.

"Oh, lucky you. Looks like Miss Sally has something to say to you," Brian says with a laugh.

"Fuck," I curse under my breath. "How do you know she's coming for me? She could be coming to complain to you about the new sidewalk construction in front of City Hall this week."

"Maybe... but, since I spent an hour dealing with that exact complaint on Wednesday when her walking group had to detour from their usual route, I think this one's for you."

I groan as she pushes other people out of her way to make her way through the crowds of people, and as soon as she's in earshot, his suspicions are confirmed when she yells, "Will Thompson, I have a bone to pick with you."

Several of the other townspeople hear her and immediately turn to watch the debacle that's probably about to unfold. I give her the biggest smile I can manage and turn toward the old woman. "I'm sure you do, Miss Sally. I'm sorry to hear that, but considering we won by more than twenty points, I don't know what the problem might—" I start, but before I can finish she cuts me off, stepping closer to me and poking her finger in my chest.

"The problem is that we should have won by at least thirty. I still don't know what the school's thinking, letting someone like you run this team. Not to mention, you let the team wear navy on Homecoming instead of the traditional powder blue," she says, seeming determined to list off whatever she's so angry about. Knowing I won't say anything to appease her, I let her continue, reminding myself that matching her energy won't do any good.

"Plus, none of your little coaching staff even bothered to show up to my knitting club's benefit, and I told you we were raising money for the youth sports program. Your whole coaching staff is full of those out-of-towners, and you all just think you're too good for us. We raised a whole thirty dollars, and y'all may as well have spit in our faces," she says, getting louder and angrier with each accusation.

"Whoa, Miss Sally. I told you when you called Tuesday afternoon and gave us a thirty-minute notice about an event during practice time in the middle of Homecoming week that it wasn't possible. Plus, we aren't even associated with the youth sports team. Remember, I told you that you'd need to contact Mr. Jones at City Hall," I tell her, trying to maintain my composure.

At my mention of City Hall, her eyes swing over to Brian, and she makes a loud hum of disapproval. "Don't even get me started on you. I swear, it's no wonder this town is going to shit. The whole place is run by incompetent, lazy children."

"Miss Sally, you do realize I'm in my thirties right," Brian asks flatly before Huey interjects.

"Sally, stop being such an insufferable old hag. Will just secured a spot to the playoffs and Brian's doing everything he can to make the updates to City Hall that have been overdue for years. Now go on and find something else to complain about."

The old woman opens her mouth, but decides better of it and turns to walk away.

"Great, we'll definitely have a slam piece in the STS before morning," I say sarcastically.

Both men laugh at that and we talk for a few more minutes before they turn to leave and I shake hands with a few more alumni and parents wanting to shake my hand or talk about the game. After about thirty more minutes, the stadium has cleared out, and I head to the field house to grab my backpack before heading home.

The field house is silent, with all the players off to the Homecoming dance in the gym and the other coaches headed back home for the weekend. After a game day, I usually can't get off campus fast enough, but tonight I can't bring myself to rush. Instead, I collapse into the chair behind my desk, and work to summon the excitement I should be feeling about the next few weeks. We have a great team and a guaranteed spot in the playoffs. I remind myself that I should feel like I'm on the top of the world, but instead I can't help the nagging feeling that something's missing.

CHAPTER 16
HANNAH

"Which one should I wear?" I ask, holding out both the tops I brought for my best friend's opinions.

Margaret and Caroline look up from where they're getting ready, inspecting the green cropped top and the black bodysuit I brought with me. "I like the green," Caroline says, standing from where she just finished her makeup, and Margaret nods in agreement.

Margaret and I came over early to help Caroline make sure she had everything ready for the bonfire tonight. I helped make sure everything was ready to go and set up some drinks and snack stations, while Margaret baked a few trays of her brown butter Snickerdoodle cookies with milk, dark, and white chocolate chips that we can't get enough of. After spending the morning working the farm by myself, I welcomed the idea of a few hours with my friends and away from my empty farmhouse.

Going with their advice, I pull the green cropped top over my head and search through my bag for my jeans just as Margaret leans over and turns on the speaker Caroline keeps in her room and taps her phone until "Any Man of Mine" by Shania Twain pumps through the speaker.

"Oh my gosh, I love this song," I squeal, already shaking my hips to the beat of the music.

I sing along loudly with my friends, taking a few minutes to dance and block out the stress of the last few days. By the time the song ends, we're all giggling, and a few minutes later, Caroline leaves the room and comes back with three glasses of peach margaritas.

"Bless you," I squeal, reaching out and taking the glass from her and taking a big sip.

"I know pregaming the bonfire wasn't part of the original plan, but what the hell. Pretty sure surviving Homecoming and spirit week deserves a little tequila," she says with a laugh.

"Amen," I tell her with a laugh, before taking another sip. "But I'm pretty sure there's no such thing as a bad time for tequila."

Caroline and Margaret laugh at that before Caroline asks, "So, Han, you look great, but don't think I didn't notice you spent the last thirty minutes curling all that hair. You hoping to catch Kent's eye tonight?"

"Wait, what?" Margaret asks, her eyes widening in surprise. "I don't know what I missed but I need all the details."

"Can't a girl just get dolled up because she wants to?" I say, rolling my eyes in Caroline's direction.

"Sure they can, but we both know how he was looking at you yesterday. Theo also might have mentioned that he said he mentioned wanting to ask you out," she replies before Margaret interjects.

"Someone please fill me in. Isn't Kent one of the coaches at the school?"

"Yeah, he's the really tall one with all the muscles," Caroline tells her.

Margaret squeals. "Oh my God, he's so cute. Did something happen between you two, Han?"

I open my mouth to tell her no, but before I can get a word out, Caroline's answering for me. "Oh my gosh, Margaret. He was totally flirting with her before the game yesterday, and he asked if they could talk tonight. I bet he asks you out."

"God, y'all are worse than our students, Caroline. He was just being nice," I tease, taking another sip of my drink. "But enough about boys. Are the two of you ready to head out?"

The girls nod, and we throw on our boots before heading outside. "The boys are already out in the field making sure the fire's ready to go, so we can take the Ranger," Caroline says, pointing to the ATV by the porch of her and Theo's farmhouse.

We pile on and huddle together in the front seat, the fall air seeming to turn colder and colder the longer we ride.

After a few minutes, we pull up to where the boys are standing beside a huge fire. Jumping off the Ranger, Caroline makes a beeline for her fiancé, who pulls her in and drops a kiss on her forehead while listening to whatever Seth was explaining to him before we pulled up.

Margaret and I make our way over to stand beside them, before Caroline says, "Quite a fire you've got going, Cowboy. I wasn't thinking it would be quite this big."

"It's all good, Sunshine. I've got a few buckets of water just in case, plus, we've got half the Springside Fire Department here as backup," he responds, causing Caroline to chuckle.

"Okay, you're right. I think we're covered. Speaking of which, is Zach here yet? I want to ask him how Bethany's recovery is going," she asks, referring to one of the firefighters that works with Theo and his younger sister. Zach and Theo started at the fire station around the same time, but they'd really formed a friendship after Zach's apartment building caught on fire, and Theo risked his life to rush in, thinking they were inside. Thankfully, they'd been down the street, and Theo made it out without too many injuries.

"Not yet, but he should be here soon. He texted me that he'd be heading this way soon," Theo responds, pulling her closer to him and wrapping his arm around her, before turning back to us. "Thanks for the help out here today. We really appreciate it."

Margaret smiles at her brother. "If you'd told me when we moved here a few months ago that you'd be willingly throwing a party, I don't think I would have believed you."

"Me either," Theo says, smiling at his fiancée. "But if being engaged to this one isn't worth a celebration, I don't know what is."

"Gag me," I tease, causing Margaret and Caroline to giggle. "I'm kidding, I'm kidding. You know we're happy for y'all. So who all's coming to this shindig?"

"Oh, not too many people. We just invited the firefighters who aren't on duty, people from school, and a few other people," Caroline replies, moving back from Theo's grasp and grabbing a solo cup from the stack on a table. "Now, who wants a margarita?"

"You women and your margaritas," Will says, rolling his eyes.

"Go ahead and drink your boring beer, Grandpa," I tell him, making my way over to where Caroline's already pouring some of the pre-made mix I brought into three separate cups and adding a few shots of tequila on the top.

Will's attention shifts to me, and I try to ignore how good he looks in the glow of the light from the bonfire. He's wearing jeans and a flannel along with a brown, worn cowboy hat, and I imagine how it'd feel to run my hand against the leather the way I used to. *Don't even think about going there tonight,* I chide myself, willing my brain away from that particular thought process.

I can tell he's about to come back with some smart-ass comment at my previous remark, but before he gets a chance, Caroline cuts him off. "Nope, don't start, you two. I don't wanna hear it tonight. We're celebrating."

Will and I both grunt in agreement, and I spend the next hour chatting with Margaret while Caroline makes the rounds, speaking to everyone who came to celebrate her and Theo.

"Another marg?" Margaret asks after a while, reaching for my empty cup.

"Sure, why not? I'll walk with you," I tell her, and we head toward the table where Caroline poured our drinks earlier.

Margaret's in the process of pouring us both another drink when I hear a voice call out from behind me. "Hannah, there you are."

I turn to see Kent making his way over from the other side of the fire. "Hey, Kent," I tell him with a wide smile. "You want a drink?"

"Nope. I'm okay for now, but thanks," he says, holding up a glass beer bottle and taking a swig. "I was worried I'd miss you, but I should have known better. Someone as gorgeous as you tends to stick out."

I try not to cringe at his attempt to flirt, pasting on a bright smile. "Nope, you found me. Have you met Margaret? She's Theo's sister," I explain, gesturing to my best friend standing by the drinks and clearly sizing up the man across from me.

"Hey, Kent, I've heard a lot about you," she tells him politely, looking at me as if she's trying to figure out if she should leave.

I give a small shake of my head, indicating she can stay. Turning back to Kent, I say, "Great win last night, Coach. Only a few more games till the playoffs, huh?"

"Yeah, that's right. We have that away game at North Hill, then Senior Night, and then another away game to finish out the season," he says before asking, "your squad has a competition coming up too, right?"

"Yep. Regionals are in two weeks, and if we get a bid to state, we'll compete there right before Thanksgiving."

"Oh, y'all will get a bid," he declares confidently just as Margaret motions that she'll be back, leaving the two of us alone. We make more small talk for a few minutes until I feel a chill run through me now that we've moved away from the fire. *Ugh, I knew this crop top was a mistake.*

"It did get a bit chilly, didn't it?" Kent asks, noticing my discomfort. "Here, you can borrow this," he adds, pulling off the jacket he had on and handing it to me.

I take it, thanking you, and after I've pulled it on he reaches out and pulls the sides of the jacket together before saying, "Yep, it looks better on you anyway."

I smile at the compliment and will myself to feel some sort of attraction toward the man across from me. He's certainly attractive and I know we'd have a lot of fun together, but just like all the other times I've tried to date in the last few years, there's nothing there.

CHAPTER 17
HANNAH

SEVEN SUMMERS AGO

"Okay, come on," I tell Will, leading the way through the trees to one of my favorite places.

"Would you please just tell me where we're going?" he groans, but the smile on his face tells me he isn't upset, despite the fact that we've been walking for the last few minutes.

"I told you it's a surprise. Come on. We're almost there." I laugh, already recognizing the familiar sight of the entrance of my creek tucked into the woods ahead of us.

We walk along in silence for a moment until we break through the clearing, and I smile as Will's jaw drops. "You definitely left this place out of the tour."

I grab his hand and pull him with me toward the water. "Yeah, I did. This place is mine, and I didn't know if I wanted to share it with anyone."

He raises his eyebrow at me before asking, "I guess you changed your mind then, huh?"

I pause for a moment before nodding. "I guess I did."

Neither of us moves for a moment until I gesture at the huge blue pond in front of us. "You want to get in with me?"

Will's eyes widen before he responds, "Uh, heck yeah. But unfortunately, I left my emergency swimsuit at the house."

I giggle before shrugging. "Yeah, me too... That's too bad." I give him a mischievous smile, and before he can say anything else I splash some water at him, soaking the front of his shirt before whipping my sweaty tank off and throwing it at him.

His surprised expression makes me laugh until he finally snaps out of the daze he was in and dashes after me, taunting, "Get back here, Scott. You're gonna pay for that."

I let out a squeal as I dash away, moving deeper toward the water. Before I get too deep, I pause and drop my jean shorts, throwing them to the shore, leaving me in my sports bra and my underwear. Still hurrying away from Will, I bob deeper in the water, waiting to see what he'll do.

I tell myself that my strip show doesn't have anything to do with the man across from me, clinging to the excuse that I'll have to walk back to the farm after we're done, and there's nothing worse than going anywhere in wet jeans. But as Will strips down to just his boxers before jumping in the water, I know that's a lie. The truth is, after spending the last few weeks together, I'm desperate to find out if Will's as attracted to me as I am to him. I've gotta say, if the new hunger in his eyes is any indication as he makes his way toward me, I'd say we might be on the same page. And sweet baby Jesus, the man is freaking ripped, I note, taking a moment to check out his muscular bare chest.

Shaking myself, I squeal again, looking for an escape route, but before I can go anywhere, Will launches himself at me, wrapping his muscular arms around me and pulling me into the water with him. I try to pull away, but his arms wrapped around me prove how useless my attempts are, so I allow my body to relax against him.

He hums and pulls me closer to him before shifting me

around until I'm facing him. "This place is incredible, Han. Thank you for sharing it with me."

We both go silent for a moment, each of us waiting for the other to say something before I can't take it anymore. I lean in and press a tentative kiss to his mouth.

For a minute, I worry he's going to push me away, but instead, his eyes widen, and he grabs my head, pulling my mouth back to his. He kisses me hard, and I let out a whimper of surprise, before threading my fingers through his hair.

I wouldn't say I've kissed a ton of boys, but I've had my share of hot make-out sessions and hookups in college, and I've never been kissed like this in my life. It feels like both of us have been determined not to cross the line with the other, not wanting to make the other uncomfortable, but now that we've started, we don't know how to stop.

"God, I could do this all night," Will growls, pulling back slightly and kissing down my neck, causing me to gasp as he nips at the sensitive skin below my ear. "I've been going out of my mind wanting you since you came out in those jean shorts my first day."

His confession sends a thrill through me, and I groan, pulling his face back to mine and teasing his mouth with my tongue. I don't know if we kiss for minutes or hours, but all I know is I don't want to stop. Will must agree with me, because by the time we pull away, the sun is setting, and the hot summer air is starting to cool.

"So much for swimming, huh?" I ask with a laugh.

Will chuckles and hums in agreement. "Yeah, but I can promise you I have no complaints. But I promised my mom I'd bring something home for dinner so I'd better go, as much as I don't want to."

I smile at how disappointed he sounds that he has to leave as we make our way toward the shore where we left our clothes before responding, "No problem. Let's get dried off, and then you can head out. We've got the rest of the summer to spend together."

He smirks at that, letting his eyes roam over my exposed, wet body before saying, "Thank God, because, Hannah Scott, I'm not even close to being through with you."

CHAPTER 18
WILL

"Will, did you hear what I said?" Seth asks, bringing me back to the present. I'm doing my best to at least pretend to be interested in the conversation Seth and Brian are having beside me, but after watching Hannah spend the last few minutes flirting with Kent, I know I'll say something I regret if I'm not careful.

"No, sorry, man," I apologize, still watching the interaction across the bonfire and trying to ignore the intense rush of jealousy I feel when Kent holds out his jacket for Hannah to take.

What the fuck is wrong with me? She means nothing to me and she can wear whoever's jacket she wants, I tell myself, but even I know I'm lying.

After everything that happened that summer, I've struggled to figure out how to coexist with Hannah. I originally hoped we could go back to being friends, but she has a way of bringing out the worst in me and my temper. I've thought about it and decided, at least for me, it's probably a result of not being able to have her, but since she's the one who shattered the future I had planned for us, I haven't been able to figure out what the hell she has to be mad about.

And now, I'm forced to watch her as she flirts with my

assistant coach, driving me fucking wild in the process. The rational part of me knows that I have nothing to be mad about, but with every passing minute, the less rational, jealous-fueled side of me becomes louder in my subconscious.

"Damn it, man. I don't know what's gotten into you," my roommate says, and I try again to refocus on whatever he's talking about. I shake my head and force myself to look away from the fire. I hate to admit it, but Seth's right. Over the last few months, I've become more and more distracted by thoughts of what should have been, and I know if this keeps up, I'm gonna lose my damn mind.

I spend the next few minutes nodding as Seth talks about his plans for the baseball season with me and one of the guys who works with Theo at the fire department. I attempt to listen to what he's saying, but most of my focus goes toward refusing to let my eyes wander across to the bonfire. I take a few sips of my beer, draining the bottle, before I throw it in the trash beside us.

"If you're getting another, bring me one," Seth says, finishing off his drink too. "I brought that cooler up and left it by that table."

"Sure," I murmur, steeling myself because the direction he pointed me in is directly beside where Hannah and Kent are still talking.

"Hey, Will," Kent says, holding out his hand to shake mine. I paste on a blank expression and nod, hoping to make a quick exit.

"You still riding the high of that win, Will? I know I am. That state championship is ours this year, I swear," he says enthusiastically, while Hannah just glares at me.

I grunt, leaning down to grab the beer from the cooler on the ground, desperate to get away. As soon as I have the thought I feel a flash of frustration with myself, knowing I'm being a dick. Kent's a great guy and I've never had an issue with him. I don't know what the hell's wrong with me.

Deciding to say fuck it to whatever is messing with my head,

I stand and pop the top off my beer before saying, "Yeah, I hope you're right. If we can keep everyone healthy and execute the way we both know we can, I have high hopes."

Hannah lets out a laugh at my statement and rolls her eyes at my statement.

"Something I said funny, Hannah?" I say, my voice tight.

"No, no. You just sound like you're being interviewed on *College Game Day* or some shit. Relax, there isn't anyone to impress here," she says, and I glare at her.

"I swear, you're fucking insufferable, Han," I growl, my voice rising. "What the hell'd I say to you, huh?"

"You came over to where I was!" she yells, crossing her arms over her chest. "How the hell is this my fault?"

Kent's eyes widen in surprise as he watches us bicker before asking, "Are the two of you always like this?"

I answer, "Yes," as Hannah says, "No," and the two of us continue to stare each other down.

"Okay," he says skeptically, still looking between the two of us. "I'm gonna go grab another drink from the truck. Hannah, you want to walk with me?"

She nods in his direction, still glaring daggers in my direction as she replies, "Sure, I'd love that."

With that, Kent holds out his hand, leading Hannah to the other side of the field where there's a row of cars parked. I watch them go, scowling at the same surge of jealousy I felt earlier.

Why the hell do I care what she does? She's not mine, and she hasn't been in years. Whatever the fuck this is, I need to let it go, I remind myself for what feels like the thousandth time, grabbing both bottles of beer and heading back to Zach.

He takes it without looking, seeming deep into a heated conversation with Theo, Brian, and Zach. I listen for a few minutes trying to figure out what the hell they're talking about. Eventually, Zach must catch my confused expression because he says, "Sorry, we're just trying to decide which would win in a fight: Theo's mean old donkey or that ostrich that lives out on old Mr. Walker's farm. You know the one that was chasing down cars on the county road last year? They're both wild ass animals, but my money's still on Petunia though."

I pause, trying to decide if he's serious or not, before letting out a laugh at their antics and trying to ignore the nagging in my gut at the jealousy I still feel.

"HEY, CAN YOU DO ME A FAVOR?" Seth asks later the following week. We're spending the evening working on Hannah's fence around the farm, and I'm pretty sure we all underestimated how big of a job this would be.

"Sure, what do ya need?" I ask, holding another piece of the new barbed wire tight as Seth loops the holder through it.

"Could you run inside and grab the big lantern light on the counter? It's getting too dark and the last thing we want is to end up with one of these ties stuck through our hands. Hannah told me it was fine, and she pulled it out for us, but I can be finished with this line by the time you're back."

"Yep, I'm on it," I say, thankful to have an excuse to stand from the crouched position I've spent way too long in as I tried to run the bottom line of wire. Grabbing the keys to Seth's truck, I head to the edge of the field and drive down the winding driveway that leads to Hannah's house.

As I walk the path to the front door, I let out a laugh as Leroy lets out a high pitched squeal from his pen and starts chasing his tail, obviously excited about the idea of having a visitor.

"I'm not here to play, bud," I tell him, turning the handle of the front door and rolling my eyes when I find it unlocked. I know she told Seth to walk in, but the idea of her coming home to an empty unlocked house still makes my anxiety rise. Attempting to brush it off, I walk through the house until I reach the kitchen. Crossing the floor and grabbing the lantern, I turn to make my way out when a stack of papers catches my eye. I tell myself that whatever it is is none of my business, but I can't help myself, instead, reaching out and thumbing through them.

I feel my eyes widen as I realize they're all bills, taking in the amounts on each of them and the red "final notice" on the top two. There has to be at least six thousand dollars' worth of bills here, ranging from farm equipment upkeep to Mr. Scott's nursing home expenses.

My gut turns at the thought of Hannah taking all of this on in addition to all her other responsibilities before dropping the bills where I found them and heading outside. My head spins as I try to determine what to make of what I just found. I think back to all the times Caroline's called us several times over the last few months despite Hannah's insistence that she had it covered. I guess that alone should have given me a sign as to how bad things were. Hannah's never been one to ask anyone for anything, and I feel like an idiot for not realizing what was going on sooner.

Shaking my head, I jump back in the truck and head back to where I left Seth, trying to figure out how to help the girl who doesn't want to help—especially not from me.

CHAPTER 19
WILL

SEVEN SUMMERS AGO

"Come on, Will. If you don't hurry, we're gonna miss it," she says as she pulls me to where my trucks parked.

I give her a questioning look before saying, "What the hell are you talking about woman? All you asked for was the check on top pasture before the end of the day. Not sure what part of that adventure we're in the process of missing."

"Well if you don't move your ass, it's not gonna matter," she replies, pushing me past Leroy's pig pen. "Leroy, tell this man to move his butt," she calls out, and her pig sticks his head out of his bed at the sound of his name. "See, even the pig is telling you to hurry!"

I laugh, throwing her the keys to an old farm truck I used to check on the horses this afternoon and letting her drive to wherever we're headed.

"You sure do have a thing for surprises, don't you?" I ask.

"What gave it away?" she teases, pausing when "Get Your Shine On" by Florida Georgia Line comes on the staticky radio. She turns it up, singing along in the most horrendous singing voice I've ever heard while she rolls down the crank window on her side. When the breeze hits her blonde hair, she yanks her ponytail down and wiggles her hips while she drives. I think about reaching out and brushing her hair back, desperate for a reason to touch her, but she looks so carefree, I don't want to do anything to ruin the moment.

It's been three days since I kissed her, but since I didn't work the last two days thanks to the weekend, today's the first time I've seen her. All weekend I fantasized about her, but now that she's in front of me, it's clear that anything I thought about doesn't compare to the real thing. Hannah Scott is the most beautiful girl I've ever seen, and I'm desperate to soak up any part of her that she wants to share with me.

I'm still lost in my thoughts when Hannah slows the truck, pulling to a stop at the top of one of the rolling hills in the middle of the pasture. I raise my eyebrow in question, waiting for her to explain what we're doing, but she just smiles.

"You coming?" she asks, opening her door and jumping to the ground.

"Uh, coming where? We're in the middle of a field, Han," I point out, wondering what in the world she's up to.

"Oh, come on and live a little," she says with a laugh, moving to the back of the truck.

Not wanting to miss whatever it is, I throw my door open and jump out of the truck, following Hannah and waiting to see where she wants to go. But instead of taking off down one of the hills, she just pulls the tailgate down and pats the spot beside her, clearly waiting to see if I'll join her.

Yeah, like I'm gonna pass up an opportunity to be close to her? I don't think so.

I walk over and sit beside her, still waiting for her to explain, but Hannah seems content to sit in silence. I give her a few minutes before finally saying, "So, do you wanna clue me in to what you were so worried about missing?"

She looks over and bumps her shoulder against mine before saying, "Don't you see it?"

"See what?" I ask, not understanding what in the world she's talking about.

She lets out a sigh before turning away from me and gesturing out in front of us. "This, Will. This is what I didn't want to miss."

I look up, expecting to see one of the animals making their way toward us or find something I missed, but all I see is miles of the pasture below us, stretching out from the barn to their farmhouse. I open my mouth to tell her I'm still lost, when I stop, taking in the sights. The sun is setting, casting the sky in shades of pink, orange, and yellow, and the breeze has picked up cooling the summer evening air. In the glow of the sunset, everything almost seems to shimmer, and I take a few minutes to pay attention to everything. From the crickets starting to chirp and the first few lightning bugs start to surround us, causing Hannah's face to light up in excitement.

"I know it's lame, but this is one of my favorite views in the world, and I thought you might want to see that this farm isn't all sweat and cow shit. I know it's a lot of work, but damn, moments like this make it worth it, you know?"

I nod, understanding what she's saying. "It's beautiful, Han. When'd you start sitting out here?" I ask, wanting to know more about her and knowing if we don't keep talking I won't be able to stop myself from kissing her. And as much as I plan to do just that before the night's over, I want her to know I'm not just looking for a cheap hookup. I've spent the last semester at school convincing myself that I wanted to be casual, but it lost its appeal pretty fast.

Hannah shrugs at my question, and I get the impression she's trying to figure out what to say before she finally admits, "I guess about the same time my parents left me here with Gramps a few years ago. Gramps and MiMi were always the best, and I'm honestly grateful I got to grow up here. But I struggled a lot when my parents just up and dipped. So I'd come out here to think and I guess it just became a habit."

She looks embarrassed that she admitted that to me, but I just nod, completely understanding what she's saying. I haven't talked about my dad in years, and before I know it, I hear myself confessing, "God, do I understand that. After my dad left, I didn't really know how to process it. Now, I just developed a temper a mile wide for a bit there, but in hindsight, sitting out in a field and taking in the sunset would have been a better coping mechanism."

That causes Hannah to smile and lean against me, resting her head against the side of my shoulder. "I remember you used to have a bit of a temper in high school. But you seem to have grown out of it."

I laugh at that before saying, "Yeah, you're right. I don't know if you know this, but Huey realized I was spiraling and kinda stepped in to help me get my head back on straight. That man's been much more of a father figure than my sperm donor ever was. He helped me get it together."

"He's such a sweet man," Hannah says before letting out a weak laugh. "You know, now that I think about it, we're really not that different, you and me."

"Oh yeah? Why's that?" I ask, wrapping my arm around her.

"We were both left by the people who were supposed to take care of us. Your dad ran out and my parents dumped me with my gramps just because they didn't feel like dealing with me."

She makes this statement so quietly, I'm almost convinced I made it up, but the look on her face tells me I didn't. I'm not sure what to say to that because she's right.

We sit in silence for a few moments, before I finally say, "Don't take this the wrong way, but your parents are fucking idiots for not realizing what they were missing."

She smiles at that and lets out a small giggle. "Yeah, I was just thinking the same thing about your dad. I just don't get it, you know? I mean I've had a great life, and I just told you how much I like living with Gramps. But I can't shake the feeling that eventually everyone's gonna abandon me."

I sit there, waiting to see if she'll say anything else. Eventually, she just shakes her head and runs her hand through her long hair. "God, I'm being such a downer. I brought you here to show you the sunset and because I hoped we could talk. But instead, I'm whining about things that happened years ago."

I can tell she's about to pull away from me, but I pull her tighter and whisper in her ear, "Thank you for telling me that, Hannah. I get it. I really do. But at least for the summer, I'm here and I'm not going anywhere. So what do you say we have some fun?"

"Hmmm, I like the sound of that," she whispers, leaning into me. "What did you have in mind?"

I pretend to be deep in thought before saying, "I don't know. You have any ideas?"

"Why don't we try this one?" she says before leaning in and kissing me hard. I'd worried I spent too much time this weekend building up the kiss we shared in our head, but one taste from her and I know that's a lie. It's just as good as the last one and I lose myself in her, kissing her and wondering who in the hell can let a girl like this go?

CHAPTER 20
HANNAH

"Okay, that's it for today. Make sure you come prepared for your test on the cell cycle. I'll see y'all tomorrow," I call out to my fifth period as the bell rings signaling the end of class.

A few students linger, asking me about the study guide I sent out until I finally have to shoo them out of the room to make sure they aren't late for their next class. As they leave, I pull my door closed and turn out the lights, desperate for a few minutes of quiet after the review game I've spent the day playing with my classes. I love incorporating fun activities into my lessons for engagement, but days like today tend to drain me more than usual.

It's been a few weeks since Homecoming, but I still feel like I've been spreading myself as thin as possible. Between competing and winning regionals with our squad and back-to-back football games, I've felt like I'm living at the school and the mid-school year slump is hitting me harder than normal.

After sitting in silence for a few minutes, I take a minute to check the spreadsheet Caroline helped me make to keep up with all the farm expenses and smile when I see that I've managed to chip away a little each week. I still feel like I'm drowning in bills, but I got a call last week that by some miracle the cost of Gramp's services had been lowered and I finally feel like I can breathe. Without that added cost, I'll be able to catch up with the bank, which takes care of the biggest chunk of debt. Caroline also convinced me to reach out to a few of the local places, and they agreed to let me use a payment plan, so while there's still a good bit of expenses, I don't feel quite as stressed.

After making sure everything's in order, I force myself to grab my planner, knowing I need to finish my lesson plans for next week. I'm flipping through the pages to find the right page when I hear a knock on my door.

I let out a groan and pray it's not Principal Hale asking me to cover for one of our classes without subs before making my way to the door. I open it, blinking back my surprise when I see Will standing in front of me.

"Hey, uh, what's up?" I ask him skeptically, knowing he tends to spend all his time in his office at the field house.

"Hey, I need you to sign off on some of these purchase orders for the state cheer competition. And I also need proof everyone's signed waivers and had physicals so I can turn it in to the state," he answers, holding out a stack of papers for me to take.

"Okay, I don't mind, but you do know Caroline normally does this, right?" I ask.

"Yeah, I'm aware. But she's out today, and I need it turned in now. So can you do it or not?"

"Chill, yes, I've got it. Give me just a sec," I tell him, turning back to walk to my desk. He follows me over, and the quiet click of the door locking behind him is deafening in the small room. I try not to let my nerves show, reminding myself that he's just here because he's the athletic director in addition to his coaching responsibilities, but the fact that we haven't been alone together since that summer has me feeling more on edge than normal.

I grab a pen off my desk and make quick work of signing the paperwork, pushing them toward him when I'm finished. He takes them from me, but he doesn't say anything as he waits for me to pull up my school laptop and print the waivers we keep on file for the girls. I send them to print and lean over when I grab them, growling as my printer jams for the third time this week.

"You've got to be kidding me," I groan, flipping the lid and hoping to see the paper causing the problem sticking out so I can get this man out of my room, but since the universe obviously hates me, that's not in the cards today.

"What's the matter?" Will asks, leaning over to follow my gaze to the printer that's obviously out to ruin my life.

"The damn thing's jammed again. I swear this thing is such a piece of junk," I answer, opening the back panel and looking for the problem.

"Here, watch out, let me look," he says, rising, and I feel him move behind me as he examines the printer over my head. My arm grazes his, and I feel my heart start to beat erratically. Sis, what the hell? I chide myself, frustrated at my body's response to him.

I move away, desperate to get away from him to get hold on where my thoughts definitely shouldn't be going. Will fiddles with the machine for a few minutes until it finally starts to spit out the paperwork he needs, and I don't know if I want to sigh in relief or mourn the fact that he's about to leave.

"Thanks," I murmur, shuffling my feet and stacking the papers as they shoot out, trying to look busy as we stand in awkward silence. God, I hate this. When it comes to anyone else, I feel confident and sure of myself, but there's something about being around Will that makes me feel like my world isn't sitting quite right on its axis.

After a few moments of standing in silence, all the paper-work he asked for is done printing, and I reach out, holding it up to him. Our fingers graze lightly as he grabs them, and I feel the familiar jolt of electricity run through my body whenever he's close. Afraid he'll realize how he's affecting me, I turn my back to him, planning to ignore his presence until he leaves.

"Han, I—" he starts, and the sincerity in those two words causes my breath to catch in my throat. It's been years since I heard anything except anger and annoyance in his tone, but the way he just said my name wasn't that at all. I'm anxious to hear what he was about to say, waiting for him to continue when the bell signaling the end of my planning period rings. The abrupt sound breaks me out of the trance I was in, and I hear kids start to move through the hallways. Thankful for the distraction, I jump up and run to the door, flinging it open and hoping he'll take the hint that I can't do this right now.

"Good afternoon. Come on in and grab your journals for the bell-ringer," I call out as a group of students make their way into my room.

From my spot at the door I hear one of the boys yell, "Coach Will! What are you doing here?"

Will chuckles before responding, "You do remember I work here right?"

"Yeah, but you don't ever leave the field house," one of his players responds.

"I'll have you know I have to do things other than create plays and watch film, okay? The whole athletic director job does take up some of my time every now and again," he responds sarcastically.

From my spot at the door, I can't hear exactly what the boys say back, but it makes Will laugh, and I strain my ears to listen to whatever they say next. They murmur back and forth before I hear Will say, "And not that it's any of your business, but since the cheerleaders are advancing to State, I needed some paperwork from Miss Hannah."

"Oh, bummer," one girl chimes in. "I thought maybe you had a crush on Miss Hannah and came by to say hi."

"Susie, I know you're new here, but Miss Hannah and Coach Will fight like cats and dogs. Even we know that. They basically hate each other. There's no way they'd ever end up together," one of the boys responds, and several of the other students laugh at that.

The bell rings and I move back into the room, and Will and I make eye contact as he moves toward the door, his usual detached look back on his face. And as he shuts the door behind him, all I can think is I wish that I could hate him as much as everyone else thinks I do.

CHAPTER 21
WILL

know, Huey, you're right," I say, pressing my phone against my ear as I look down at the mess of wires from the old fence I just cut down at Falling Oaks Farm. "I'm sorry, but since we're in the playoffs, I haven't had a single damn moment... You're right... Okay, yeah... Okay, see you then."

I shake my head as I hang up, rolling my eyes at Huey's insistence on making sure that I'm taking care of myself. We normally grab a beer a couple times a month, but over the last few weeks, pretty much every moment has been spent in my office or on the football field. I know I need to chill, but I really think we've got a shot at state this year, and I've become pretty focused on that.

But here you are working on Hannah's fence in the damn dark instead of watching film or doing any of the shit I need to do around the apartment I share with Seth, my subconscious reminds me, and as much as I want to ignore it, I know it's true. Ever since I found that stack of bills a few weeks ago, she's been on my mind even more than normal. I've told myself it's just because I care about the farm and her grandfather, but I know that's not the truth. It's really not about the money at all. It just makes me angry to think of her struggling with all of that on her own.

Which is how I'd ended up on the phone with the billing department for the nursing home and covering the costs of Arthur's stay for the next two months. Part of me still wondered what I'd been thinking, but I pushed it aside, knowing it was the right decision, despite making the nurse promise not to tell anyone what I'd done.

Turning back to the fence, I blow out a breath as I grimace at the mess I managed to make before my phone rang. Seth and Theo both had other plans tonight, so I came by myself, telling myself that I needed to help get some of the project knocked out. But if I'm honest, I think I came here because I haven't been able to stop thinking about Hannah. Since that summer, she hasn't been far from my mind, but over the last few weeks, this shit's gotten out of control, and I feel like a man obsessed. But really, the joke's on me because when I went to grab the materials from the barn, I realized she wasn't even home, and now I feel like an even bigger idiot than before.

Shaking my head to remind myself to get back to work, I grab the new fencing and hold it up, trying to maneuver the heavy wire roll by myself. *Fuck, I did not think this shit through at all.* After a few minutes, I'm cursing and ready to say fuck it, but I know I can't leave this huge damn hole in the fence so I've got to figure something out.

I'm debating calling Huey back to see if he can ride over and help me when I see a pair of headlights pull down the driveway. Between the glow of my headlights I'm using to give me enough light to fix the fence and the ones coming down the drive, I can't see the car, but I know no one else should be coming this way, so I throw my arm up, waving Hannah down. Her car slows to a stop, and she steps out of the car, squinting in my direction.

"Will? What the heck are you doing?" she asks, walking toward me and reaching out to help me hold the awkward roll of wire.

"Um, did you forget we're redoing your entire fence, Han?" I ask, leaning down and attaching the new wire to the post.

"Of course I didn't. God, you're such a smart ass. I meant why are you out here by yourself in the dark? I mean, I'm not complaining…but this fence is decades old, an extra day or two isn't gonna hurt it," she says, moving to help me stretch the roll so it's easier to attach.

"Just thought I'd get some of this knocked out," I mumble, trying to change the topic. We work in comfortable silence for a few moments, until I try to move around her the way I need to, and I catch a whiff of her familiar vanilla scent. Suddenly, the fence is the last thing on my mind and all I can think about is pressing her hot skin against me. She moves closer, trying to make sure the wire is straight, and her mouth hovers close enough to mine that I feel her breath against my cheek.

I shift, without even thinking, until our mouths are centimeters away from each other, and we both freeze, waiting to see if either of us will breach the short distance. We stay like that for a long moment, and just when I'm about to say fuck it, I catch some movement out of the corner of my eye. Both of us turn to see one of the cows walking over, inspecting the work we're doing. It's nothing out of the norm around here, but it's enough to ruin the moment we're having and I want to growl in frustration.

"Hey, Cletus," Hannah coos, reaching out and patting the bull's head. "Buddy, whatcha doing, huh?" She steps closer and wraps her arms around the animal's neck, and I have the fleeting thought that I'm really fucking losing it because I'm jealous that a cow's getting her attention rather than me.

"Jesus, Hannah. You do realize that these aren't little pets. That bull weighs over three thousand pounds, and you just dote on him like he couldn't trample you in a fucking second," I sneer, sounding much more annoyed than I intended.

"Will, I swear. You act like I don't know how to run this place. Newsflash, I can. Spending a few weeks here that summer doesn't mean you know every damn thing. I don't need your help for fucking everything," she growls, and we both stop because it's the first time either of us has referenced anything that happened that summer since the night she tore it all to shit in my truck.

We stare at each other for a moment, and I think she's going to finally acknowledge the way we used to be but instead, she just turns back to the bull. "Plus, Cletus would never hurt me, would you baby? No, you know you're my favorite, don't you? I know, but don't tell the others I said that."

Turning my back to her, I make quick work of finishing up the section of fence line I tore down earlier and throw all the tools in the bucket they were stored in. There's really no reason for me to still be standing here, but I can't force myself to leave. Between visiting her in her room at school today and now, this is the first time in years we've been alone, and I can't ignore the desire I have to try to force her to talk to me. This secret between us has been like a cancer, spreading through our lives and keeping us both from moving on. I open my mouth, trying to decide what to say, but just before I start, her phone rings.

She steps back from where she was still petting Cletus and answers. "Hey, Caroline. The paper with the new counts for those stunts? Yeah, it's in my backpack from practice. Let me grab it."

And just like that, she walks away, barely throwing a hand up in my direction as she heads to the house. Shaking my head, I grab my tools and throw them in the truck, pausing when I realize the spot in the driveway looks familiar. I push down the pang in my chest as I stare at the place that used to be ours, before turning and slamming the tailgate closed in frustration.

God, how the hell did we fuck this up so bad?

CHAPTER 22
WILL

God, this feels like a bad idea.

It's after eleven and I'm sitting halfway down the driveway to Hannah's house, waiting for her to sneak out and meet me. Tomorrow is her twenty-first birthday, and when I'd told her I wanted to start the day with her, she'd immediately suggested a late-night date by the creek.

Part of me feels ridiculous, acting like a couple of high schoolers when I'm about to start my senior year of college, but I have to admit that there's something a little exciting about sneaking around with her. In reality, I know her gramps really wouldn't care, but telling him we were spending time outside of work would also come with more questions. Plus, he's technically my boss for the summer, so I can't help feeling like we might be playing with fire.

But, judging by the fact that I haven't been able to stop thinking about Hannah since I started, I don't think I really care if I get burned. Something about these last few days have been a special type of torture. If I'm really honest, I have to admit that I'm falling fast for this girl, and I don't know what to do about it. The more time I spend with her, the more I want to know about her. Not to mention the fact that she's hot as hell and the way she's kissed me has had all sorts of fantasies running through my head.

Before I can let that train of thought go for too long, I see Hannah running toward my truck in the moonlight, and I can't help but smile when she jumps in the truck and immediately leans over to plant a quick kiss on my mouth.

"Hey, birthday girl," I tell her, smiling as I reach out to pull her to me, wanting another taste of her, but she pulls back and winks in my direction.

"Uh-uh. Not too fast. If we start all that up here, I won't want to stop. Let's get down to the creek, then we'll see about another kiss," she teases, before leaning over and dropping another peck on my cheek.

I let out a groan before turning on the truck, leaving the headlights off as I turn off the drive and cut through one of the pastures to avoid getting too close to the house. We sit in comfortable silence for a few minutes as we bump through the fields until I can't stand it. Keeping my eyes on the field, I reach out and pull her across the front seat of my ancient crew cab Ford. She slides across eagerly, sliding herself under my arm and leaning against me as I drive.

"So, where'd you tell your mom you were off to?" she asks, sliding her hand across my lap to pull herself closer to me.

"Just told her I was going to see some friends. Honestly, with all four of my siblings, she's got her hands full," I tell her, slowing as I pull through the opening of the trees to get to the pond.

"I bet. How are your siblings? Gosh, I bet they're so old now."

"Yeah, it still catches me off guard sometimes. They're good. Ollie's getting ready for his senior year, and then Andrew and Luke are starting their sophomore year, and Kit's about to be in the ninth grade."

"That's wild. I know they're happy to have you home for the summer," she says, and I nod.

"I guess so. You know the middle three are typical teenagers so I don't know that they're happy about much of anything, but I've enjoyed it. We've tried to do dinner all together at least once a week despite everyone having an incredibly busy schedule, and I've enjoyed spending time with them. At least Kit's always excited to see me."

"I remember when she used to dress up in a little Springside cheerleading outfit and cheer with us at the games. She is so precious," Hannah says, and I laugh at the memory.

"God, I remember that. Mom used to have to bribe her to take the stupid thing off long enough to wash the grass stains out."

We both laugh at that as I pull up at the creek and back my truck in so we can sit on the tailgate and look out at the water. As soon as I'm parked, Hannah's jumping out of the truck and kicking off her shoes to dip her feet in the dark water.

"Damn, Han. You know there could be snakes in there right?" I ask, shaking my head and grabbing the blankets, and a few things I brought to surprise her.

"Oh, come on. Don't be such a grandpa," she teases, splashing some water in the direction of the truck.

The moon is full in the sky above us, and the way it casts a glow on the water and the woman in front of me is probably my new favorite sight. She continues splashing in the water and humming to herself as I set the blankets across the tailgate and pull out the birthday cake I got from the Piggly Wiggly to surprise her with and the bottle of champagne I grabbed to pair with it.

After a few minutes, Hannah looks up and must notice that I'm up to something because she starts to make her way over, asking, "What are you up to over here? Don't tell me you–"

Whatever teasing retort she was about to make immediately

dies on her lips, and her mouth opens as she looks at everything that's spread in front of us.

"Oh my God, Will! What the hell is all of this?" she asks, and I smile at the surprised tone of her voice.

"I wanted to surprise you. It's not every day that you turn twenty-one," I tell her, and I look over at her, expecting her to tease me about this being cheesy or lame. But instead, I'm caught off guard when I see tears filling her eyes.

"Whoa, whoa, what's the matter, Han? Did I do something wrong?" I ask, immediately regretting this whole thing. I should've known was probably a stupid fucking idea.

"Wrong?" Hannah asks, letting out a watery laugh. "Are you kidding? This is the nicest thing anyone's ever done for me!"

I look down at the cake and wine in front of her and the two small presents I have set off to the side and shake my head. "You don't have to try to make me feel better, Hannah. I didn't mean to—" I start, trying to figure out what to say when she runs at me, throwing her entire body into me, and I stop talking, just pulling her to me.

"The last three years that I lived with my parents, they didn't even remember my birthday. There were no presents, no cards, no cake, and definitely no party like the rest of my friends. And then when I moved in with Gramps, he and my MiMi would always make sure I had something I liked for dinner and they'd put a little bit of money away for my college fund. But never anything like this," she says, waving at the setup in front of us.

I sit there for a moment, not sure what to say before she leans back and kisses me hard. "Thank you, Will. Seriously, this is so special."

"You're welcome," I tell her, still trying to get over my surprise. Our birthday celebrations definitely got a lot smaller after Dad left and Mom had to save every penny she could, but she's always gone out of the way to make the day special for my siblings and me. "So, you want cake or presents first?"

"Presents?" she asks, looking around the tailgate until her

eyes land on the boxes I attempted to wrap at home earlier. "You didn't have to get me anything, Will. But I do love the Christmas paper."

"Hey now, that's all I could find at home okay?" I say with a laugh.

"It's perfect. And where on earth did you find a cake?" she asks, already reaching across the bed of the truck for the presents.

"The Pig. I didn't have them put your name on it because I knew that'd definitely start the rumor mill, but I wanted to surprise you."

"Well, you certainly accomplished that," she says, holding up one of the boxes. "So, can I open this one?"

"Go ahead," I tell her, sitting beside her and leaning against the side of the truck and smiling as she tears into the box like a kid on Christmas morning.

She laughs as she pulls out a pair of cheap, plastic champagne flutes that say "Pop the bubbles, it's my birthday" on them I found while I was picking up the cake. "For your first legal drink," I tell her, grabbing the bottle of champagne I brought and popping the top to pour us each a glass.

"Okay, wait, forget the cake. Where the hell did you find champagne in Springside?" she asks, reaching out and taking the glass from me.

"Surprisingly, also at the Pig. But honestly, it was on sale for four dollars a bottle, so my hopes aren't super high," I tell her sheepishly, and we both laugh at that.

We both take a sip, and wince. "Shit, that stuff's terrible," I say, sputtering at the taste.

Hannah laughs harder at that. "It's not that bad. Definitely better than the cheap liquor from the frat parties. Plus, it's the thought that counts."

"Okay, whatever you say," I say, sitting my flute to the side and grabbing the other present. "Go ahead and open this one."

She takes it from me, and tears into it much like she did the other present. She's grinning as she tears into it, but as soon as she opens the small black box, her eyes widen and she looks up at me, "Will, what the hell is this?"

She pulls out the silver necklace with the small ruby pendant I picked out from the jewelry store in Saddle Ridge and just stares between me and the necklace.

"The guy said a ruby is your birthstone, and I just thought you'd like it," I tell her, suddenly feeling vulnerable at the way she's not saying anything.

"Will, this is the most beautiful thing I've ever seen," she says, and my stomach sinks as I see tears in her eyes again. "But it's way too much."

"Well, too bad. I wanted to surprise you, so you're just gonna have to deal," I tell her, trying to cheer her up.

She opens her mouth to protest again, but I pull her to me and silence her with another kiss. "So, I think it's about time for some birthday cake?"

She rolls her eyes at my clear attempt to change the subject and just nods before saying softly, "Thank you, Will. You seriously don't know how much this means to me."

I kiss the top of her head softly and murmur, "Of course. I just wanted to make you smile. Happy birthday, Han."

And as she kisses me back, I realize there isn't much I wouldn't do for this girl.

CHAPTER 23
HANNAH

'm gonna make you feel so good, baby," he growls in my ear, coming up from behind me and wrapping his hands around me. He pushes me against the kitchen counter, tracing his fingers up my leg under my skirt until he reaches my panties.

Pulling them to the side, he starts to tease me, barely even touching me as he runs his fingers up and down my core. He continues for a moment, ghosting his fingers everywhere but never applying the pressure he knows I want.

"Will, please," I pant, throwing my head back against his shoulder and rolling my hips, trying to force him to stop teasing me.

Instead of giving me what I want, he pulls back and presses a kiss to my neck before biting me softly, causing me to moan. "Uh-uh-uh, you promised you were mine, but then you ran off on me. But you're mine again, so you're gonna be a good girl and take what I give you. Do you understand?"

My body heats at his words, and I open my mouth to say something smart, but instead, he turns me around and kisses me hard, cutting off whatever I was about to say.

With me facing him, he snakes his hand between us and wraps one of my legs around his hip, pulling his body flush against mine so that I can feel how hard he is for me.

"Fuck, angel, I can't wait to be inside you again. You're gonna feel so fucking good," he whispers, resuming his teasing.

My legs start to shake with the desperation I feel, needing him to give me more, but he continues, kissing me hard until finally, he grazes my clit. I let out a loud moan and wrap my leg around his hip to pull him closer. Giving in, he starts to slide his fingers in and out of me, leaning down and groaning. "God, I've missed this."

"Will," I moan, feeling my orgasm start to build. "Please don't stop."

He continues to fuck me with his fingers, kissing my neck hard until he stops and pulls back to murmurs, "Tell me you're mine, Hannah."

"I—I—" I moan, lost to the climax that seems just out of reach.

"Come on, baby. You want to come? Just say it."

"I'm yours. I'm yours. I'm sorry, just, please," I tell him, rolling my hips as his fingers start to slide in and out again, until my body tenses and I'm right there...

Beep. Beep. Beep.

I wake with a start, gasping as I realize what just happened. There's no fucking way I just had a sex dream about Will Thompson. That hasn't happened in years, but between feeling like my heart's gonna beat out of my damn chest and the desire running through my veins, there's no denying that it did.

Determined to forget about it, I throw myself out of bed and stomp into the bathroom to get ready for the day. After I'm dressed in a pair of jeans and a sweatshirt, I pull my hair into a messy ponytail and throw on an old Springside High baseball hat before making my way to the kitchen. As I'm fixing Ruby's bottle, I start to feel my mind drifting back to my dream, but just when I remember how real his fingers felt as they brushed across my clit, a flash of red and pink catches my eye outside, and it hits me that something's off.

"There's no fucking way," I whisper to myself, squinting out the window and continuing to stare for a minute before grabbing Ruby's bottle and walking outside.

I make my way over to the temporary pen I built last week until Ruby was strong enough to go back and socialize in the pastures, and stop when I realize I wasn't hallucinating.

Looking down at the pen, I see Ruby curled up, sleeping on the hay like she normally does. But unlike all the other mornings, she's not by herself. Instead, Leroy is laying his head on Ruby's hip, snoozing away without a care in the world.

"You two have gotta be shitting me," I say with a laugh, reaching out and patting them both on their sides gently to wake them up. "Rise and shine, my little troublemakers."

Both of them stand and start to nuzzle into my hand, causing me to laugh when they move with such excitement. I've got to admit it looks like they both resemble overeager puppies wagging their tail as opposed to farm animals.

"Here, Ruby girl, I've got your food right here. Leroy, you're gonna have to wait okay?" I coo at him, gently pushing his huge frame out of the way so I can start to feed Ruby. Instead of moving, he blows out a breath in my direction and comes over to plop down by my feet.

"I know, this is just such an inconvenience, isn't it, big boy?" I say to him as Ruby starts to eat from the bottle in my outstretched hand. "But really, how in the world did you manage this one? I mean out of one cage and into another? For an animal without thumbs, you sure are a crafty son of a bitch."

At my question, the pig looks at me before turning his body over and offering me his tummy, waiting for me to pet him. I laugh at him, murmuring, "I swear to God, Leroy, I don't know what the hell I did that made you think you were a damn dog, but sometimes, it's a little fucking weird."

Continuing to feed the calf, I shake my head and look around the pen, trying to put together the way Leroy managed to pull this off. My eyes land upon a pile of dirt on one side of the enclosure I built for Ruby, showing me where Leroy clearly used his snoot to dig a hole large enough for him to fit through to wiggle his way in.

"Mischievous little fucker," I murmur under my breath as Ruby finishes her breakfast. Pulling the bottle away, I reach out and nuzzle her nose, giving her some attention as she wiggles happily under my hand. After a moment, Leroy stands and joins her, the both of them rubbing against each other and letting me pet them.

"You two are so silly," I tell them with a laugh. "Come on, Leroy, let's get you back to your pen."

Both Ruby and Leroy glare at me, as they lay down, cuddling their bodies together in a clear sign of defiance. Rolling my eyes, I throw my hands in the air and shake my head. "Fine. I don't have time for your nonsense today. I guess you can stay here. I'm sure Leroy will find his way back if he wants to anyway. I don't know what I'm gonna do with either of you."

Grabbing Ruby's empty bottle, I turn and relock the gate before heading inside. After checking the clock, I realize I only have twenty minutes before I need to leave, so I head back to the bathroom, throw on some makeup, and yank the hat off my head, twisting my hair in a bun and hoping it looks presentable.

Running out of my room, I grab my backpack and an energy drink from the fridge before heading out to my car. Just as I'm sliding in the front seat, I hear my phone ping with a text. Throwing the car in drive, I reach around the side pocket of my bag where I'd dropped my cell earlier, pulling it out to check my texts while I speed down the driveway.

> CAROLINE: I don't know about y'all, but I'm so excited about tonight.

> MARGARET: Same! I can't believe it's been months since we were last at Boot Scooters! Maybe I'll have better luck finding a man to spin me around this time.

I laugh at my friend's usual chaos and throw my phone in the cupholder as I race to school. By the time I pull into the parking lot, there's a long thread of texts, both the girls talking about outfits and logistics. Tucking my phone in my pocket, I rush into the building barely making it inside on time, and unlock my door before throwing my bag down. After making sure everything is ready for the day, I pull out my phone to respond to my friends.

> HANNAH: I'm excited, but I can't believe that Will is dragging us to a high school football game on the first Friday in months that we haven't had a game.

> MARGARET: I know, but I think it'll be fun. The boys agreed to leave early, so we'll be ready to dance by nine.

> CAROLINE: Yeah, it'll be fine! Plus, I'm pretty sure the game in Saddle Ridge is the only way we convinced the boys to drive us. We're really just lucky that Pike's Corner got caught with ineligible players this late in the season and gave us a bye for the playoffs this week.

> HANNAH: Okay, okay, fine. You're right. But I don't have to like it.

> CAROLINE: Relax, Han, you just need to blow off some steam tonight. Are you SURE you don't want to reconsider inviting Kent? I bet he'd love to come.

I roll my eyes at my best friend's not-so-subtle attempt at matchmaking. I told her after the bonfire that Kent asked for my number and asked to go out sometime, but I just couldn't do it. He's such a nice guy, but no matter how much I want to, I don't feel a spark and I don't want to lead him on.

> HANNAH: *eye roll* I'm good, thanks. I just want a night out with my girls. I'll see y'all around 5!

After pressing send, I throw my phone down just as the bell for homeroom rings, and students start piling into my room.

Grabbing my Expo marker and my computer, I stand to take roll, and add the bell ringer on the board before turning and smiling at my seniors. "All right, guys. Happy Friday. Let's get started."

"OH MY GOSH, what a game! Saddle Ridge is definitely gonna give us a run for our money next week," Caroline says, wrapping her arm around me and Margaret as we walk out of Saddle Ridge's stadium. We convinced the boys to leave at the end of the third quarter since Saddle Ridge was up by four touchdowns, meaning our biggest rivals will be heading to Springside for the next round of playoffs this week.

"Yeah, yeah, you're right, but that's the boys' problem, not ours. And I don't know about either of you, but I'm ready to dance!" I say, shimmying my shoulders and causing Margaret and Caroline to giggle.

After a short walk to Will's truck, we pile in to make the short drive over to our favorite dive bar. Line dancing under the neon signs to nineties country music always makes me feel like all my problems fade away for just a little while.

"Let's go, girls," I say, grabbing their arms and pulling them inside with me, leaving the boys to follow behind us. Before we make it inside, I can already hear "Sold" by John Michael Montgomery blaring through the speakers, and the smell of beer and grease from the kitchen makes me feel like I'm back in college heading out for a night with my friends.

As we walk inside, Caroline pauses and turns back to the boys. "We're going to the bathroom. Can you get us drinks and we'll meet you over there?"

Theo nods, and Caroline pulls us through the packed dance floor. After finding the dark bathroom and freshening our lipstick, we make our way back over to where Theo, Will, and Seth are leaning against the bar holding out a beer to each of us. I take a long sip, moving my shoulders to the beat of "Copperhead Road" before grabbing Margaret's hand and pulling her to the dance floor to join the line dance.

"Hannah, I don't know what the hell I'm doing," she says with a laugh, trying to catch on to the footwork. I see Caroline and the boys laughing at her as I start calling out the steps for her to pick up on. "I swear, I always feel like I missed out on a class in high school or something when we come here."

I laugh at her sarcasm as Caroline comes over to join us, kicking and turning with us. After a moment, the band comes on stage and starts playing a newer release, and everyone starts to disperse, some still dancing and singing on the dance floor while others move to get a drink or return to a table. Caroline, Margaret, and I move closer to the stage, singing at the top of our lungs while we sip on our beers. Theo comes up behind Caroline, wrapping his arms around her. I lose track of time as I sing and dance along to the music with my best friends until the others hold up their drinks and motion that they need another.

"I'll grab you one if you save our spot," Caroline yells over the sounds of "Neon Moon" blasting throughout the bar, and I nod in agreement as they make their way toward the bar.

They haven't been gone long when the music changes to a slower song and everyone starts to slow dance around me. I scoot up, trying to get out of the way when a man walks up, holding out his hand to ask me to dance. I take him in, rolling my eyes when I see the way he's dressed like he's going to church and not a dive bar, but eventually decide to say fuck it and give him a chance. Placing my hand in his, he immediately tries to spin me, catching me off guard and almost causing me to stumble.

We continue to sway to the music with him stepping on my feet every few steps until he pulls back to take a sip of his beer. In the process, he steps on my foot again and stumbles, pouring beer all down the front of my pink sweater. For fuck's sake, is this guy for real?

Normally, I'd tell this guy to get lost, but I just don't have the energy to risk making a scene tonight. Hoping my friends will be back soon, I try to tamp down my frustration. I let my mind briefly imagine that he was someone else, but as always, it doesn't work and I'm left feeling empty.

CHAPTER 24
WILL

The music shifts, and I watch the band perform on the stage in front of the room. I lose myself in the music for a few minutes, before looking around as something catches my eye across the room.

The first thing I notice is the sight of Hannah's neon pink sweater, and I start to smile at the way she's dancing around until I realize she isn't alone. Instead, a man I don't recognize is holding out his hand, pulling her closer to him as the song speeds up.

You've got to be fucking kidding me. First Kent and now this?

I feel like fire's coming out of my ears, and I struggle to get a hold of myself. On the dance floor in front of me, Hannah stays pressed against another man as he pulls her hips to him and moves to the beat. Where the fuck did Margaret and Caroline go? And why the hell is she dancing with a man who looks like he belongs on Wall Street. The asshole is wearing a button-up to a dive bar, for fuck's sake.

The rational part of my brain reminds myself that I have no claim on Hannah Scott, but I can't seem to calm myself down from the jealousy racing through me.

Finally, after watching him spill his beer all down the front of her sweater, my resolve snaps. Unable to stop myself, I stride over, reaching out for her arm and pulling her toward me.

"What the fuck, Will," she cries out, while the man she was dancing with holds up his hands in a sign of surrender before stepping aside and lets me pull her away.

"Sorry, man, I thought she was single," he says, ignoring the beautiful girl in front of us who scowls at him before walking off in search of another woman to dance with.

What an idiot, I think to myself, ignoring her protests as I pull her outside so we can talk before murmuring in her ear. "Chill out, Han."

"Don't tell me what to do! Let me go," she growls, trying to jerk her hand from my grasp but I ignore her and continue pulling her toward my truck. "God, you have some fucking audacity, Will. I know you hate me, but can I really not just have fun with my friends?"

"First of all, I don't see your friends around, Han. I saw some dickwad who you would tear to shreds in two minutes if you weren't trying to be nice. I mean really, he spilled his beer all over your shirt, for fuck's sake," I say before realizing what she just said. I pause, pushing her against the cab of my truck and asking, "What do you mean I hate you?"

"Will, are you serious? We've barely been able to be in the same room for the last few years without arguing. I know you don't want me to be happy, but damn. Just let me go. I was having fun, and I want to be able to dance with my friends."

I glare at her for a moment, refusing to back away and give her some space. *God, we're a fucking mess.* I shake my head, glaring at the woman who has been the center of almost every fantasy I've had over the last seven years and try to process what she just said. This beautiful, headstrong, smart-ass woman standing in front of me like she has no idea how much I fucking want her. She legitimately thinks I hate her and don't want her to be happy? I know we've had our differences and we argue more than two people should, but I've always thought she knew that deep down I cared about her. Plus, it's not my fault she ended us that summer…

I study her, waiting for her to say something else, but she just glares at me, crossing her arms over her chest. She's serious, I realize, and I feel like the biggest idiot in the world. Yes, we've argued, and yes, she completely broke my heart when she walked out on me that summer with no explanation, but I never wanted her to be this fucking unhappy.

To be fair, the thought of her happy with another man makes me pissed as hell, but I don't say that. Instead, I look down at her, caged under my arms as I press her against my truck. Her body shifts and brushes against mine, her eyes widening when she grazes against my hard length.

Unable to stop myself, I lean in and whisper against her ear, soaking in the feeling of having her near me. "Does that feel like I hate you, Han? You can call me all the names you want, but I've never stopped wanting you."

Her breath catches at my words, and she shifts closer to me again, trailing her hand down my front.

I know we're playing with fire, but I can't find it in myself to care. If playing with fire means I get to have her back, I'll burn the whole fucking world down. She's all I've thought about since she stormed out seven years ago, and the feel of her in my arms feels like heaven. I trail my nose against her throat, soaking in her vanilla perfume.

"What if I don't want you?" she questions breathlessly, still teasing my chest with her fingers.

"You can pretend all you want, but you and I both know that isn't true. But if you want to pretend, I won't kiss you until you're begging for my mouth on yours," I whisper, leaning in closer to tease my mouth down her neck.

"Fuck you, Will. I've never begged for a damn thing in my life and I'm not about to start now," she growls, jerking back from me.

"That's fine," I tell her with a smirk. "Then go on back there and dance with whoever the hell that asshole was and when I drop you off tonight, you can use those sweet fingers to get yourself off wishing it was me."

She leans back, shocked at the turn this conversation's taking, but she doesn't push me away. Instead, she presses her hips back into mine, keeping her torso pulled back to see my face. "Yeah, like I need your little dick to make me come."

"Hannah, let's be real here. You can say whatever you want, but we both know that every time I was inside you, you were screaming my name," I whisper, and she moves her hips a little against my cock, feeling how much I want her. She lets out a breathy moan and it's all I can do to keep my promise not to kiss her.

"Will," she says, wrapping her leg around me and pulling me closer. I lean down and ghost my mouth against her neck, never quite touching her the way she wants.

"When's the last time someone made you feel good, Hannah?" I ask against her neck. I don't know what the fuck we're doing, but I know I never want to stop.

Her eyes widen in alarm and she stammers, ""That's—that's none of your damn business."

"Fine, you want to know the last time I fucked someone? Or the last time I let someone wrap their lips around my dick? Or the last time I tasted someone's sweet pussy?"

She moans, continuing to rub against me, before shaking her head. I lean in closer and whisper in her ear, "Seven years ago, baby. I haven't touched another woman since you walked out on me that summer, and I don't give a fuck if you claim you don't want me. I know the truth. And if you just want sex, that's fine. Use me, baby, because I'm fucking desperate for you."

She whimpers at my confession before pulling back, her eyes full of surprise before groaning, "Fuck it!"

And before I can stop her, she launches herself at me, wrapping her legs around my waist, and kissing me hard.

CHAPTER 25
HANNAH

Our mouths collide and I groan at the feeling of finally tasting him again. I might not be able to have all of him after everything that happened, but if he's offering this, I'm sure as fuck going to take it.

Part of my brain tries to remind me that the reason I ended things hasn't gone away, but I tamp that down, refusing to acknowledge it right now.

Without breaking contact with my mouth he reaches around and grabs my ass, hoisting me up against him. He pulls back just a bit and sends me one of his signature smirks, before whispering against my ear. "I thought I told you to beg, Hannah."

"Fuck that, Will," I say, pulling him in and kissing him again. "Don't even try to act like you don't want this as much as I do. Now kiss me before I realize how much of a mistake this probably is."

At my words, I see his eyes darken in the low light from the street light above us before he's back, kissing me with even more ferocity. He nips at my lip, and I roll my hips against his hard length between us, moaning as he hits me the way I'm craving, even through the fabric between us.

If I come like this, I'm pretty sure he'll never let me live it down, I think briefly before deciding I couldn't care less, pushing the thought from my mind and wrapping my arms around his neck.

"Does that feel good, baby?" he asks, lifting my hips and helping me move against him faster. "You want to come like this, or you want more?"

"More," I moan, pulling his mouth back to mine.

Fuck yes.

"This doesn't mean anything, though. We just fuck as many times as we need to to get whatever the hell this is out of our system. No drama, no feelings, and no one has to know," I say, knowing I'm fucked as soon as I suggest it. Is it really what I want? No. But it's better than nothing, and it's all I can give him right now.

I think I see a flash of hurt in Will's eyes at my suggestion, but as soon as I notice it, it's gone and I tell myself I must have imagined it. He doesn't reply at first, kissing me hard and running his hand under my shirt to pinch my nipple through my bra.

"God, Will, please," I beg, feeling the zap of electricity go straight to my core at the way he's touching me.

"I got you, baby," he whispers, nipping my neck while continuing to drive me wild with his fingers and the friction from rubbing against his cock.

Just as the words leave his mouth, a car pulls out of one of the spots beside us, and the light from the headlights reminds me of where we are. I suddenly become hyper-aware of the cars beside us, and I pull back, alarmed that I let it go that far without thinking about the fact that we're basically in public.

"Will, we can't do this here. Somebody could see and if you think we're too far from Springside to end up on the STS like this, you don't know Miss Ethel."

"Shit, Han, don't talk about Ethel when you're grinding that sweet pussy against me," he groans, before wiping a hand over his face. "And if you think I'm above pulling you in the backseat of my truck in this parking lot, you are sorely underestimating how fucking bad I want you."

It's on the tip of my tongue to tell him I'd be okay with that when I hear Caroline's voice cutting through the parking lot. "Hannah? You out here?"

My eyes widen in alarm at the idea of her finding us like this, but she's far enough away that she can't see anything from that distance. "Let me down," I whisper, trying to get him to put me down. "Neither of us are ready to explain this right now."

Will lowers his voice, not letting go of his hold on my ass. "You may be right, Han, but this isn't over. You offered yourself to me, and I can promise I'll be coming to collect. Don't even bother pretending it's not what you want. We both know better."

And with that, he drops me to my feet, moving away from me before calling out, "Hey, Caroline, we're over here."

A few minutes later my best friend finds us, pulling Theo along behind her. "Oh my gosh, Han, I was so worried about you. What are you doing out here?"

"Oh, I was getting a headache from the noise, so I stepped outside. I couldn't find y'all so I made Will come out with me. He thought he had some Tylenol in the truck," I say, the lie feeling bitter on my lips.

Caroline reaches out, hugging me before turning her concerned gaze on me. "Are you feeling better? We can go if you're ready!" Her worried tone makes me feel even worse for lying to her, but there's no way to explain everything to her right now, so I try to push it down.

Part of me doesn't know why I've kept all of this from her for so long. She's my best friend and I know she'd support me no matter what. But I know that once I start trying to explain everything to her, she'll convince me to try again with Will, and as much as I wish we could go back to how things were, I can't.

"Nope, I'm good now. Let's go dance!" I tell her, pasting on a bright smile and leading her back inside without looking back at Will.

CHAPTER 26
WILL

Hannah Scott is gonna be the fucking death of me.

I watch her on the dance floor, laughing and singing with Caroline and Margaret as the band plays "Dust on the Bottle." I'm still rock hard from finally tasting her and feeling her against me again. All I can think about is pulling her back outside and fucking her hard.

I hadn't intended to tip my hand and reveal as much as I had, particularly that I haven't been with another woman since we were together last, but fuck it. Sure, I could have screwed around when I went back to school, but it just hadn't felt right, and by the time I moved back to Springside, I didn't want to take on the small town rumor mill just to get my dick wet. Plus, trying to have any credibility as a head coach in my late twenties meant I stayed as far away from all that as possible. But just like everything else, none of that mattered when it came to Hannah.

"Will, I swear you have been completely out of it lately," Seth says, bumping me with his arm and waiting for me to look up. "What the hell's up with you?"

"Oh, uh, sorry man. Football's just taking up a lot of my time right now. Pretty sure you get this dialed in during baseball season, Coach," I remind him, hoping he won't push the topic any further.

"Fine," he says. "But I asked if you could help me at Hannah's this week. I want to get that knocked out before I get too far into the projects at Margaret's bakery."

"Yeah, man, sure. I mean after practice or whatever, I'll be there," I tell him, trying to keep my eyes from drifting back to Hannah.

"Thanks... You know, if you'd told me when he moved here that he'd be out there dancing instead of over here drinking a beer, I would have told you you were full of shit," Seth says, gesturing to where Theo's dancing with Caroline. He doesn't look particularly excited about it, but every once in a while, Caroline leans in to whisper something in his ear or kiss his cheek, and he smiles like he's won the damn lottery.

"You're right about that," I say, trying to force a laugh and ignore the pang of jealousy I feel in my chest. Not because of Caroline—I was definitely never interested in her like that; instead at how easy it looks for them. They're fucking perfect together, and there's nothing keeping them apart. Sure, they have their own share of shit, but they take all of it on together instead of the way Hannah and I have spent the last few years.

Maybe tonight is a start toward that for us, or maybe it's just the start of some really good sex, but either way, I know that if I get Hannah Scott back, there's no way I can let her go again.

"ALL RIGHT, guys, our first game of the playoffs is Friday. Any ideas on how we're gonna beat Saddle Ridge again this week?" I ask the coaches as they spread out across the living room of my apartment.

"You know, we beat them by a touchdown right at the end

early in the season, and it looks like they've made a lot of changes since then," Jason says, pointing at the film we've spent the last hour combing through.

"Yeah, their special teams has completely changed," Kent says, leaning back from his spot on my couch. "And they're running a much faster offense too."

"I noticed that when we were there Friday. I think we're gonna need to build in some extra conditioning this week to make sure we're able to keep up with them. Thoughts?" I ask, and the rest of the men nod.

"All right, good. We're also gonna run a couple of the new plays we talked about last week during practice and see if we can get those ready to go. Anybody have anything else?"

Everyone shakes their heads, and I stand, grabbing another beer now that we're done with our strategy discussion. Sitting back down, Kent asks, "So, where's Theo today? I know you mentioned he couldn't make it."

"Apparently, he's got his hands full. He originally told me that he might be late because Petunia tried to start a fight with one of the calves this morning, and the momma didn't take too kindly to it. He was trying to get them separated when the fire station called in for help."

"Who the hell is Petunia?" Kent asks, raising an eyebrow in question.

"It's this ass that Ol' Mr. Willy convinced him to take when he sold him his cattle a couple months ago."

"Ass? Like the animal?"

"Yeah, and trust me, I don't think there's an animal out there that lives up to its name more," I say with a laugh. "She's terrible, and he's had nothing but trouble with her since he got her. But everyone else around here knew better than to take her in, so he's kinda stuck."

"God, I swear, just hearing y'all talk about this farm shit wears me out," Kent says, and I just glare at him. Immediately, my thoughts turn to Hannah at his words.

"Yeah, they're a lot of work," I say, trying to ignore the pull I feel to text her. Kent, Jason, Marcus, and Seth chat about the new parts house that's supposed to be opening next month, but just like all the other conversations they've had recently, I tune them out, before eventually giving in and pulling out my phone to text Hannah.

> WILL: Pretty sure I haven't thought about anything but you since Friday.

I debate sending the text for just a moment, knowing I'm probably coming on a little stronger than I should, but I'm fucking desperate for this girl. As soon as I press sent, my phone immediately pings with a response, and I grab for it, smiling at the screen.

> HANNAH: Is that a good thing or a bad thing?

> WILL: I'm not sure, but I know I'm gonna lose it if we don't finish what we started soon.

I sit my phone down when there's no reply for a moment and I worry again that I'll end up scaring her away. After a minute, my screen lights up and I lurch for it, fumbling with it for a moment as I try to get the damn thing unlocked.

Out of the corner of my eye I can see Seth giving me a strange look, but I ignore him, swiping at my screen to see what she said.

> HANNAH: *sigh* Me either. But if we're gonna do this, it's gotta be just sex. No strings. No promises. Just sex.

> HANNAH: And none of our friends can know. If Caroline gets a hold of this, I'll never hear the end of it.

I feel a rush run through me at her text as I think about how it'll feel to slide inside her again after all these years. The rush is accompanied by a brief pang at her request, wishing I could understand why she's so determined to set boundaries like this. I have the thought that there's no way this will end well for us. There's too much history and too many feelings for us to pretend like the way we feel about each other is purely physical. But the part that's horny and desperate for whatever part of her that she'll let me have wins out.

WILL: Sounds like a plan.

CHAPTER 27
HANNAH

"God, this is the only way to end a Monday," Margaret says, shaking her shoulders as she sips on her peach margarita the next Monday.

"Amen. I don't know about y'all but today was an absolute shit show at school," Caroline groans, grabbing the pitcher from the center of the table and refilling her glass.

"Right? Whoever thought having a school-wide assembly and a fire drill on a Monday during a full moon was seriously delusional," I agree, before turning to Margaret.

"So, I need a bakery update. How long until I can spend all my money on coffee and those delicious cookies you make?"

She smiles at the question, and her eyes light up in excitement at the mention of her new business. "Oh my gosh, I'm so excited. It's still gonna be several months before I'm ready to open because the space needs so much work. But, I do have some exciting news to share in the meantime. Mayor Brian called me this weekend to ask if I'd be interested in running a pop-up through the holidays at Deer Valley Inn!"

"Oh my gosh, that's incredible Margaret!" Caroline squeals and I nod in agreement. Mayor Brian's family has run the small inn and winery in town for as long as I can remember, but I heard he was trying to upgrade several of the services since he took over last year following his mom's death.

"I know, I'm so excited! I've been testing out some new holiday drinks and treats all weekend. Seth also told me when I saw him bringing in his groceries that he'd help me get a head start on the building over winter break too, so I'm keeping my fingers crossed for a spring opening," Margaret continues, grabbing a handful of chips and dipping them in the queso.

"Hmm, is that right? Do you run into Seth often?" I ask, raising my eyebrows in her direction.

"What? Not really! I mean, you know he and Will are my neighbors now that I live in Caroline's old apartment, but he was just being nice!" she says, her eyes widening at my implication.

"Right..." I say, still eyeing her skeptically.

"That's it. Plus, we all know after how my last relationship worked out, I'm not exactly looking for someone to complicate my life with," she adds.

"Okay, that's fair, but just because your ex didn't know how to keep his dick in his pants doesn't mean you can't have some fun with someone else," I remind her, feeling another wave of hatred for the man who broke Margaret's heart before she came to Springside. He was some high-powered attorney from the city, and she'd been waiting on him to propose until she walked in and found him with his dick down some other girl's throat. It turned out he'd been sneaking around with one of his clients for months, and their breakup had prompted her to join her brother in his move for a fresh start.

Ignoring me, she launches into her recipe for a caramel gingerbread latte that honestly sounds heavenly, and I feel my phone vibrate in my pocket. Pulling it out, I see a text from Will on my screen.

> WILL: What are you doing after the game Friday?

I feel my heart start to race at the idea of finally spending time alone with him after all these years.

> HANNAH: I don't have any plans. What'd you have in mind?

WILL: Don't worry about it. I'll meet you at the farm when we're done.

> HANNAH: Fine, but remember the rules... No strings, no emotions. Just sex.

He doesn't reply to that, and I roll my eyes. I don't know what the hell I'm thinking. Can I really convince myself that I'm okay with just sex after the last few years? There's a part of my brain that tries to scream that there's no way that'll ever be enough for me, but I tamp it down. This arrangement may have been my idea, but it was the only way I could convince myself that I might get a little bit of the happiness I've been missing since I pushed him away.

"HEY, Gramps, what are you up to?" I ask as I enter his room Friday afternoon. I had to push my visit this week thanks to the extra cheer practices for state next week and Caroline and I staying behind to work with Maggie. The weeks keep getting busier the closer we get to the end of the season, and I'm exhausted. Plus, I haven't been sleeping much, anxious with the thought of finally spending time with Will again.

"Hey, my Hannah Banana!" Gramps calls, smiling from his chair. "Come on in. I wasn't expecting you today!"

"I know, but I wanted to swing by before the game and check on you. I haven't seen you since Sunday, and I feel terrible!"

"None of that nonsense now," he tells me, reaching out and squeezing my hand as I sit beside him. "You have way more to worry about than visiting an old man like me."

"But, Gramps, I love spending time with you. This competition season on top of playoffs has just been a lot," I admit, leaning my head against the back of the chair. "I'm sorry I missed our usual visit."

He waves me off, obviously deciding he's done with that line of conversation. "Tell me about this competition. Are your girls ready?"

I smile at the question, knowing Gramps doesn't know the first thing about cheerleading, but he genuinely cares because it's something I love. "Yeah, they're getting there. I definitely don't know if we'll win, but they're excited and I think they've had a lot of fun getting everything together."

Gramps nods before saying, "Oh, y'all are gonna win. I just know it. I hate that I can't travel to see it, but make sure you get a video to show me, okay?"

"Pretty sure you sat through your share of these when I was in school, so I think you've more than filled your quota, old man. But I'll get a video if it makes you happy."

He smiles, rocking back in his chair before asking, "So, Saddle Ridge tonight, huh? You think we'll move on after this one?"

"I think so. You know we went and watched them play last week since we had a bye, and they were pretty good. But I still think Will and the other coaches have it under control."

"Speaking of Will, how's he doing?" Gramps asks, and I swear he narrows his eyes at me in suspicion, but I know I'm just being paranoid.

"Uhh, he's fine, I guess. A pain in my ass as always," I tease, even though I know that's not the truth.

"Hmm, whatever you say, granddaughter. I always thought there was something between you two, but I guess I was wrong, huh?"

"What?" I stammer, completely caught off guard by that statement. "No, there's definitely nothing between us. At all. Ever. Nope."

He raises his eyebrow at my babbling before just nodding. "Okay, my mistake."

"Yeah, so, how's Gladis doing?" I ask, needing to change the subject.

"Oh, she's okay. She's been having trouble with her hip in this colder weather after her hip replacement last spring, but other than that she's good."

"The two of you have a hot night of bingo ahead of you, right?" I tease, and he laughs at my question.

"Yep, there's a twenty-dollar prize this week, and we're teaming up to take Silas across the hall down."

"Look out. Isn't he the one with the leg cast all the way up to his thigh?" I ask, shaking my head, not surprised to see his competitive nature hasn't changed over the last few months.

"So what? He's still going down, Hannah Banana."

"I'm sure he is, Gramps. I'll need a full update on that one this weekend."

"BLACK, BLUE, WHITE! FIGHT, SAINTS, FIGHT!" I cheer along with the squad, looping my arm through Caroline's as the ball flies through the air at the end of the second quarter.

It seems like the whole stadium holds its breath as we wait to see if Blake's pass to one of his receivers is good. We're already up by one touchdown, but it's been a rough fight, with both teams fighting hard. The receiver catches the ball, and the Springside sideline cheers at the sight of another touchdown.

"Oh my God, he did it!" Caroline cheers, throwing her arm around both me and Margaret.

The squad below us dances to the fight song, and we shake our shakers with the beat. I'm trying to focus on the game as the kicker lines up for the extra point, but I can't stop myself from letting my gaze stray to the sideline where Will's standing with Theo and a few of the other players. He's so focused during these games, and I feel the same pull I've been trying to ignore for the last several years toward him as I watch. But this time's different because I know that tonight, I'll get to be with him again. It doesn't mean anything, but the thought of having him inside me after all this time has me thinking about...

"Earth to Hannah," Caroline says, waving her hand in front of my face. "You good? I've been calling your name for the last few minutes. It's time for us to go down for half time."

"Oh, yeah, sorry. Lost in my own little world," I say, forcing an awkward laugh.

Caroline gives me a funny look before just nodding and leading us down to the field while the team runs into the locker room for half time.

"All right, girls, are you ready?" she asks as Saddle Ridge's squad takes the field.

"I feel like I'm gonna throw up," Maggie says, and the rest of the squad laughs.

"You're all gonna be great. This is your last trial run performance before state next week, and you just need to go do everything like we've practiced," Caroline says, and I nod my encouragement.

"That's right. Just keep those motions sharp and remember not to pull those libs until 3 instead of 1, okay?"

The girls nod and grab their poms, just as the announcer comes over the speaker. "And now, please welcome to the field your regional champions, the Springside Saints Cheerleaders!"

Caroline and I yell and cheer along with the crowd before taking our usual performance position, grabbing hands and squeezing as the girls wait for their music to start.

A few seconds later "High Hopes" blasts through the speakers, and the stands cheer as the girls throw their first set of basket tosses to the beat of the music.

"Those have gotten so much better," Caroline whispers, neither of us taking our eyes off the field. "Come on, hit this pyramid now."

I squeeze her hand in agreement, holding my breath as the music changes to a remix of "Thunder" by Imagine Dragons, and Maggie flips through the air in a back handspring sequence before loading into the newest pyramid. She flies up, hitting an extension and reaching for the tops and connecting grips before flipping forward then backward and landing back in a lib.

The stunts hit, and Caroline and I both let out loud cheers of excitement as they dismount and move to their cheer formation.

"Blue... White... Are you ready? Are you ready? Are you ready to fight?" they cheer, and the crowd cheers along with the signs the girls hold up, causing me to smile.

"Okay, last part! You got it," Caroline cheers as they move to their ending dance formation. The music clicks back on with "Blah Blah Blah" by Kesha pumping through the speakers, and as the girls throw their last tumbling pass, I can't help but smile because I can already tell they're going to hit before they even load the new stunts. We'd adjusted the last formation wanting to maximize the scoresheet for state, and this is the first time they've performed them outside of practice. Their energy and enthusiasm is off the charts, and I'm so damn proud of how fast they've come.

Caroline and I both lean forward just a bit, squeezing the circulation out of each other's hands as the libs go up before water falling into reloads and hitting the ending formation, yelling "Springside... Saints."

As soon as they hit, Caroline and I are screaming, cheering them on as they run off the field to hug us. It's just a halftime performance, but I know that moment gave them the confidence they needed going into state and I'm so happy they hit it.

"Oh my gosh, Miss Caroline did you see us?"

"Miss Hannah, did you see my back tuck? I think that's the best one I've ever done!"

"I need to see a video of our basket toss. I'm pretty sure that's the highest we've thrown all season."

I smile as they all talk at once, helping them gather their things as we move off the field for the game to restart. When I turn, I see that Will and the rest of the team are standing right behind us, and I smile at him as we make eye contact, feeling my excitement rise at seeing him tonight.

One more half.

CHAPTER 28
WILL

I pull into Hannah's driveway after the game, grinning like a fool between the high of the win and the knowledge that I'm finally going to have her to myself again. I haven't been able to think about much of anything else this week, and I've fought the urge to ditch Seth and steal her away every time I pulled into her driveway to help on the farm.

I've just jumped out of the truck when I hear a squeal and hear something running toward me in the dark. I tense, trying to figure out which direction it's coming from when I feel a heavy weight of something hitting my legs.

"Leroy, you little fucker," I say with a laugh, patting the pig's head as he weaves himself between my feet over and over before rolling over for me to scratch his belly.

"Let me guess, Leroy got out again?" Hannah calls, stepping out the front door and squinting out at us from the porch.

"Sure did. Have you ever considered that maybe he doesn't want to be pinned up? Cause he sure as hell gets out all the damn time," I point out, straightening and making my way toward the house.

"Trust me, I know," Hannah says, rolling her eyes at me. "I tried letting him roam where he wanted, but he likes his bed and his little piggy house. Plus, he's a damn escape artist, and he's stubborn enough that he's gonna get what he wants."

"Sounds like someone else I know," I tease, walking up the stairs, and stopping in front of her. Leroy follows and runs at her, trying to hold his huge body up on his tiny back legs to get her attention.

"I see you, ya stinker," she coos, rubbing his ears and laughing as he tries to lick her face.

"I swear you have the weirdest fucking pig I've ever seen. I mean he really thinks he's a dog." At my statement, she turns to look at me with disgust before leaning down and dropping a kiss on Leroy's head.

"Don't you insult my baby," she says, continuing to love on the pig.

"Fine, fine," I say, holding up my hands in a sign of surrender.

"Okay, Leroy, we're gonna be inside, okay? Go get in your pen or go play with Ruby, okay?" Hannah says, standing back up and opening the front door to let me in. "So, I guess I should tell you that you coached a great game."

I follow her inside, accepting the beer she's holding out for me and popping the top before taking a sip. She fiddles with her bottle, picking at the label and looking a little uncomfortable. "Thanks," I tell her with a smile, walking over and pulling her in my arms before dropping a kiss to her mouth.

"This is all I've thought about for the last week," I admit, kissing her again and feeling her start to relax in my arms. "I thought about dragging you out of the house, but I'm pretty sure both of us are exhausted from the week. So why don't we put on a movie and you let me see how many times I can make you see stars?"

Her eyes widen at that and I feel her breath against my neck quicken. I know she gets off on the way I talk to her, so I continue, testing the waters to see how she'll react.

"That's right, Han. You told me I could have your body, and I intend to take my time relearning every fucking inch of you."

She just stares for a moment before leaning down and kissing me frantically. I kiss her back before pulling away and picking her up, wrapping her legs around my front as I stalk over to the couch. Sitting down, I position her in my lap and kiss her for a while, before trailing kisses down her neck. On the way back up, I whisper in her ear while my hands tease her pussy through her jeans. "When's the last time someone touched your sweet pussy, baby?"

"I—I—" she stammers, and I continue kissing and teasing her, waiting to see what she'll say. I don't know why I asked, knowing the answer will probably make me jealous as fuck, but something in me needs to know.

"Hmm?" I prompt, continuing to tease her with my fingers and with my lips on her neck.

"Will, please," she begs, and my dick hardens even more at hearing those words from her.

I wait for her to answer, but one never comes, so I lean in and nip her neck.

She's silent for another moment before she whispers so quietly I'm not sure I hear her. "You, Will. It was you."

We both freeze, and I wait for her to laugh or tell me that she's kidding, making fun of me for my admission the other night. But one never comes. My blood heats, and I feel the last remaining bits of control I was trying to maintain snap.

Suddenly, any ideas of taking it slow are out the fucking window as our mouths clash, and I run my hands under her sweater, yanking it off her and freeing her from her bra in one quick motion.

"God, Will, please," she moans, grinding her hips against mine as I kiss a trail down her neck before sucking one of her perk nipples into my mouth. She whimpers at the contact, bucking her hips against mine more frantically like she needs to feel me as badly as I need her.

Pulling back, I push her to her feet, and I don't miss the look of hurt that briefly passes over her face. "I know you don't think I'm done with you, Han," I say, letting out a low chuckle. "I'm just gonna lose my fucking mind if I don't get you naked right now."

She nods, helping me unbutton her jeans and shimmying out of them and her panties all at once. I yank her back into my lap, kissing her hard and trailing my hand down her center. I let one finger dip through her core, letting out a moan when I feel her.

"God, you're fucking soaked," I groan, kissing her again. "So fucking perfect. I'm gonna make you come tonight and later we can take this slow, but right now I need to be inside you."

"Yes," she whispers, grinding her hot pussy against my still-clothed cock. "Quit talking about it and fuck me, Will."

"Always so damn bossy, aren't you?" I respond, undoing my pants to free my dick. She stands to her feet, yanking my jeans down before crawling back in my lap. I pause for a moment, taking in how damn sexy she is before murmuring, "Please tell me you're on birth control, because I don't want anything between me and this sweet pussy."

"Yes, just get inside me," she growls, and I lean against the back of the couch and palm her ass to pull her closer.

Giving in, I lift her up so she's open for me, before lining myself up with her entrance and impaling her on my cock with one quick thrust. She whimpers as I enter her, and I feel my breath catch in my throat at how fucking tight she is. And I know right now, there's no way I'm giving this up ever again.

CHAPTER 29
HANNAH

Over the last seven years I've tried to convince myself that sex with Will Thompson wasn't anything special. I've told myself I wasn't missing out on anything and what we shared hadn't meant a thing. But as soon as I feel him start to fuck me like we're the same people we were that summer, I know that's not true.

"Shit, Hannah, you feel so good," he groans, leaning down to kiss my mouth while he flexes his hips in and out of me.

I don't say anything, channeling all my desire into kissing him back while his cock starts to hit the spot inside me that always made me see stars.

"Did you miss riding my cock all these years, huh, Han?" Will growls, pulling back from our kiss to trail his mouth down my throat. "How many nights did you use those pretty fingers on this cunt trying to convince yourself you could make yourself feel as good as I'm making you feel right now?"

His words throw kerosene on the desire already building between us, and I pull his mouth back to mine, trailing my fingers down his back hard enough that I know he'll have marks for the next few days.

"Yes, baby. Mark me up however you want. Just know that you may not be ready to admit it yet, but this pussy is mine. And I'm gonna take my time over the next few weeks reminding you of all the ways I can make you come."

"But it's just sex," I remind him, wrapping my legs around him harder and using the new leverage to control his pace. He complies, letting me fuck myself on his cock for a moment before reaching between us and rubbing my clit with his fingers.

"God, yes, Will. Yes. I'm so close," I murmur, my movements losing rhythm as he teases me, letting me chase my orgasm.

"Come on my cock, baby. This pussy's gonna look so good dripping with my cum, sweetheart."

That mental image pushes me over the edge, and I come with a loud cry. Will doesn't stop, continuing to rub my clit through my orgasm before grabbing both my hips to pull me closer to him.

"You're so fucking beautiful when you come," he whispers, tightening his grip on me, before he picks me up and starts moving me up and down, fucking me hard on the length of his cock.

God, that's fucking hot, I think to myself as he continues to lift me over and over, groaning each time he bumps my sensitive clit when he slides into me.

"I'm close," he warns, and I feel myself tighten at the desperation in his tone. "Gonna fill you so good, baby."

He lifts me faster and faster before finally slamming me down and grinding against me. I feel his cock twitch inside me, coating me with his cum the way he promised, and I feel my second orgasm rip through me.

"Yes, angel, yes," he groans, shifting against me as I ride it out before collapsing on his chest.

Neither of us says anything for a while, and I lie on top of him, keeping him inside me while he brushes his hands through my hair. I don't know how long we stay there, with both of us refusing to move as if we're both scared that when we do, all of this will disappear.

Finally, after a long while, he leans down and pulls my mouth to his, dropping a soft kiss on my lips. "That was incredible, Han. Now, throw on my shirt and come into the kitchen. I'll fix us something to eat and we're gonna do that again."

CHAPTER 30
HANNAH

SEVEN SUMMERS AGO

WILL: I'm here whenever you're ready.

HANNAH: Okay, on my way!

I look down at my phone, smiling at the text before tucking it into the back pocket of my jeans and quietly slipping out the front door. Making sure the screen door doesn't creak, I close it behind me before tiptoeing my way down the porch steps. It's about a quarter of a mile down the driveway where Will always waits for me, and I try to calm the nerves I always get right before I see him.

It's been a couple of weeks since my birthday, and it's safe to say we're crazy about each other. We spend almost every day together around the farm, plus all the nights we sneak away to meet at our creek. I'm exhausted from all the nights we've stayed up, whispering in the moonlight and dreaming about the future under the stars, but it's completely worth it.

True to his word, we've taken the physical side of our relationship slow, and I'm desperate to finally feel him inside me. We've fooled around, but every time we got close to saying fuck it, he stopped us and told me he wanted to make sure I didn't feel rushed. It was sweet at first, but as time's gone on, I've become more and more needy. He hasn't even let me touch him, just fingering me and tasting me until I come and then kissing me and holding me under the stars. I asked him about it last week because I was starting to worry he wasn't into me, and he told me he didn't trust himself not to fuck me once he gives in. But I've spent the last few days dropping hints and teasing him as we worked around the farm, and I think tonight's finally the night.

Walking up to his truck, I throw myself in the cab and kiss him hard before saying, "Hey! I missed you this evening. Did you have fun at the movies with your siblings?"

"Yeah, it was nice. We went to Saddle Ridge to watch the new *Spiderman*. It was pretty good, but all I could think about was this," he murmurs, pulling me over to straddle his lap and kissing me hard.

I groan as he kisses down my throat, nipping and teasing the skin right below my ear, and rolling my hips against his lap to tease him.

He lets out a low groan, before whispering, "Fuck, baby, you're driving me nuts."

"There's an easy way to fix that," I tease him, sliding off his lap and motioning for him to drive.

He looks at me for a few moments, before asking, "Are you sure that's what you want? Because once I get to feel you, I'm never gonna have enough."

"Hell yes, I'm sure," I breathe out, my heart picking up at his words. "Now fucking drive."

He laughs at my eagerness and throws the truck in drive, driving through the pasture a little faster than he normally does. Neither of us say anything, not wanting to ruin the moment, but we can't seem to keep our hands off each other, constantly reaching for the other in the darkness.

When the creek comes into view, he makes quick work of reversing into our usual place, and before the truck's even in park, I have my door open ready to jump out and get to him.

Will seems just as eager, throwing himself out of the truck and meeting me at the tailgate. He thankfully remembered to grab a couple of the blankets so the plastic ridges won't dig into my back, but I'm so eager to feel him, I don't really think I care.

As soon as he has them down, we're reaching for each other, and our mouths clash as we kiss hard.

"Are we finally doing this?" I ask, pulling back as he picks me up and sits me on his tailgate before leaning in to kiss me again. I can feel my heart about to beat out of my chest, and I try to take a breath to slow it down.

He brushes a piece of my hair out of my face and gives me one of his signature golden boy smiles. "Well I guess that's really up to you, Han. You know how I feel about you. What do you want?"

"Honestly, I want you to fuck me," I say, kissing him hard. But just as I'm about to give myself over to him, I pull back, fear suddenly gripping me out of nowhere. "But what do you want? God, these last few weeks have been incredible. But we're living in a bubble—sneaking out and stealing kisses isn't anything close to a real relationship. What happens when Caroline and the rest of the town find out?" I ask, my anxiety rising. God, way to kill the moment, Hannah, I think to myself.

"Do you not want them to know?" he asks, obvious concern flashing in his eyes.

Gazing into his blue eyes, I murmur shyly, "Well, we're both about to move away again. You have to go back to Southbrook soon. I don't want things to be weird if we don't work out."

His eyes turn more serious than I've ever seen them before and he says, "Han, we are gonna work out. I've never been as obsessed with someone as I am with you. But if you want to wait to tell them for a few weeks, we can wait."

I hear the sincerity and determination in his voice, so I nod and say, "Okay, but until then no one has to know. I want to wait and explain it to Caroline in person. I know she'll understand, but this was supposed to be our boy-free summer."

He nods. "Sure, until you're ready no one has to know."

I smile and throw myself at him, my anxiety vanishing as suddenly as it came. "All right, then what are you waiting on?"

His eyes never leave mine as he pulls back and slides my jean shorts down, watching me to make sure this is what I want. Deciding he needs some encouragement, I reach out and rub my hand against the front of his jeans, teasing him until he stiffens under my hand and groans.

Giving in, he yanks my shirt over my head and moves in to kiss me hard. I wrap my legs around his waist, desperate to feel him as close as I can, and let out a soft moan when I feel his cock press against my center.

"God, you feel so good," he murmurs, pulling back enough to let me yank his shirt off over his head. I hum in agreement, already reaching for his belt and yanking his jeans down too. I take a moment to admire how incredibly hot he is, reaching out and running my hand down his abs. He gives me a moment to tease him before he loses control again and pulls me back to kiss me hard.

I don't know how long we kiss for, but I know I'm completely lost in him. I still feel a touch of nerves, but they're majorly overpowered by the desire I feel to be with him. I don't know why having sex with Will seems like such a big deal. I've had a few hookups at school, but none of them have ever meant anything. I can't help but feel like being with Will is either going to be the best high I've ever experienced or it's going to break my heart.

Pulling back, I reach out and slide my hand inside his boxers, pumping his dick with my hand a few times to encourage him. He lets out a moan pumping his hips into my hand a time or two, and I feel him lengthen even more. God, he's huge. I knew he felt big whenever I teased him the last few weeks, but finally feeling him under my hand makes me even more desperate to feel him inside me.

"Lie back, baby. I need to get you ready for me," he says, pushing my shoulders until I'm lying flat on the tailgate with my legs dangling off the front. "Just relax, we've got all night."

I open my mouth to make some sort of smart remark at that, but he pulls my panties to the side and runs his tongue through my center, causing me to completely lose my train of thought. He takes his time, flicking my clit with his tongue and wrapping his arms around my hips to pull me closer to him.

"God, Will, you feel so good," I moan, threading my fingers through his hair and rolling my hips against his tongue.

He continues to lick and lap at me, until he moves his arms and runs one hand down my slit until he slips two fingers inside me. I moan as he alternates between moving his fingers and flicking my clit until I feel my orgasm start to build.

"Oh my God," I whimper. "Please, Will, I need more."

At my request, he adds another finger inside me, and I let out another loud moan. I feel him smile against my core as he murmurs, "That's right, baby, do you feel me stretching you and getting you ready to take my cock? You're already fucking soaked for me, baby."

I just moan, unable to form a coherent thought with the way he's teasing me. My orgasm is still building, and I feel like I'm dangling right on the edge of something.

"Please, please, please," I chant, trying to roll my hips to gain the friction I need.

Right when I think it's about to happen, Will pulls back, and I cry out in disappointment. He leans down and kisses me softly, brushing the hair out of my face.

"I promise I'm just getting started, Han. But the next time

you come is gonna be around my cock," he growls, and I just whimper in acknowledgment. I've never been this turned on in my life and I need him to stop teasing and fuck me.

"Will, I swear to God if you don't hurry the hell up," I whisper, but he just laughs at my threat, pulling his boxers down and freeing his hard dick. I moan a little at the sight, wrapping my legs around him and trying to pull him closer.

"Hmm, someone's a little needy all of a sudden, huh?" Will says with a laugh, bending down and reaching for his jeans.

"What are you doing?" I ask, sitting up on my elbows and fighting the urge to cross my arms over my chest like a toddler throwing a tantrum. I'm not normally like this, but God, he feels good and I'm annoyed he's taking so long to give me what I want.

"Give me just a second to grab a condom, baby. You're not on birth control, are you?" he asks, already digging through his pocket.

"Ugh, no. I got off of it a few years ago because my hormones got out of whack. I've been meaning to make another appointment, but I hate going to the doctor," I admit, suddenly regretting that decision. I want nothing more than to feel him slide inside me bare.

It hits me that if he hadn't thought about it, I would have let him do it tonight, consequences be damned, but I know he's right. He reaches to pull a condom out of his pocket, tears the packet open and slides it down his cock quickly. Leaning down, he kisses me again, and I feel my desire ramp right back as he teases me with his mouth.

He pushes me back until I'm lying flat against the tailgate and he helps me wrap my legs back around him. Reaching down, he teases my clit a few times with his dick, causing me to roll my hips against him again, silently begging him to hurry.

"God, Hannah, I can already tell you're gonna fucking ruin me," he growls before pulling back and lining himself up with my entrance. He starts to slide in slowly, and I whimper at the way he's stretching me. He's so much bigger than anyone I've ever been with, but I love the slight pain I feel as he sinks inside me.

He takes a moment, pushing inside me until he's all the way in, and pausing once he bottoms out. "You okay, baby?" he asks, looking at me in the dark for a sign that I'm ready for him to move.

"Yes. Will, please. I need you to move," I beg, and he immediately starts to oblige, shifting in and out of me slowly. He pumps into me using the same slow rhythm for a few moments until he must decide I really do want this because he eventually speeds up, sliding all the way in and out of me and causing my quiet whimpers to turn into near screams.

"You…feel…so…fucking…good," he groans, punctuating each word with a thrust inside me. His movements get faster and more frantic as I feel my climax build again until he reaches down and strums my clit. "I need you to get there, baby. We'll take this slow next time, but you're so fucking tight. Come with me, Han," he begs, and with his words, he rolls my clit harder, teasing it over and over as he fucks me until I feel myself tighten with an orgasm.

"Oh my God, Will, I'm coming. Don't stop. Please, don't stop," I moan, not even really knowing what I'm saying, lost to the sensations of my orgasm.

"Shit, Han. You're so fucking perfect. I was right. You've fucking ruined me, and I don't even care. Hell, you feel so good," he says, praising me as he moves his hips faster and faster inside me until I feel him finish.

We both go still, and we just stay there for a moment with him still inside me. After a moment, he leans down and kisses me gently as he pulls out. "Well, I hope you're still sure about us, because after that I'm not sure I'm letting you out of my sight for the next few weeks. You may have created a monster because that was fucking incredible."

"I couldn't agree more," I tell him, grabbing my shirt and

throwing it on while he pulls off the condom and throws it in a trash bag from the truck. After he tugs on his jeans, he crawls up beside me, pulling me in close to him and holding me tight.

And as we lie there in the silent summer night, looking up at the stars, all I can think is I don't think I'll ever want to let him go.

CHAPTER 31
HANNAH

"Okay, girls, just a few more squads and we're up," Caroline says, motioning the squad over from where we just finished running through our last practice run. "Everything looks great, and you've worked so hard for this moment. So go out there, smile, and kill it like I know you can!"

"State champs here we come," Maggie says, causing the other girls to cheer in agreement.

"Han, do you have anything to add?" Caroline asks once the girls get quiet again.

"Remember to point your toes during the jump sequence and catch high on those basket tosses. And remember, this is supposed to be fun. Springside's never even placed in regionals, and y'all won the dang thing! So just go have fun and enjoy the experience," I tell the squad, smiling at their anxious and excited expressions.

Caroline nods in agreement, before saying, "Yes, we're already so proud of all of you. Now, let's get ready to do this thing! Does anyone have any questions?"

One of the freshmen raises her hand and asks, "Is it true most of the football team came to watch us?"

Some of the other girls start to talk amongst themselves, and

Caroline holds up her hand to quiet them back down. "First of all, it doesn't matter who's in the stands. All that matters is the twelve of you on that mat. But, Coach Will did organize for several of the coaches and some of the sports teams on campus to come support us today since we spend so much of the year supporting them."

Several of the girls squeal at that, and Caroline and I shake our heads at their antics. After making sure no one else has questions, everyone stands and Maggie leans in and puts out her arm, waiting for us to join her in our huddle. Once everyone's in, she calls, "One, two, three, Saint's on me! One, two, three…" and we all yell "Saints" as the girls smile and jump around.

"Good luck, girls!" we tell them as one of the announcers calls out that they're next. Leaving the squad behind, Caroline loops her arm through mine as we walk over to the small area reserved for coaches. While we wait for the girls to be called, I turn around, taking in the crowds of people, and notice Margaret sitting close to the front, waving a pom-pom at Caroline and me. As we both wave to her, I catch the sight of Will behind her, and our gazes meet. He mouths "good luck" in my direction.

I feel a rush run through me at the sight, but I try to remind myself that I do not have time to be distracted right now. Between our extra practices for this weekend and him staying late at school all week to get ready for the playoff game last night, I haven't seen him in person—other than the game last night in Birmingham, which the Saints won in a landslide victory—since he left my house last week. I feel a rush run through me at the sight, but the sound of the announcer's voice crackles through the speakers, bringing my attention back to the present.

Despite my best effort, I'm a little lost in my thoughts when Caroline chimes in. "So, call me silly if you want, but is there something going on with you and Will? He didn't bring the team to watch us last year, and I'm pretty sure he hasn't taken his eyes off you since we walked out here."

I freeze, panicked as I try to figure out what to say. Thankfully, I'm saved by the sound of the announcer's voice crackling through speakers, bringing both of our attention back to the mat in front of us.

"Competing in the small varsity division, please welcome the Springside Saints."

Caroline grabs my arm as the girls run out cheering and spiriting, and I feel the nerves I've been trying to ignore all morning hit me hard.

"Oh my God, why do I feel like I could throw up all of a sudden?" Caroline groans, rubbing her other hand over her eyes.

"Same," I tell her, pasting on a smile. "But we've done everything we can, so we've gotta just hope they hit now."

"You're right. I really don't even care that much about placing this year. I just want them to hit zero," she says, and I place my hand over the one she still has in her grip.

"Me too," I tell her just as the girls finish getting set.

"Good luck, ladies, your music's on," the announcer calls out, and Caroline squeezes my hand hard as everything goes silent.

When the opening to "High Hopes" starts to blast through the speakers, their baskets soaring through the air right on cue; I let out a loud whoop of excitement.

We continue to watch, squeezing hands and counting silently as the music shifts to the pyramid sequence. Maggie flips through the air, and we both squeeze each other harder, refusing to jinx their performance by saying anything.

The music cuts as the girls move to their cheer formation, yelling, "S-A-I-N-T-S! Saints, Saints, Saints" before getting set and starting, "Blue... White... Are you ready? Are you ready? Are you ready to fight?"

The crowd cheers along, and the energy in the room is so infectious I want to pause and soak it in, but the music starts back, and I'm back to feeling like my heart is in my throat. The first few girls throw their tumbling passes, and I hear the group of Springside fans cheering over the sound of the music when they land their back handsprings, back tucks, and fulls before moving to the last formation.

"Come on, girls, finish it," Caroline yells, as they load the libs and waterfall down to the inversion handstands.

"I can't watch," I mutter, holding my breath and fighting the urge to cover my eyes. Caroline squeezes my hands in agreement just as they pop the girls up to land on their feet for the final pyramid yelling, "Springside...Saints!"

"Oh my God, they did it!" I mutter as Caroline starts jumping up and down, before pulling me into a hug.

"Han, that was incredible! They hit! Our squad hit at state! And I couldn't have done it without you!" she yells, and I can tell we're both holding back tears.

Before I can respond, the squad runs over, basically tackling us both with their excitement. "We did it!" they yell, and Caroline and I both smile at their excitement.

"Great job, girls! Despite what the results say, I couldn't be more proud of you!" Caroline says as we walk back to the waiting area outside.

"Yeah, what she said!" I say before smiling. "But a trophy sure wouldn't hurt, right?"

CHAPTER 32
WILL

"Okay, I don't know shit about cheerleading, but I'm pretty sure that was freaking incredible," Seth says, leaning forward in his chair so Theo and I can both hear him.

"Yeah, it was," I admit absentmindedly, but all my focus is on Hannah as she and Caroline jump around, hugging and screaming for the squad as they dismount their stunts before moving out of view for the next squad to get set. *God, she's so fucking beautiful.*

I haven't been able to think about anything but the way she felt riding my cock last week, and the sight of her smiling in excitement below has me wishing I could pull her out of this arena and keep her to myself for a couple of hours.

"Coach Thompson, how long until they announce the winners?" Blake asks from his seat in front of us, interrupting my thoughts.

"Uh, I think there's only one or two more squads left," I tell him, checking my watch. "Another thirty minutes tops."

He nods, turning back to the front as Seth and Theo make small talk about a project on Theo's farm that I halfheartedly attempt to follow while we wait on the results. It sure as hell doesn't seem to work because I find myself distracted by the thought of finally getting her alone again.

"All right, who's ready for some results?" the voice over the loudspeaker booms, and the squads that are starting to line up across the mat scream so loud, I swear my ears start ringing.

I smile when I see Hannah and Caroline standing with their squad on the corner, huddling together and whispering. *She's so damn gorgeous*, I think, watching as her long blonde hair falls in her face while she wiggles around impatiently.

"First of all, we want to say congratulations to all the teams here. And thank you to all the coaches, parents, and school districts that make this possible," the announcer says, and everyone claps.

She continues on for several minutes, talking about the tough job the judges had thanks to all the talent until Seth finally leans over to whisper, "Damn, I'm not even the one competing, and I'm getting anxious."

I nod in agreement, just as the woman in the front of the room starts, "Without further ado, coming in third place in the 3A small varsity division, we have the Bulldogs from Brookside High School."

The squad standing next to Hannah erupts into cheers, screaming and hugging while one of the girls goes to grab the trophy. After a few moments, the arena goes silent again, until the announcement continues, "And in second place we have the Wildcats from Saddle Ridge High School!"

The girls on the opposite end of the arena cheer as Seth leans over. "So either they won, or they didn't place…"

I nod, feeling my nerves heighten as I watch Caroline and Hannah squeezing each other's hands so hard I'm scared they'll break.

"Surely they won," Theo mumbles. "My fiancé is their freaking kick-ass coach."

Seth and I chuckle at that, as everyone around us goes quiet. There are at least twelve other squads on the mat, and they all look like they're about to lose it as they wait for the announcer to finish.

"And finally, your 3A small Varsity division state champions are...the Saints from Springside High School!"

"Hell yeah!" Theo yells, causing a few of the parents from other schools that are sitting near us to turn and give him looks of disapproval. He shrugs in apology, and I let out a whoop of excitement. In the rows in front of me, the football team jumps up and starts high-fiving each other, as the squad on the floor screams and hugs each other while Maggie runs forward to grab the trophy.

As soon as it's in her hands, she runs back, holding it up while the squad all but tackles Caroline and Hannah. Most of the girls are crying, and I smile when I catch sight of Hannah, who's always pretended she doesn't cry, wipes a stray tear.

"Those girls really love Hannah and Caroline," Seth says, watching the scene below us.

"Yeah, they do," I agree, wishing that I could go pull her into my arms and congratulate her. But considering that everyone here thinks we can't stand to be in the same room, plus the fact that the school would definitely frown upon it, I stay put, watching her and wishing she was mine.

"ALL RIGHT, guys, we have the Huntsville Hornets away on Friday, so in addition to the game, we also have a huge travel week," I say, sitting down on my sofa with a beer Sunday afternoon to comb through the film I have pulled up.

"Shit, I am not looking forward to that ride on the bus," Kent groans, and we all nod in agreement.

"Yeah, I can't say it's something I'm excited about either, but the boosters have offered to help us cover the cost of staying in a hotel outside of Huntsville for the night. Apparently, Blake's dad has a connection and they were willing to give them to us pretty cheap. It's not what I'd normally do, but depending on how late the game goes it could be after three in the morning before we got back, and I'm not comfortable being on the road that late after a game."

"Hell, I can't say I'll complain about that," Jason agrees, reaching out for a handful of chips off the coffee table.

The other coaches nod in agreement, and I grab the remote to start the first few plays of Huntsville's last game.

I let the video play for a while, pausing them every so often to point out the things I noticed when I previewed this game last night. "I really think we need to think about moving Drew over here on the offense line when we run the new '24 dive' play," I suggest to Kent, just as I hear my phone ping with an incoming text.

> HANNAH: Hey, are you coming by tonight? I wouldn't mind a repeat of Friday

I smile at the text, before pausing and resisting the urge to curse at the realization that by the time I get everything ready for the week, it'll be close to midnight.

> WILL: I wish… As much as I'd love to, there's a ton of stuff I have to get done tonight. What about tomorrow?

> HANNAH: You know it's Margarita Monday.

> WILL: Crap, that's right. And I have a booster club meeting Tuesday night and then Thursday, I agreed to drive the bus for the volleyball team since their coach has an appointment.

> HANNAH: Wednesday is our late practice day this week.

I growl in frustration at the texts, feeling the good mood I felt when I saw her name on my phone drifting away.

> WILL: Damn. I don't know if I can make it this week.

> HANNAH: I mean technically we made it the last seven years so I think we'll survive...

> HANNAH: I guess I'll also admit that I'm a little sad about this. I was looking forward to sliding my mouth up and down your thick...

> HANNAH: But never mind... I'll just have to take care of myself. ;) See you Friday!

"Will, why do you look like you're ready to punch something?" Marcus asks, looking over at me in concern. "Is there something wrong?"

I blink up from my phone, feeling all the coaches staring at me. "Oh, uh, no, I'm good. Just fired up for the game Friday," I tell them, the lie sounding lame even to my ears.

"Oh, okay," Marcus says skeptically, before sharing a look with all the other coaches.

Eventually, they all turn their attention back to the film, and I struggle to get my frustration under control. It figures that now that we both want to be together, even if she claims it's just for sex, we'd have a full schedule. Eventually, I push those emotions to the side and grab my phone again to respond to Hannah.

> WILL: Tease me all you want, but I'm coming for you on Saturday and I promise you'll be begging by the time I'm through with you.

CHAPTER 33
HANNAH

"Oh my goodness, you're getting so big," I coo at Ruby as I open the gate to her pen on Thursday night. She lets out a happy *moo* and comes over to where I'm holding the bottle I just made out for her.

"Such a sweet girl," I say, reaching out and petting her soft head while she eats.

I hear my phone ring in my back pocket, and I reach for it, almost dropping the milk bottle in the process.

"Hello," I answer, without checking the caller ID.

"Hey, Hannah, this is Dr. Ava from the emergency vet; how are you?" the voice on the other end says.

"Hey, Dr. Ava," I reply. "How are you?"

"Oh, I'm good! I was just driving by your farm after I got called out over this way, and I wanted to check in on how you and your calf were doing. I know it's been a couple of weeks since I talked to you, and I just wanted to see how you were holding up."

I reach down for my calf, giving her some love while she finishes her bottle before responding. "We're good. She's such a sweet thing, and I haven't noticed any of the things you warned me about when we talked a couple weeks ago."

"Great, I'm glad to hear it. All the other animals doing okay?" she asks, and I smile at her question. The vets before her definitely didn't call to do wellness checks on the farm, and I love how helpful she is.

"Yeah, Leroy's as big of a pain as ever, but we both know I love him to death for it," I tell her, causing her to laugh. "And all the cows and the horses seem to be doing great. I tried that new feed you suggested, and they love it."

As I talk, Ruby finishes her bottle, so I take it from her and toss it over the side of the pen before sitting down in the fresh hay I put out a few minutes ago to love on her for a few minutes. Watching me, she bounces around on her hooves in excitement while I reach out to nuzzle her nose.

"Leroy's certainly a handful, but he's such a sweet little fella. I fell in love when you brought him in for his yearly check-up this summer. And I'm glad to hear that..." Dr. Ava pauses, just as the calf lets out another loud moo of contentment. "Oh, I must have interrupted dinner time, huh?"

I chuckle while Ruby attempts to get as close as she can to me until she's almost in my lap. "You're fine! She just finished and now she's seeing how close she can get to me without standing on me."

Ruby continues to snuggle closer to me, and I pat her gently before pulling the phone back to whisper to her, "Sweet girl, you know I love you, but you do weigh a couple hundred pounds."

"Calf cuddles are probably one of my favorites," the doctor says, before adding, "but anyway, I won't keep you. I've been meaning to call and check on everything for the last few weeks, but we've been slammed. I know you've got your hands full, but I'm always here if you need something. After I got divorced last year, I realized how hard it is to do all this stuff by yourself."

"Oh, Dr. Ava, I really appreciate it. It's been a lot, but we're getting there. Let's grab dinner or something soon?"

"Sure, I'd like that. Anyway, I've gotta run, but I'll talk to you later," she answers before ending the call.

Putting my phone to the side, I rub my hands over Ruby's hair, mumbling to her, "You know, sweet girl, I know it feels like it's us against the world sometimes, but I really think we're gonna make it."

Ruby moos in agreement, and I lean my head back against the gate, looking out at the farm that stretches for miles around us.

"I don't know about you, Rubes, but I wouldn't want to be anywhere else either. We've got everything we need right? Don't we, girl?"

"OH MY GOD, WHAT A GAME!" Caroline says as we step onto the bus Friday night. We just came out on top against the Huntsville Hornets and we're officially headed to the semi playoffs.

"Right? I can't believe that pass Blake made at the end of the third! And that we went into triple overtime! I've literally never experienced anything like it! It was fun, but I'm freaking exhausted!" I tell her, leaning my head against the back seat of the bus.

"Oh, same. I'm just so glad the boosters worked out hotel rooms for this one. I can't imagine making the four-hour drive tonight! It's already almost midnight!"

I look down at my watch and see she's right. Considering I've been up since five and spent the whole day teaching, it's no wonder I feel dead on my feet.

We ride for a few more minutes, and I smile at the fact that it's completely silent on the bus for once. Clearly, the girls are as worn out as we are, and by the time we pull up to the hotel, several of them are already asleep.

"All right, girls, I know it's been a long day, but we're here. Grab your stuff and meet us in the lobby. We'll give you your keys and head up from there," Caroline announces, and I stay behind to help them while Caroline goes in to get the keys before the team gets here.

Once we're all inside, she gathers the girls around and says, "Okay, I'm about to pass out the keys, and I expect you all to go straight to the room and stay there until breakfast at eight in the morning. Do you understand?"

The girls nod, and I add, "Remember, we're trusting you because it's such a long way from Springside, but if we hear one word about you being out of your rooms or doing something you aren't supposed to be, you'll be dismissed from the team and face disciplinary actions at school. Is that clear?"

The girls all say, "Yes ma'am," and Caroline hands me half of the keys to pass out. Once we're sure everyone knows where we're going, the girls head upstairs, and she hands me an extra key.

"Since Taylor's sick and Jenny wanted to stay in a different room instead of being alone, we have an extra. I know we were gonna share, but there's no use in leaving it empty."

"Thanks," I say, reaching out and slipping the key into my pocket. "You think we're gonna have any problems out of them tonight?"

"Honestly, I'm not worried. I mean I know they're teenagers and that usually comes with some questionable choices, but they know we're serious about removing them, and plus, they all looked pretty dead on their feet. We'll keep an ear out, but I really think it'll be fine."

"Yeah, that's kinda how I'm feeling too," I admit. "And I'm as wiped as they are so I'm about to head up. But I'll make sure my phone ringer is on loud so you can call and wake me up if you need me."

"I will. I'll see you in the morning, Han," she says, reaching out and wrapping her arm around my shoulders.

"See ya then," I tell her, getting on the elevator just as the bus carrying the football team pulls up.

Once I get to our floor, I make sure all the girls are in their rooms and have everything they need before letting myself into the room number Caroline gave me.

After changing my clothes and getting ready for bed, I grab my Kindle and my cell before collapsing into bed. I was exhausted on the ride over, but now that I'm in bed I feel a little more restless than I expected. I scroll through my Kindle, figuring I can find something to read to help settle me down. I download a second chance romance about a football coach in a town called Baker Oaks and spend a few minutes getting lost in the story. I'm so absorbed in my screen, that the sound of my phone pinging almost makes me jump out of the bed. I turn it over and feel my eyes widen at the sight of Will's name on my screen.

> WILL: You feeling as wide awake as I am?

> HANNAH: Yep. I don't know what's the matter with me. I was exhausted on the ride over, but now I can't sleep.

> WILL: Same. You end up with a room by yourself?

> HANNAH: Yeah... you?

Instead of responding, my phone rings and I look down to see his name. Hitting to accept the call, I press my phone to my ear and answer. "Hello."

"Hey, Han." His low voice fills the empty room, and I snuggle under the covers, wishing I was with him.

"I take it you ended up without a roommate too, huh?"

"Yeah, a couple kids had parents that signed them out so all the coaches ended up getting their own."

"Well, that worked out I guess. Congrats on the win."

"Thanks, I really can't believe we're headed to the semifinals," he admits, and I smile at the excitement in his voice.

"Yeah, it's awesome. I'm so proud of you," I say, and the phone goes quiet for a minute.

Finally, I'm about to check and make sure my phone didn't die when I hear him whisper, "God, I wish I could be with you right now."

"Sure, Will, that'd be a great example," I say sarcastically, pausing before continuing, "but I kinda wish you could too."

I swear I hear him smile through the phone at my admission, and I suddenly realize that probably didn't fall under the "just sex" category. I open my mouth to make a comment that brings us back to safer territory just as he says, "I've missed you like crazy this week, Han. I know I've seen you at school, but it's not the same. Now that I've touched you, I need you all the time."

My heart speeds up at his admission, and I smile at the sincerity in his voice. "Yeah, I know what you mean. I guess I've kinda missed you too. Or at least, I've missed your cock."

He laughs at that before saying, "Whatever you need to tell yourself. But tomorrow afternoon, you're mine."

"That sounds good. Good night, Will," I tell him, afraid that if I don't end this conversation soon, I'll end up giving away how badly I want more than I should from him.

"Good night, Han. Sweet dreams," he replies, and I pull the covers tighter around me, trying to convince myself that I don't want more with Will Thompson.

CHAPTER 34
HANNAH

"You know, I think this is becoming an addiction," I tease as Will pulls out of me, shrugging back on my clothes and waiting for him to join me in the tailgate. Curling up in Will's arms under the stars has become an almost nightly ritual since we finally had sex last week, and I still can't get enough of him.

He crawls up beside me and drops a kiss on my lips, pulling me against him before responding, "You know, I was thinking the same thing, but fuck it. There's worse things to be addicted to."

"You're right," I tell him, wrapping my arms around him to pull him closer despite the heat of the humid late July air. I panicked when I looked at the date this week and realized we only have a little longer left in the bubble we've built around us. I feel like this summer's slipping through my fingers, and no matter how hard I try, I can't hold on to these moments. The thought of going more than a day or two away from Will makes me feel on edge, never mind the thought of not seeing him for weeks.

Shaking myself out of my spiral, I lay my head on his chest and remind myself to soak up every moment I get to have with him.

We don't say anything for a while, content to just hold each other in the quiet night until Will finally asks, "So I know we're ignoring reality for a little longer, but I just need you to know there's no way I'm letting you go when the summer's over. I only have a year left of school, and it's only two hours between Southbrook and Tuscaloosa."

I smile at him, shaking my head because I'm convinced the man's a mind reader. "How in the hell did you know that's what I was thinking about?"

"Because I know you, Han. And I haven't been able to stop thinking about it either," he admits, and I feel my heartbeat speed up a little at his admission.

"God, I'm obsessed with you," I tease, trying to hide how true that statement is.

"Back at you," he says, kissing the top of my head. "So, I know you're getting your degree in education, but after that, what's next?"

"Um, well. I'm not exactly sure," I admit, feeling a little sheepish at my admission. "I'm probably going to go for my master's as soon as I finish my bachelor's degree since there's such a pay difference. And after that, I'm thinking about moving back here. I didn't ever see myself moving back home after school, but my gramps can't run this place by himself, and this place means a lot to him, you know?"

Will nods in understanding and brushes his hands through my hair. "Yeah, I get that. I'm thinking about moving back too, to coach. I figure they'll let me start at the bottom of the coaching staff and see what happens. My youngest three siblings will still have a couple years of school, and I want to be able to support them when I can."

I nod in agreement, smiling at the thought of both of us teaching at our old high school. "So we both want to move back here?" I ask, not believing that we could actually want the same thing.

"Sounds like it. I told you, we'd find a way to be together," he teases, brushing his hand softly over my lips.

I roll my eyes at him, ignoring the way that his admission makes me feel. "Okay, fine. But we can't agree on everything. What else do you want?"

I feel his eyes on me, and I look up, expecting him to make some joke about the future, but instead, he looks more serious than I've ever seen him. After a moment, he whispers, "A family, Han. I want the family I didn't get after my dad left. I want to have a house full of kids. A house full of chaos, laughter, and dirty clothes. I know it's too fast but, God, is it really? We've known each other for a while. I just needed the time alone with you to realize how perfect we are together. I've thought a lot about where this might be going, and I've decided to just say fuck it. I can't stop thinking about how much I want to do it all with you."

My heart stops for a moment at the serious turn our conversation just took, but I can't help the smile that spreads across my lips at his admission.

"Are you serious?" I whisper, waiting for him to act like it was all some big joke, but he doesn't. He just nods, opening his mouth, probably to apologize or try to take back part of what he just admitted, but before he can, I throw myself at him, kissing him hard.

"You literally just described everything I've ever wanted, Will. I watched all of my friends growing up with these wild, fun families, but it's always just been me. I mean, I want to finish school first, don't get me wrong. I actually called and made an appointment to get on birth control later this week, but the idea of raising a family on this land just feels like everything I've ever wanted," I admit quietly, realizing I've never even told Caroline all of this.

He smiles at me, kissing me again, before holding me tighter against him. "I'm glad we're on the same page, Han, because it's all I want, but I don't want it with anyone else."

CHAPTER 35
WILL

WILL: I'm heading your way.

Hannah: Sounds good... I'm in the middle of something in the barn, but you can just wait inside the house.

Reading her text, I throw my phone in the seat beside me and tell myself not to speed too fast down the country roads toward Falling Oaks. I'm pretty sure this has been the longest week of my life, and I'm so ready to finally spend some time with Hannah. Every spare moment has been consumed with thinking about her, and I've had to fight the urge to skip out on some of my coaching duties to see her.

After pulling into the driveway, I veer off toward the barn knowing there's no way I'm giving up any time with her after staying away all week. I throw the truck in park just as I hear the sound of a loud shriek coming from inside. My heart stops, and I sprint inside, feeling my anxiety rise at the idea of finding Hannah hurt.

The door is latched from the inside, so I pound on it, desperate to make sure she's okay. It doesn't budge, and I growl in frustration as the screeching continues. Finally, I lean back and run at the door, hitting it hard and knocking the hook off the back. I look around the large space, trying to find the sound of the noise before hearing Hannah yell, "Leroy, stop it!"

Running toward her, I'm completely confused about what's going on until I'm close enough to take it in the scene in front of me, and I can't help but laugh at the absurdity.

Hannah is standing over Leroy and holding his front hoofs in her hands as he wiggles and throws his head back and forth, trying to get away. As soon as he sees me, he lets out another ear-splitting squeal like he's begging for me to save him.

"Leroy, you're so damn dramatic. You know I've got to trim your nails before they start hurting you," she says, gently using a small set of clippers on his hooves as he continues to wail away. "I've never been so glad to not have neighbors. I swear if we did —Oh, Will! What are you doing here? I told you that you could wait at the house," Hannah says, finally noticing me standing in front of her.

"Yeah, well, I pulled up and heard the ruckus, so I came to make sure you were okay," I admit, trying not to feel silly about the misunderstanding. "Did you really not hear me trying to get in? I broke the lock off trying to get through the damn door."

Hannah lets out a laugh at that, finishing with Leroy's last hoof before straightening and letting him go. As soon as he's released he darts toward the open door and runs off into the darkness while Hannah reaches up to pull a set of earplugs out of her ears. "Not a hundred percent sure what you're saying because even with these stupid things I'm pretty sure my ears will be ringing for the next three business days. But I'm sorry that you were locked out. If I don't close off all the exits, Leroy tends to get ideas about becoming a runaway. "

"Sorry, I was just worried something was wrong," I admit sheepishly.

"It's fine. I'll just have to reattach that latch sometime over the next few days."

"I'll take care of it," I tell her, walking over to pull her into my arms. "But first, I need to kiss you for a while. I've been thinking about tasting that sweet mouth against mine for the last week."

Her eyes widen for just a moment before she runs at me, all but tackling me to the ground and kissing me hard while she threads her fingers through my hair.

I manage to keep my footing, wrapping her legs around my hips before moving backward to let her lean against the wall of the barn.

"God, you're perfect," I groan, dropping a trail of kisses down the column of her neck.

She whimpers at the feel of my beard against her sensitive skin, and I feel my dick harden in my jeans at the sound. I tell myself to stop this and at least get her in the house, but after spending the week unable to touch her, I can't make myself pull away.

"Will, please, fuck me," she murmurs, reaching down to undo my belt and unbutton my jeans.

"I do love it when you beg, baby girl," I tease, grabbing her shirt and yanking it over her head. "I haven't gotten to taste this sweet pussy in years, and I can't wait any longer."

"Yes," she pants, leaning against the wall of the barn as I tear her leggings off her.

As soon as she's bare, I grab her ankle and hook it around my shoulder so she's open for me before leaning in and running my tongue through her center. "Damn, you're fucking soaked, Han."

She opens her mouth to respond just as I lean in and start teasing her clit with my mouth while sliding my fingers inside her, and whatever she was about to say dies in her throat. Her hips start to shift against my face as I tease her, and I pull back, kissing down her leg but continuing to tease her with my fingers before whispering, "That's right, baby. You're gonna come on my tongue before you slide onto my cock."

She moans at my words, and I kiss back up her leg, continuing to touch and taste her until she tightens around my fingers, yelling, "Yes, please, don't stop, yes, Will."

Just as she's starting to come, I nip at her clit lightly, and she screams, bucking her hips frantically as she loses it. As she rides out her orgasm I moan, desperate to be inside her again. "God, you're so fucking beautiful when you come apart," I whisper, pulling back to stand and grabbing both legs to wrap them around me. "But I need to be inside you now."

She's still a little out of it as she comes down from her climax, but she nods eagerly, leaning her shoulders against the wall to give me room to slide inside her.

As soon as I line myself up with her entrance, I know I'm not gonna last long. The feeling of having her this close after wanting her all week, combined with the way I can feel her dripping down my cock, has me ready to spill inside her already.

"Please, Will, I want to feel you," she begs, and I snap, pushing into her in a quick thrust. Grabbing her hips, I help lift her up and down on my cock, fucking her hard.

"So good, Han. You're so pretty when you're filled with my cock," I praise, knowing I'm close. "I'm nowhere near through with you. You're all I've thought about all week."

"Yes," she moans, and I lose it, rocking into her faster until my orgasm hits me. I pump my hips harder, filling her with my cum. She continues to whimper as I finish, and eventually, I slowly help her stand, pulling out of her, and groaning when I see my cum running down her leg.

"Come on, baby, let's get inside. I'll cook us something to eat, and then we're doing that again."

"OH MY GOD, Caroline, the house looks incredible!" Hannah

says, busting through the door at Caroline and Theo's farmhouse Thanksgiving afternoon.

"Thanks, Han. I got a little too into the decorations this year, but I think it turned out cute," Caroline replies, hugging her before gesturing to the kitchen. "And you already know that Margaret did most of this."

"Damn, Marg, you do remember there's only six of us, right?" Hannah teases, taking in all the dishes spread across the counters and the bar across the kitchen. I follow her gaze, still shocked by the amount of food Theo's sister prepared for today. There are two turkeys, ten sides, and at least six different deserts, in addition to the things we tried to contribute.

After sitting down the dish of corn casserole she brought with the rest of the food, Hannah turns back to us, already rambling. "I'm sorry I was running a few minutes late. I took Merle out for a ride this morning because I haven't had time to do that lately, and we totally lost track of time."

"You're fine! I just took the turkey out less than five minutes ago," Margaret says, coming over to hug Hannah. "And Will and Seth didn't get here too long ago."

"Oh, that's right. You went to your momma's, huh?" she asks Seth from where he's sitting on the couch with Theo's lab, Bear.

"Yeah, we did. She told me to remind all of you that you're always welcome, but I refuse to subject anyone else to her health shit on Thanksgiving," he says with an eye roll. "Will's used to it by now, but I can promise that it's nothing like what Margaret's done here."

"It's not that bad," I lie, trying to be nice. Seth's family has always welcomed me with open arms after my mom moved up north a few years ago when the last of my siblings graduated. She wanted a fresh start after spending the last twenty-seven years raising kids, and I completely understood.

"Whatever, man. I love her to death, but it was literally turkey, green beans, and a salad. She didn't even make the rolls like she normally does. What kind of Thanksgiving is that?" Seth complains before slumping dramatically into the side of the sofa.

"You're such a drama king," Margaret says with a laugh, leaning down to pull a pan of rolls out of the oven. "But don't worry, I've got us covered. Y'all ready to eat?"

"Let's do it," Caroline says, handing each of us a plate. "You all know where everything is. Have at it."

Everyone moves to fix their plate and it doesn't take but a few minutes until we're all gathered around the table. Hannah's the last one over, and I fight the urge to smile when she sits her plate down beside me.

"Hold on, let me grab the wine I brought," she says, stepping back across the kitchen and returning with a bottle of Moscato. After filling everyone's glass, she sits and holds up her glass.

Caroline grabs hers too and looks around, waiting for us to all follow suit, and then she says, "Thanksgiving has never been my favorite. Since my parents moved away, it's always just been a day for Hannah and I to watch trashy TV and share a frozen pizza on her couch while we watched everyone around us spend time with the family that we didn't have. But over the last year, I've realized that family doesn't just mean the one we're born into. It's about the people I know I can count on every single time. It's the ones who walk through the fun stuff and the really hard shit. And I've just gotta say, I'm just really grateful that y'all are mine."

Hannah and Margaret both look at her like they're about to cry, and Seth, Theo, and I just make eye contact across the table, unsure of what to say. Finally, Hannah shakes herself out of whatever she's feeling and teases. "Damn, Caro, enough of the sappy shit. You already know we love you. Now, let's eat."

We all laugh and Margaret adds, "Yeah, please do. You know I need all the feedback on these recipes."

"Like you don't already know that they're incredible," Caroline says, rolling her eyes, before turning to me while everyone starts to eat. "So, Will, speaking of family, I've been meaning to ask, how are your siblings doing?"

"They're good. Kit loves her school in Georgia, and the twins are still attending school in Wyoming. Ollie's got some new job in Indianapolis and he seems to really like it too. I hate that I don't get to see them much, but we check in as often as we can. And Mom loves living in Maine. She's running her own art business now, and last I heard, I think she might have found herself a boyfriend."

"That's great. I'm so happy she's doing something she loves," Caroline replies, and I nod in agreement.

"So, Seth, when will you start practice for baseball?" Theo asks, and I listen to the two of them start to talk about the season before Hannah slides her hand over to place it on my leg, squeezing my leg under the table.

What the hell is she doing? I wonder, trying to keep my face neutral, waiting to see what else she'll do. But she just rests her hand on my thigh and continues eating with her other hand like she just wants to be near me. *Damn, what I'd give to be able to pull her into my arms right now.* Across from us Theo and Caroline are huddled together while they eat like they can't stand to be away from each other, and I feel a flash of jealousy—not at my best friends—but at desperately wanting that with Hannah.

I know she keeps saying that whatever this is between us is just sex, but I know, at least for me, that couldn't be further from the truth. I'm completely gone for this girl, and there isn't anything I wouldn't do to keep her.

CHAPTER 36
WILL

SEVEN SUMMERS AGO

I walk in the house after a long day on the farm and smile when I see my siblings all sitting around the kitchen table talking to Mom. I've been spending so much time with Hannah, I don't know the last time I was home for dinner.

Pulling off my boots at the back door, I call out, "Hey, kiddos. How was your… Wait, what the hell is wrong?"

I feel my panic rising as all of my siblings and my mom look up at me and I see tears and anger in all of their expressions.

No one speaks for a moment, and I look around, waiting for one of them to say something. Eventually, Ollie breaks the silence. "Mom just got something from Dad's lawyers. He's filing for sole custody of us?"

"What?" I roar, feeling anger surge up in me like I've never felt before. "Why the hell would he do this, Mom?" I ask, looking down at the paperwork she's holding in her hands. Tears are streaming down her face, and she just looks up at me, looking more hopeless than I'd ever seen her.

"My bet is he thinks he can get out of paying child support since he got in trouble for not making payments over the last few months. I guess he thinks forcing them to live with him will save him some money."

"That's bullshit," I yell, feeling a fury at my shithead father I haven't felt since I first caught him cheating on my mom all those years ago.

"Language, honey," my mom scolds me, but there's no heat behind her words.

"Aren't we old enough to get a say?" Ollie asks, looking as angry as I feel. "I don't want to move to Crestview for my senior year. I've been in Springside my whole life."

"Yeah, I just finally made the varsity cheer squad, and if we have to leave, I'll miss out on a whole year," Kit cries, tears streaming down her face.

Andrew and Luke just nod in agreement until finally Luke says, "Yeah, I have no desire to live with that asshole. Plus, there's no way we're leaving you here alone, Mom."

She smiles at that despite the tears in her eyes, and she just nods at them, trying to look hopeful.

I take the papers from her and flip through them to see if anything sticks out. Ollie only has two months until he's eighteen and can make his own decisions, but the others have a couple years left of high school. It figures that my fucking dad wouldn't take any of that into account before making this decision.

"Okay, everyone, calm down. This isn't happening. Mom, call your lawyer in the morning and see what he says. I don't know of any judge who would make this decision, but I'm gonna do what I can to make sure it never gets there. I'll go see Dad next week and try to figure out what the hell he thinks he's doing. I think I can figure out what he's actually after."

My mom's eyes widen in surprise, before she argues. "Will, baby, you don't have to do that. This isn't your battle."

"No, it isn't but it shouldn't be yours either. It's not your fault you married an unfaithful and selfish bastard," I tell her, and she cringes.

"But, Will, you haven't seen him in over five years. I can't ask you to do this," she says, and I look at my siblings to see a mixture of fear and anger along with a little bit of hope at my declaration.

"Good thing you didn't ask then, Momma," I tell her, giving her a quick hug before turning back to the table. "All right, enough of this crap. Let's eat."

CHAPTER 37
HANNAH

"Hey, Gramps! How ya holding up today?" I ask, making my way into his room after leaving Thanksgiving at Caroline's.

"Hey, Hannah Banana! I guess I'm okay for an old bastard like me. They had to change up a few of my meds, and you know how that messes with me sometimes. But enough about me, how are you?"

"Oh, I'm good. I brought you some of Margaret's desserts. Everyone told me to tell you they said hi," I tell him, holding up the Tupperware that Margaret insisted I bring with me. "The pie is good, but the cookies are to die for."

"Hand it over," he says eagerly, holding out his hand. "That last batch of cookies you brought didn't last through the night. I shared some with Gladis, and we both 'bout made ourselves sick on 'em."

I laugh as he yanks off the lid and takes out two of the cookies, inhaling them both before I can even sit down.

"I'll let her know they were a hit," I say, settling into the chair across from him.

"How's that bakery of hers coming?" Gramps asks, putting

the lid back on the container and throwing it out of his reach before adding sheepishly. "Gladis will be furious if I eat them all without her."

"It's coming along. Seth's offered to help out a lot over the break, and she's hoping for an opening around the end of the spring."

"Seth's a good guy," Gramps says, nodding in approval. "I'm sure he'll have her up and running in no time."

"Yeah, and Mayor Brian asked her to do a pop-up at Deer Valley Inn through the holidays too so that'll be going soon," I add.

"Oh, that's great. I know Brian's got his hands full, but he and his cousin Bridget have put a lot of work into that place over the last year since his momma passed. Gladis was telling me that they were featured in some hotshot wedding and winery magazine this week. It was the talk of the town at Bingo night."

"Oh, I haven't heard that, but that's awesome. Margaret's really excited to do some holiday specials too. I've lost track of how many recipes she's tested out for the next few months."

"Well, tell her if she ever needs someone to sample them, I'm completely up for it. And, tell her once she opens, she needs to add delivery too. This place will keep her in business," he says enthusiastically.

"Okay, Gramps, I'll tell her, but I'm not sure the nurses will like y'all eating all that sugar."

"Listen, I'm almost eighty years old and I've had more surgeries in the last couple years than I ever wanted to have. So if I want to eat some cookies, that's what I'm gonna do, ya hear me, Hannah Banana?" he says, shaking his finger at me, causing me to roll my eyes at his dramatics.

"Fine, fine," I tell him, holding up my hands in surrender. "I'll pass the message along for you,"

"Thank you. Now, have you been keeping an eye on this weather? The girl on WKOA said we could be getting some serious snow over the next few days. Can you believe it? It hasn't snowed here in years."

"Yeah, I heard something about it, but you know they say this all the time and we never get any. I think it'll be fine. It's still football season for goodness sake," I tell him before adding, "at the game last Friday, we were literally in shorts."

"Well, I know, but just promise me you'll pay attention. The farm is enough work without all that extra chaos."

"I'll watch it," I promise.

"Good. And if you need help, I'm sure Will would be happy to come help you. The two of you worked so well together that summer. I always thought y'all would end up together, but judging by the fact that you can barely stand to be in the same room with him, I guess I was wrong."

I'd just raised my bottle of water to take a sip, but as soon as the words leave his mouth, I can't resist rolling my eyes. "Not this again, Gramps. Are you gonna bring this up every single time I visit?"

"No, but will you at least explain why you're trying so hard to act like there isn't anything there?" he asks, and I have to look away at the confusion on his face.

"Gramps, I don't know what you think you saw, but there's never been anything there," I tell him.

The lie gets caught in my throat, and my gramps gives me a disbelieving look like he knows I'm full of shit, but he lets it go.

"Like I said, I guess I'm wrong. And that's fine. I just want you to be happy, Hannah. I know it probably wasn't how you saw your life going and I'll never forgive my son for giving up the opportunity to be a dad to you, but you've made this old man so proud to call you his. Just promise me that you'll let the right person in when it's time. I know you think you have to hold it all together, but it's okay to need someone. Just promise me you won't shut everyone out forever."

I feel my throat tighten at his words and tears fill my eyes, but I push them down. Reaching over, I grab his hand and squeeze it, before saying, "I promise, Gramps. I love you always."

He smiles and pulls me around the table to hug me. "I love you too."

I hug him back, and eventually he pulls back, leaning back in his recliner. We sit there for a while, talking about everything from the farm to the Iron Bowl and the upcoming semifinals Springside will be playing in next week, but all the while, I can't stop thinking about what he said about Will.

Do I really shut everyone out? My first response is no, thinking about everything I've shared with Caroline over the years, but I pause, remembering there's so much I haven't told her. And despite the fun I'm having with Will, I still haven't told him why I ended everything between us.

Pushing the thoughts aside, I try to snap myself out of it. *No one can fix any of it, and there's no use in becoming either of their charity cases. If the train wreck with your parents taught you anything, it's that everyone leaves, and there's no use in pretending otherwise.*

"OH MY GOD, I can't believe this shit," I tell Caroline on the phone the next afternoon. "If I wanted to put up with this crap, I wouldn't live in South Alabama."

I'm finally headed toward the house after spending the last few hours making sure the cows have plenty of hay and checking on the horses and chickens at the back of the property. I look out, shaking my head in disbelief at the fields that are completely covered in snow. It started falling around lunch and hasn't stopped for the last few hours.

"I know, I've literally only seen snow in Springside twice in my life, and it's definitely never been this much. Theo and the rest of the fire department got called in because the town's a disaster. Cars are all over the place, and he said he's lost track of the number of trucks they've had to help pull out of the ditch," Caroline says through the speaker just as I walk into the yard, heading to make sure Leroy and Ruby have plenty of hay to keep them warm.

"God, what a disaster. So you're alone too?" I ask, looking around and pausing when I realize Leroy isn't in his pen

"Yeah, he said he'd try to be back tonight but we'll see. But Bear's keeping me company," she says, referring to Theo's grumpy chocolate lab. "I hate that our farms are so far apart or I'd come keep you company. Binging reality TV and reading on my Kindle while I drink a full bottle of wine is about all I have planned for the night."

"Ugh, I know. But I'm pretty sure your fiancé would end up pulling you out of the ditch trying to get here and we'd never hear the end of it," I tell her, wrinkling my eyebrows when Ruby isn't in her normal spot either. There's a large hole in the ground, and I shake my head at the absurdity of what I'm seeing.

"Ugh, Leroy, I seriously do not want to deal with your shit this morning! Did you seriously dig a hole big enough to get Ruby out too?" I groan, looking around the snow-covered ground for a sign of my pig. "I gotta go, Caroline. Leroy's escape artist skills strike again, and apparently, he's decided to make Ruby his accomplice this go around."

She lets out a laugh before saying, "Good luck with that one. Let me know when you find them."

"Will do," I say before hanging up and walking around the house. "Leroy, here boy! Ruby, come here sweet girl."

I walk by Leroy's normal spots, noticing it's about to get dark. "Shit, you two are gonna make me lose it."

I'm starting to get worried, but I try to push that thought down, deciding to go grab a flashlight before it's too late so I can keep searching for them. "Leroy! Ruby! Come here sweet—" I pause as I walk up on the porch, before bursting into laughter at the sight in front of me.

My calf and my pig are both curled up on my doormat passed out and looking like they're waiting for me to come home and let them in.

"Are you serious?" I ask, bending down to pet them both and causing them to wake with a start. "You both broke out of your pens, huh? I know it's cold but you can't be doing that!"

They both roll on their backs like they're waiting for me to rub their stomachs, their tails beating the wood porch in excitement.

"I swear, you both think you're dogs," I tell them, shaking my head at their antics. "Come on, let's go back to our pens," I say, and they both just look at me, still lying on their backs and making no move to stand and follow me. "Ugh, y'all, come on. You both weigh a couple hundred pounds, angels. I can't carry you over there."

They still refuse to move, and I throw my hands up, before opening the door, intending to grab the flashlight so I can figure out how to get them back to their pens. Instead, the two animals dart into the house, immediately running to the living room and lying in front of the fire.

"You cannot be serious! Cows and pigs are not allowed in the freaking house!" I yell, but it's clear neither of them is listening.

I blow out a frustrated sigh, before finally admitting defeat. "Fine, but just because it's snowing. I'll build you two a little pen by the fire, but if either of you shit inside my house, it's over."

Making quick work of using furniture to make an enclosed area for my sassy animals. When I'm done, I snap a picture and send it to my group chat with Caroline and Margaret, and before I can think any better of it, I send it in a separate message to Will.

I sit my phone down, planning to change into some pajamas and grab my Kindle, but before I can step away, my phone's ringtone fills the room. Will's contact shows on the screen and I answer, feeling my heart start to race before I even hear his voice.

"Han, is there really a cow and a pig in your house?" he asks, skipping any greeting and jumping straight to the point.

"Yeah, there is," I say with a laugh. "I know, but they're stubborn, and it's freaking cold out."

I hear him chuckle through the line, and the sound sends a spark through me. "Never a fucking dull moment with you, Hannah Scott. How you holding up with the snow?"

"Oh, I'm okay. I can't believe we actually got some though," I reply, walking to my bedroom to change clothes.

"Yeah, I don't think I've ever seen this much snow," he says, lowering his voice. "So what are your plans for tonight? I wanted to come by, but clearly the weather wasn't on board with that."

"I would have liked that," I admit, putting my phone on speaker and throwing it down on my bed before whipping off the first of the multiple layers I had placed on to go outside. "No real plans. I'm about to put on some sweats and cuddle up with my Kindle and a bottle of wine. It'll probably take me at least twenty minutes to get all these layers off though."

I expect him to laugh at that, but instead Will murmurs, "God, I already want to be there, Han. You're torturing me thinking about watching you strip right now."

My breath catches in my throat and heat rushes to my core at his words. Neither of us speak for a moment, and before I can stop myself, I blurt, "Who says you can't?"

Before I can change my mind, I lean across the bed to grab my phone and click to change the call over to FaceTime. His face fills my screen, and I feel a rush at the way he's looking at me.

"Hey, baby," he mutters as I prop my phone on the dresser. Before I can talk myself out of it, I reach to pull both layers of the remaining sweaters off. Throwing them across the room, I force myself to straighten my shoulders, ignoring the chill from standing in just my bra while glancing back at the screen.

"God, Han, you're so fucking beautiful," Will says, leaning closer to the screen. "I knew I should've come over this morning."

"Yeah, and what would you have told Seth when he asked why you weren't home during the biggest snowstorm Springside's had in the last century?" I tease, running my hands down to sit on the band of my leggings.

"Hannah, you know I don't give a shit about any of that. It was your idea to keep this a secret. Otherwise, I wouldn't give a damn who knows that you belong to me."

I freeze at that, feeling a panic that I can't explain clawing at my chest at his words. Why does he keep trying to make this more? A part of me wants to jump at the opportunity to make this into something more than sex, but I know there's no way that will end well. Desperate to remind him why that can't happen, I say, "Will, stop being silly. You know we can't go public even if we wanted to. What would the school say?"

"Baby, you're more important than any of that. I'm a grown man, and I don't care how much I love my job. If it comes down to you or the job, I'm picking you every time. Rules or policy be damned."

My mouth goes dry, and neither of us speaks for a few moments. Finally, Will breaks the silence by murmuring, "Are you gonna stand there, or are you gonna keep showing me that perfect body?"

I shoot him a dirty look, while reaching for my phone. "Actually, now that I think about it, I'm pretty tired. Maybe I'll just go on to bed and take care of it myself. I bet my fingers feel just as good as yours would," I taunt.

"Hannah," he warns, his voice serious, and my stomach dips at the warning in his voice and the desire on his face.

"Fine, but no more of the serious stuff tonight," I say, throwing my phone down on the bed and sliding my leggings off.

"Hannah, as nice as your ceiling is, I'd much rather see you," Will adds, and I see him roll his eyes on the little phone screen.

Grabbing my phone, I hold it up to let him see my mostly naked body, and he freezes. "Damn, baby. You're so fucking sexy."

I smile at that, lying across my bed and trailing my phone down so he can see all of me. "God, I've never hated the snow more in my life," he groans, as I trail my fingers up and down my body, teasing him by pulling my panties down at my hips a little more each time.

"You gonna be a good girl and take those off for me? I want to see what's mine" he growls.

I answer by sliding the waistband lower and lower until I pull them all the way off, leaving me completely bare.

"Fuck, yes, baby," he growls, and I hear his sharp intake of breath as I lower the phone to let him see all of me.

"Are you gonna touch that perfect pussy for me, baby?" he asks, and I pull the phone up so I can see his face.

The look of raw desire makes heat rush to my core, and I whisper, "You want me to?"

"Hell yes, Han. Touch yourself, and let me watch you come apart wishing it was me."

I let out a moan at that, moving the phone down so that he can see my fingers trail down my stomach before brushing softly against my clit.

"That's right. Tease that sweet little clit of yours. But you don't come until I say so," Will demands as I focus on following his instructions. I don't remember ever feeling this desperate to find my orgasm, and I groan with need each time my fingers brush across my sensitive clit.

"Now show me how wet you are for me, Hannah. Slide your finger inside, and tell me if that pussy's dripping for me yet," he instructs, and I immediately do as he says.

"Shit, baby, that's so fucking pretty," he groans, watching

through the screen as I slide a finger inside myself. "How wet are you, baby?"

"So wet," I whimper, moving my finger in and out as I feel my orgasm starting to build.

"Han, you're gonna make me come," he growls, and I look down at my phone to see the feral look in his eyes. He's lying back on his bed and I can tell he's fisting his cock as he watches me touch myself through the screen. "Fuck that sweet cunt of yours and let me watch you come apart for me."

His words drive my desire even higher, and I lose myself in his command. Reaching down with my other hand to tease my clit, I slide another finger inside my pussy, fucking myself faster as the orgasm I felt building earlier threatens to overtake me.

"Yes, come for me, baby. I want to hear you," Will urges, and apparently his words are all the encouragement I need because, at that, my orgasm overtakes me.

"God, yes," I moan, writhing my hips against my fingers as I come, barely aware of Will continuing to praise me on the other end of the line. It takes me a moment to come down, and when I do, I reach for my phone, smiling at the satisfied grin on his face.

"Damn, that was sexy," he mutters, and I can't help but laugh.

"Did you finish?" I ask, realizing I was so lost in the moment, I have no idea if he's still expecting something in return.

"Yeah, baby, hottest damn thing I've ever seen in my life," Will says, shaking his head in disbelief. "I enjoyed that, but this snow shit needs to go because if I don't get inside you soon, I'm gonna lose my damn mind. This time tomorrow, I don't care if I have to walk the fifteen miles to your house, I'm gonna be in your bed."

I laugh again, nodding in agreement. "Yeah, yeah, whatever you say."

"I mean it. You better get your rest tonight, because tomorrow you're mine," he growls.

"Hmm, sounds good to me. Good night, Will," I say.

I ignore the pang in my chest at having to say goodbye, despite the fact that I'm dead on my feet and there's no reason for us to keep talking now that the sex is over.

"Good night, Han. Sweet dreams," he says, shooting me a smile before he ends the call.

I take a minute to wash up and get ready for bed, before collapsing back on my mattress, pulling the covers up around me. The house that has always been my refuge suddenly feels oddly empty in the silence, and I blow out a sigh at the feeling of loneliness that threatens to overtake me.

CHAPTER 38
HANNAH

SEVEN SUMMERS AGO

"Are you okay?" I ask, noticing that Will looks upset as we load the truck for the last Farmers' Market of the summer. He doesn't respond at first, so I give him a moment before calling out to him again, "Earth to Will. You okay, babe?"

He smiles at me, but I frown when I realize it doesn't quite meet his eyes. "Sorry, I'm just distracted today. What'd you ask me?"

"I was just asking if you're okay. You've looked upset today," I tell him, bending down and grabbing one of the boxes of corn to load in the truck.

"Yeah, I'm okay. My dad's just being an asshole, but there's not really anything new," he says, and I nod in understanding.

"I get it. You don't have to apologize. I just want you to know you can always talk to me about it if you want."

Will looks up to meet my eyes, and I see whatever defenses he was trying to build crumble. "I know, I'm sorry. I'm being an ass. I'm just used to working through this shit on my own. I tried to call Huey this morning on the way over here to talk through it but he was out on a fire call, and I'm just in my head."

I run my hand over his arm, wanting to be close to him before saying, "I'm sorry, baby. And there's no pressure because I'm certainly no Huey, but I'm here if you want me."

Will's eyes soften at that, and he reaches out, pulling me into his arms. "God, you really are perfect for me. I'm screwing this all up. I found out last night that my dad filed for sole custody of my siblings."

At that admission, I feel my jaw drop, and if the moment wasn't so serious, I'd be fighting not to laugh. Not because it's funny—quite the opposite, actually. It's more because even I know how absurd that request is. "But your dad's been gone from Springside for years. What the hell does he want now?" I ask, trying to figure out what it is that I'm missing.

"Apparently, he wants to force my siblings to move to Crestview for the rest of high school. Not really sure why yet. My mom thinks he wants to get out of paying child support," Will admits, and I feel my anger at Will's father rising even more.

"What the hell, Will? Why the fuck would he do this?" I ask, knowing it probably isn't the most helpful question at the moment, but I can't help myself.

He just shrugs his shoulders, and I hate how frustrated he looks. "Other than the fact that he's a selfish bastard that only cares about himself? That's all I got. But I told Mom I'd go try to talk to him next week since he's been ignoring our messages."

My eyes widen at that statement. "Wait, I didn't think you'd seen him since the divorce."

Will just nods before murmuring, "Yeah, that's right."

The weight of what he's saying all crashes into me, and I pull him to me, reaching out to place a soft kiss on his mouth. He pulls me into his arms again and even after we pull back from the kiss, neither of us moves, clearly content to just stay in each other's arms. After a while, he pulls away and gestures toward all the veggies and fruit lying at our feet.

"Enough of all that. My dad's been a disappointment for years, and I'm not going to let him ruin our day. We're almost done here, and I took care of those last bales of hay this morning. What do you want to do when we finish?" he asks, and I smile at the excitement in his question despite all the negativity he's dealing with.

"Well, I actually have a little surprise for you," I tell him, watching his eyes widen in surprise.

"Of course you do. You and your surprises," he teases, dropping a kiss on the top of my head. "So do I get to find out now, or do I have to wait until we get all this other shit done."

"Well," I tell him, drawing out the word to tease him, "I was originally going to make you wait, but since you asked so nicely, we're doing something I promised you at the beginning of the summer. Any guesses?"

Will pauses, probably thinking through some of our earliest conversations before shaking his head. "I'm trying to think, but honestly, I've already gotten everything I wanted this summer."

He winks at the end of that statement, and I roll my eyes in mock annoyance. "Aww shucks, aren't you just the sweetest? But as for what we're doing today, I thought I'd teach you how to ride a horse. I know you've been around them a pretty decent amount this summer to feed them and help clean out their stalls, and I think you'll really like it."

"That sounds fun, Han," he says, dropping one more quick kiss onto my mouth before pulling back and grabbing some of the boxes to pile into the back of the truck. "Let's get this knocked out, and then we'll go. And then tonight, when I have you alone, I'm gonna fuck you until we both forget about all this shit, okay?"

"And they say the perfect day doesn't exist," I tease, sliding up on my tiptoes to kiss him one more time.

CHAPTER 39
WILL

"Yeah, the county just posted that all the roads are passable again, so I'll be there in five," I tell Hannah late the next afternoon as I walk to my truck. The remnants of yesterday's snow is melting as we speak, and I can't wait any longer to get my hands on her.

"Okay, if you're sure it's safe," Hannah responds. "I just finished checking on the horses and the cows, and I'm in desperate need of a shower. I won't be long but just come on in and make yourself at home when you get here."

"Sounds good. I'll see you in a few," I say, pulling out of the parking lot and stepping a little harder on the gas than normal at the thought of her naked and wet for me.

The sight of her teasing her pretty pussy over FaceTime is permanently ingrained in my head and I need to finally feel her again. It's only been a few days since I was over here before the holidays, but every time I'm away from her, the more and more I crave her.

I drive in silence, reminding myself not to speed too much with the questionable road conditions, but my desire to see Hannah still has me making the fifteen-minute drive to Falling Oaks in just under ten. As I turn into the driveway, I force myself to slow down, despite the fact that my body is humming with the need to touch her again.

After pulling up to the farmhouse, I get out of the truck, shivering at the barely above freezing temperature as I head inside. Walking in the door, I shake my head at Leroy and Ruby cuddled in front of the fire before bellowing, "Hey, Han. I'm here."

"Oh, hey. Give me just a few minutes, and I'll be out of the shower. I had to wash my hair, so it's taking me a little longer than planned," she yells, and I follow the sound of her voice into the master bedroom.

The door to the bathroom is not quite closed, and as I make my way over I groan at the sight of her naked back. She's got her head tipped back as she rinses the shampoo out of her hair, and the sight of the suds streaming down her tanned back snaps the remaining shreds of control I'd been trying to maintain.

Kicking my boots off, I push the door open further, already pulling my shirt over my head. At the sound of my entrance, she turns and laughs. "Hey, you. I told you I'm almost done. Don't you want to watch a movie until I'm done or something?"

"If you think I'm gonna sit on your couch and watch TV while you're in here soaking wet and naked, you clearly don't understand how badly I want you right now," I growl as I drop the rest of my clothes and pull the door open to join her in the steamy shower.

Hannah opens her mouth to respond, but I stalk over to her and reach for her legs, lifting her body to mine and letting her wrap her legs around my waist as I press her back against the wall and drop my mouth to hers. She lets out a hiss as the cold tile meets her back, and I take advantage of the opportunity to deepen the kiss, threading her tongue with mine.

"Damn, I've missed you," I groan, continuing to kiss her before reaching down and teasing her clit to make sure she's ready for me.

"I missed you too," she admits, rolling her hips against my fingers. "God, that feels good."

I tease her clit for a few more moments, before running my hand through her center and fighting the urge to growl as I feel how wet she is already. "Such a good girl for me, Han. You're already ready to take my cock in this sweet pussy, aren't you?"

She rolls her head back against the wall to look at me, and I don't miss the need in her expression. "God, yes. Please fuck me, Will. Please, please, please." She rolls her hips against me again, trying her best to grind against my cock.

"Someone's a greedy girl tonight, huh? Damn, you're fucking dripping for me," I mutter, running my fingers through her core again. "Such a dirty girl, aren't you? Begging to take this cock while your pussy leaks for me," I tease. As soon as the words are out of my mouth, she stills and drops her gaze, refusing to look at me.

I thread one of my hands through her hair, pulling just hard enough that she has to bring her gaze back to mine. "Baby girl, you listen to me and you listen good. I'm fucking gone for you, and the sound and feeling of you begging for my cock is the sweetest fucking thing I've ever heard, you understand."

Her eyes widen and she reaches up to thread her hands through my hair, pulling me down to kiss her hard. As soon as our lips touch, she resumes her grinding against me. "As much as I want to savor this, I need to be inside you, Han. After this, I promise I'll spend the rest of the night taking it as slow as you want, but please, let me fuck you hard and fast first."

She nods eagerly, and I reach down to line my cock up with her entrance. I inch in a bit, trying to make sure I don't hurt her, despite the warning I just gave, but as soon as the tip meets her hot pussy, she tenses her legs around me, forcing me inside her with one deep, quick thrust.

"Fuck," I curse, and she just moans in response, already trying to use the wall for leverage to fuck herself on my cock. "You're so damn perfect."

Using one hand to keep her firmly against the wall, I let the other one trail to her breasts, rolling one of her rosy nipples in my fingers to tease her. She continues rocking against my cock, until I surprise her by pinching her sensitive peak in my fingers. She gasps at first before the surprised sound morphs into a moan.

"God, yes, Will. Harder," she begs, and I oblige, moving my hips faster as I slam into her hard, before sliding my hand down from her breast to toy with her clit again. I roll it in my fingers for a few moments, feeling the grip on my control fading fast.

"Come on, baby. Come for me," I beg, continuing to play between her legs. She throws her head back, chanting, "Yes, more."

Moving in and out of her faster, I continue teasing her until I can tell I'm about to lose it. Needing her to get there, I slide my fingers around her clit and tug lightly. The change in pressure tips her over the edge, and we both lose ourselves in the orgasm that overtakes us.

"You...feel...so...fucking...good," I grunt as I thrust into her hard, spilling my cum inside her.

She moans in acknowledgment, continuing to ride out her orgasm. After several moments, we both still, and she leans her head back against the tile.

"You know, I thought last night was really hot, but it turns out nothing compares to riding your dick," she teases, pushing me back gently so she can stand. In the process, my cock slides free from her pussy, and I growl at the sight of my cum starting to run down her legs.

"Fuck, baby. You look so damn pretty with my cum inside you," I murmur, sinking to my knees in front of her. Running my hand up her leg, I collect as much of it as I can and gently slide my fingers back inside her, fucking her with my release.

"Damn it, Will. Oh my God," she groans, trying to pull back for a moment before leaning back against the wall for balance and letting me have my way.

I continue pushing my cum back inside her for another moment, until her body recovers and she starts rocking against me, begging for more. "Yes, baby."

I add another finger, moving them faster as her breath begins to quicken again. "That's right. Come on my fingers the same way you came on yours last night," I encourage. "Ride my hand. Give me one more before we get out of the shower, and I take you to the bed."

"Will, yes. Don't stop," she begs, and I smile as I feel her pussy start to clench around my fingers.

"Whose fingers feel better, Han? Mine or yours? You like to tease me, but I think we both know who owns this perfect body," I taunt.

"Fuck you, Will," she mutters, moving her hips faster.

At her words, I still my fingers, keeping them inside her, but refusing to give her what she wants. "Come on, Hannah. Just admit it, and I'll give you what you want."

"Fine," she groans. "Yours are way better, okay? Just please make me come," she pleads, and I can't hide the smile at her words.

"Yes, ma'am," I mutter, moving my fingers faster and leaning forward to press a kiss against her clit. As soon as my mouth makes contact with her pussy, she screams, and I feel her clench even harder around my fingers as she rides out her second orgasm.

After a few seconds, she stills, leaning against the wall of the shower and letting out a sigh. "I think you broke me," she mutters. "And by the way, you're an asshole."

"Maybe, but you love it," I tease, rising to my feet and pulling her into my arms under the water. "Let's get you rinsed off and then we're gonna spend the next few hours doing that again."

"You're trying to kill me," she mutters, leaning her head back to resume rinsing her hair.

"Nope, just can't get enough of you," I reply, leaning down and pressing a kiss against her cheek. "Now, let's get you clean."

CHAPTER 40
WILL

SEVEN SUMMERS AGO

"Hey, My name's Will. I'm here to see Charles Thompson," I tell the receptionist at Dad's office in Crestview. My skin feels like it's crawling just thinking about having to see the man who's wreaked such havoc on my family over the last few years.

"Oh, hi. He's with a client, but if you don't mind waiting, they should be done shortly," she says, smiling widely at me and twirling a piece of her hair around her finger.

"Fine, I'll be over there," I respond, pointing to the sitting area by the door.

"That's fine, but you're welcome to stay here and keep me company," she flirts before winking at me. God, I do not want to be here.

I take a second to glance at the receptionist, and I have to admit that prior to this summer I would have thought she was my type—short dark hair and an even shorter skirt. But on top of having no interest in anyone associated with my father, all I can think about is how much I prefer Hannah's sweet smile and long blonde hair. I just glare at her for a moment before moving to sit on the couch against the wall without a word.

After about forty-five minutes of waiting, I finally see my dad walking to the front with the woman I'm assuming is the client he was helping. But after watching them for a moment, they don't look very professional. His hands on her lower back, and she leans into him as she walks like she needs to be closer to him. He chuckles at something she says, and I feel the familiar mix of rage and disappointment I've felt every time I thought about him over the last few years.

Apparently, one affair wasn't enough, huh? I think to myself as I wait for him to notice me.

It takes a few more minutes, but eventually he looks up as he leads his "client" to the door, and the shocked expression would make me laugh if I wasn't so desperate to be out of this place.

"Will?" he asks, looking at me as if he can't decide if I'm really here.

"Good job, you remembered my name," I say sarcastically as the woman he was with walks out the door. "I wasn't sure if you forgot over the last six years."

"Well... I—I—I haven't heard from you either," he replies, and I fight the urge to roll my eyes at that response.

"You're right. My mistake for thinking you'd be an adult and reach out. But nope, it was on me as a sixteen-year-old kid who caught you cheating on my mom to fix our relationship. But anyway, that ship sailed a long time ago, and that's not why I'm here."

The office is silent at my outburst, the secretary's eyes wide as she takes in what I just said.

"This isn't a good time, Will. Plus, it's not appropriate to have this conversation at work," he replies, rubbing his eyes as if I'm the problem.

"Hmm, that's rich considering what I just saw walking out of there. I'd say I feel bad for Sandy, but it's not like she didn't know how you were when y'all ended up together," I reply, causing my dad to growl in frustration.

"Okay, fine. Go ahead and tell me whatever it is you came to tell me. Ask whatever you need to ask. But do it quickly; I have work to do," he says, his voice tight with frustration.

"Yeah, I'd hate to inconvenience you," I say sarcastically before reaching into my pocket, pulling out the custody paperwork, and holding it up for him to see. "Can you just explain to me what the hell this is?"

He rolls his eyes at the paper in my hand and shakes his head. "Un-fucking-believable. Did your mother make you come? This is between her and I and it's really none of your godda—"

"Stop right there," I growl, not wanting to hear any more of the bullshit he's about to spew. "You really don't get it, do you? This isn't about Mom at all. It's about my siblings who are terrified you're gonna come in and cause them to lose everything they love about their life. Plus, it's not like Mom ever did anything but try to love you. You're the one who destroyed our family. She's just spent the last six years trying to pick up the pieces."

He rolls his eyes again, and I fight the urge to reach out and shake him for being so damn selfish. "Son, you're still too young to understand, but—" he starts, but I can't listen to him anymore.

"Enough. We're not doing this. And don't call me your son. You gave up the right to call me that a long time ago. Just tell me what you want, so we can put this shit behind us."

"Ugh, fine. Do you know how much it costs to pay child support for all four of them? I'm sick of spending all of that money each month. I talked to my lawyer about it, and he said if I could get custody I wouldn't have to pay it anymore," he whines, sounding like a petulant child.

"That's what we figured. Damn, we'd hate for you to have to contribute to cover costs for your kids. And if you get custody... you do realize that you'd still have to pay for shit right?

Extracurriculars, sports, food, clothes..." I say, reminding myself to keep my temper under control.

"Says who? Your mother has spoiled you and your siblings. All the sports and extra shit isn't necessary. Plus, they're all old enough to get a job," he answers, shrugging his shoulders.

I wait for him to say something else or let on that he's joking, but nothing ever comes, and I feel my control start to fade.

"Oh my God, you're fucking serious..." I mutter, staring at him as hate feels my chest. "First of all, you make triple what mom does, and you're still complaining about having to send a couple hundred dollars to take care of the kids you wanted. I bet the suit you're wearing costs three times what you're being asked to pay each month. And I know you probably don't know this since you haven't seen her in over six years, but Kit's only fourteen. She's not getting a fucking job."

He just glares at me as I talk before finally saying, "Fine, but she can still help Sandy with the baby. Having a live-in babysitter would definitely be nice."

I freeze at his words before laughing coldly at him. "For fucks sake, do you even hear yourself? You are by far the most selfish person I've ever met. No, you don't get to move my sister away from her friends and her school because you decided to have another kid. You can't even take care of the ones you have, but whatever. You certainly don't get to move them all in together and act like one big happy family."

My father glares at me, and I feel the heat of hatred on my skin. Too fucking bad. I'm over this shit. "Yeah?" he questions, continuing to glare at me. "And what exactly are you going to do about it? We both know my lawyer's better than that cheap ass billboard attorney your mother hired."

I feel a new wave of hatred running hot through my veins when I say, "If you don't drop it, I'm gonna go to Sandy and tell her about the woman who just left out of here. And I'd be willing to bet she's not the only woman you've been sneaking around with because you just can't seem to help yourself. And when she divorces you and takes this new baby with her, you'll have another eighteen years of paying child support you don't want to pay. Drop all this shit, and you only have a little over three years."

I hate resorting to his tactic of making this about money, but since that seems to be the only thing motivating this whole shit show, I decide to go with it, ignoring the pang of guilt I feel at what I'm doing. And clearly it works because he narrows his eyes at me in frustration before throwing his hands in the air.

After a moment, he blows out an annoyed breath and growls, "Fine, I'll call my lawyer off. But the deal's off if you go to Sandy. Are we clear?"

"Fine," I agree, smiling as he tears the legal paperwork that's caused my mom so much heartache over the last few days down the middle.

"Now get the hell out of my office," he says, looking angry and annoyed at me as if I'm the one that started all of this bullshit.

"Fucking gladly," I tell him, turning and striding out of the door without looking back.

CHAPTER 41
HANNAH

"So not only did I have my observation the Monday that we came back from Thanksgiving break, but right as Principal Hale was finishing my observation, one of my juniors asked if I thought Jay Gatsby's parties would have gone viral on TikTok. Then when I said maybe, he added that Gatsby needed to get over Daisy because he could have had and I quote 'mad bitches with all his money'," Caroline says, using her fingers for air quotes while Margaret and I giggle. "I mean, I swear this kid has barely said anything all year and then decides to say that!"

"Hey, at least your observations are done though! I always dread them until they're over. And let's be honest, there's an eighty percent chance Principal Hale didn't even realize what was going on," I admit with a laugh, taking another sip of my margarita.

"Yeah, you're right. Honestly, I just feel like we're crawling toward Christmas break. That freak snowstorm we had this weekend combined with the excitement about the state championship has completely ruined any momentum going into these next few weeks," Caroline says, and we clink our glasses in agreement.

"Anyway, enough about school," I declare, turning toward Margaret. "I want to hear all about your pop-up in Deer Valley. How's it going?"

Margaret's eyes light up in excitement before answering, "Oh my gosh, it's been incredible. I've sold out of treats before ten every day this week. And I found two people from town to help me work the counter so now I have some flexibility in my schedule."

"Margaret, that's incredible!" Caroline says, and I nod in agreement.

"Yeah, I mean I'm not the least bit surprised, but that's great news. I just know that when you get your storefront open you're gonna have more business than you know what to do with," I tell her, bumping her shoulder with mine as I refill my margarita.

"You're the sweetest," she says, smiling at me. "But I've got to say I underestimated just how much town gossip I'd overhear while I'm making coffee. Did you know there's a woman living with the mayor?"

"What?" Caroline asks, looking shocked. "Brian's never dated anybody."

"No, they're not dating. She got stranded when she totaled her car during the snowstorm, and Huey found her. Apparently, Helen had just quit to move back home, and the new girl's helping with the Christmas events. They gave her a room at the inn, but there was some issue, and now she's living with Brian."

"Watch out, Miss Mabel, we have a new town busybody," I tease and Caroline chimes in, "Yeah, next thing we know, you'll be sending in our secrets to the STS."

We all chuckle at that, before I tell her, "On a serious note, I thought my grandfather was going to hurt himself on those desserts from Thanksgiving last week. He told me that everyone in the nursing home is willing to fight over your sweets."

Margaret smiles before responding, "They're just so sweet.

I'll have to remember to take them a few surprises once I'm closer to opening downtown."

"They'd love that," I encourage her, and Caroline nods in agreement.

"You know, I just really love this town," Margaret says happily, grabbing her glass. "Moving here was the best thing I could have done."

"Yeah, I've got to admit we're not too sad about it either," I tease.

CHAPTER 42
HANNAH

"Okay, yes, I'm walking in now. Yeah, it shouldn't take long. I'll call you as soon as I'm done," I tell Will as I walk into the front door of the town's OB office.

Hanging up, I take a deep breath, trying to shake the nervous pit I always feel in my gut when I have to step foot within a thousand feet of a medical practice. I know it's just a checkup and an appointment for birth control so I have nothing to worry about, but I feel my anxiety rise anyway. After a quick mental pep talk, I make my way over to the reception desk in the center of the room where a receptionist is sitting and answering the phone that seems to ring on repeat.

"Hey, my name is Hannah Scott, and I'm a new patient under Dr. Millwood," I say, trying to paste on a bright smile.

"Great, just go ahead and fill out this paperwork then. We'll get you back as soon as we can," she says right as the phone rings again.

I grab the stack and fill it out as quickly as I can before returning to my seat. Looking around the room, I can't help but smile at all of the families in the waiting room—the pregnant women with their husbands holding their hand, whispering about the future, and the sweet little families with their newborns cooing quietly in their arms. The sight makes me think about the conversation Will and I had last week and the way his eyes lit up when he talked about starting a family.

While I'm not ready for kids yet, I can't help the thrill that runs through me thinking about all that the future with him.

I'm still lost in my little dreamland when one of the nurses calls me back. I follow her through the halls until she puts me in a room and instructs me to undress while I wait for the doctor.

I follow her instructions and roll my eyes at the little paper blanket they left for me to cover my lap. I'm just getting settled onto the table when I hear a knock at the door. "Come in," I say, crossing my arms over my chest, crinkling the paper as I try to block the chill from the air conditioner.

A short, elderly man enters the room and grabs the rolling stool before taking a seat at my feet. "Good morning. Hannah, I take it?"

"Yep, that's me," I reply, shifting nervously on the paper covered table.

"Okay, what do you need done today?" he asks, still looking at my presumably empty chart.

"Umm, well I came to see about birth control and to get my first yearly out of the way," I tell him, trying to ignore the nerves I feel continuing to rise.

"All right, fine," he says without making eye contact, turning his back and grabbing a packet of utensils off the counter. "Let's get this done then."

I frown, unsure why he's acting like this is such an inconvenience but I lay back and let him get the exam portion over with. Thankfully, the pelvic exam goes quicker than I thought, but when he rises and starts pressing on my stomach, I can't help the squeak of discomfort.

"Hmm, okay then. I guess that's uncomfortable for you?" he

asks, pressing harder, and I have to take a moment to try to catch my breath.

"Yeah, it is," I say, wincing as he continues to press on the side of my stomach.

"Are you always this tender?" he asks, pushing into my other side with even more force.

"Uhh, I don't know," I answer. "I don't have people pressing on my stomach that often."

He gives me a glare that tells me he doesn't appreciate my response, before turning back to press under my belly button and asking, "Do you normally have stomach pain without the pressure?"

"I mean, I have really bad cramps sometimes and I've been noticing some bloating lately, but I thought that it was just something I was eating," I explain, reminding myself that having an attitude with him won't solve anything.

"Are your periods normal?" he asks, before pressing his whole hand down hard in the middle of my stomach, and I let out a cry.

"Sorry, that really hurt. And I guess? I don't know. Like I said, I cramp really bad, and some months I don't really have one," I tell him, not really knowing what he's looking for.

"I see. Well, this level of discomfort isn't normal, Miss Scott. So we're gonna do an ultrasound to see what's going on. Get dressed and give me just a minute to make sure the room's empty and the tech is ready for you," he says, and just like that, he's gone and I'm alone.

Umm, okay, this is definitely not how I expected today to go, but I try to remind myself it's probably nothing. He was pressing really hard, so it doesn't seem like such a big deal that it hurt, right?

After redressing, a nurse knocks on my door and leads me down the long hallway to a room with a big sign that says "Ultrasound" on the door. The nurse lets me into the small, dark room and introduces me to the ultrasound tech, and they both step out for me to undress from the waist down again. I try to take a few calming breaths as I settle on the table, and after a few minutes, the tech comes in.

"Hey, my name's Sam and I'll be doing your ultrasound, okay? Just lie back and we'll get this done quickly," she says, giving me a reassuring smile.

I try to ignore the cold of the wand as the tech inserts it, and a grainy picture comes up on the screen. I squint at it, but since I have no fucking idea what I'm looking at, I wait for her to say something.

Immediately, I know something's wrong by the look on her face. After a moment, she says, "I'm gonna grab Dr. Millwood, so he can see this in real time."

She comes back a minute later with the doctor who walks in and looks at the screen. After a moment, he breaks the silence. "Oh my."

I stare at him, confident he won't leave a statement like that hanging, but he doesn't say anything.

"Uhh, sorry, Doc, but do you want to clue me in?" I ask, and I hate how nervous my voice sounds even to my own ears.

"Oh, sorry. I've just never seen a case this bad before," he says, still looking at the screen. My stomach plummets at his words, waiting for him to continue, but he seems lost in the ultrasound. The tech and I make eye contact, and I feel my frustration rising at her apologetic grimace.

"Okay, I need someone to start filling me in now please," I say, trying to keep my words calm.

"Right. Do you see this right here?" he says, pointing at the screen.

"Yes, I do, but I have no idea what I'm looking at," I admit.

"It's your ovary. But normal ovaries don't look like that. They're about half that size, and do you see all those dots? The ones making your ovaries look like Swiss cheese? Those are cysts," he explains simply.

I just glare at him as the tech continues moving the ultrasound probe, and I will myself not to cry at the way he's talking to me. "Okay, so what does that mean?"

"Well, we'll need to run some other tests, but my guess is PCOS. You can look it up later," he says, brushing me off.

"All right, fine. But what do we do about it?" I ask, feeling my patience sliding away rapidly from the combination of his brushing me aside and his lack of bedside manner. Did he really just suggest I WebMD whatever the hell this is?

"Well, you were already coming in for birth control, so we put you on that and hope it manages the symptoms," he answers.

"Okay, and then it goes away?" I question him.

"Uh, no, probably not. There's no cure for PCOS, if that's what it is. The cysts may fluctuate, but we just won't know."

I feel my throat tightening, and I will myself not to cry. "Okay. But what about kids? Will I still be able to have them?"

The room goes silent for a moment before the doctor shrugs. "Uh, judging by this, I wouldn't count on it. I mean maybe I guess, but as bad as your ovaries look, I'd say no. But since you were coming for birth control, that should make you feel better. Anyway, let's make sure we're getting good pictures of this," he says, turning to the ultrasound tech like he didn't just destroy the future I've built up with a few words. "This could be great for that presentation I'm giving later this year."

I blink at him a few more times, but he just continues looking at the damned screen. I look down at the tech, but she just gives me another apologetic wince.

"Anyway, I'll get the nurse to make sure we get that birth control called in for you to whatever pharmacy you have on file and see if we can squeeze you in for some blood work. But the lab's been a headache lately, so you may have to wait a few weeks. She'll call you with results to confirm sometime in the next two weeks, but unless we find anything concerning, we'll see you next year," he says, and without another word, he's gone. As soon as the door closes behind him, I feel tears start sliding down my cheek.

"Oh, honey, I'm so sorry. Dr. Millwood isn't the best with bedside manner," Sam says as she takes out the wand and starts cleaning everything off. "It'll be okay."

And despite the fact that I know she's just trying to be nice, her words cause my tears to turn into body-wracking sobs because I'm pretty sure that after today, nothing will ever be okay again.

CHAPTER 43
WILL

"All right, guys, great practice!" I tell the team later that week. It's Wednesday afternoon and we just finished running the last of the drills for the day. "Get some rest tonight and study those plays some more because I promise you that Williams County is one of the best teams we've played all year. We're gonna have to bring our A game if we want a chance at that state championship."

The team chimes in with variations of "yes, sir" and "yes, coach" before I motion for them to be dismissed, and they turn and head back into the locker room.

"I think that was a pretty good practice," Theo says, watching them go. "You feeling okay about Friday?"

"Yeah, I think we're as ready as we can be," I answer, and the other coaches nod in agreement.

"I agree, I think it's kinda up to them at this point," Marcus chimes in.

"You're right. It's been a long week, so you can all go ahead and head out," I say.

"Sounds good, see you tomorrow," Theo says, and they all turn to head to their trucks, leaving me alone.

After making sure all the gear from practice is put away and double checking that all the kids found a way home, I grab my stuff and jump in the truck. It's Wednesday, so I'm headed to visit Mr. Scott, despite the fact that I feel a little more guilty each week about what Hannah and I are hiding from him.

I make the short drive over to his nursing home and smile at the nurses on the way inside before knocking on his door.

"Come in," I hear from the other side, and I enter to find him setting up the checker board for our weekly game.

"Will, son, how are ya?" he asks, pausing and walking around the table to give me a hug.

"I'm good. How are you feeling this week old man?" I tease, making sure he gets settled into his usual seat before sitting across from him.

"Oh, you know, same old, same old," he says with a laugh.

"Well, you look better than you did last week. Did they get your meds fixed?" I ask while setting out my checkers on the board in front of us.

"Yeah, I've had a better week this week. But nobody wants to hear about how this old bag of bones is falling apart. How's your week been? The boys all ready for the game this week?" he asks, making the first move.

"I think we're as ready as we're gonna be. I feel bad saying it, but I'm ready to get this one over with, you know? Not that I want the season to end. It's just like we've done everything we can, and until Friday we're just waiting. We're so close to state next week, and I really hope we can pull it off."

"That makes sense. I hope y'all make it. It's been years since Springside made it this far, and I'd sure like to see that big trophy headed back this way," he says, as I jump his first piece.

"You and me both. Anyway, how's Gladis this week?" I ask, waiting for him to make his next move.

"Oh, she's good. They've put together a little outing for some of us to go see the lighting of the Christmas tree later this week and she's so excited. Pretty sure she's gonna try talking me into staying out all night," he says with an exaggerated eye roll.

I laugh at his antics and shake my head. "You wild kids. That sounds like fun though. What else is going on around here?"

"Well, you know there's always some gossip going around this place, but that's not what I wanted to ask you about," he says, looking between me and the checkers board.

"Okay, what's up?" I ask, expecting him to ask me about the farm or something else at the school.

"Do you want to tell me why I found out this week that you're paying for me to stay here, Will?" he says, and I feel like all the air in the room is suddenly gone. Neither of us move, and I blink at him for a moment, trying to figure out what to say.

"Uh, what are you talking about?" I ask hesitantly.

"We both know what I'm talking about, Will. I heard some of the other residents saying that their monthly costs were going up, and I started wondering about mine. I know my grand-daughter would lie to me if I asked her about it, so I had them pull the records. I mean, I'm not trying to sound ungrateful, but I can't let you do that for me."

"Yeah, you can. You gave me an opportunity several years ago when I needed it, so just think of this as me repaying the favor. Just don't tell Hannah," I tell him, trying to focus back on the board in front of us.

"We'll come back to the money discussion the next time I see you, but since you brought her up... Are you ever gonna admit that you're in love with my granddaughter?" he asks, jumping one of my pieces before leaning back to give me a knowing look.

I blink a few times, trying to decide if he actually just said what I think he did before eventually stuttering, "What? I—I don't—"

"Come on now, Will. I may be old, but I ain't stupid. You've been in love with her since you two spent that summer sneaking around the farm. I know y'all thought I was oblivious, but even I couldn't miss the way you two looked at each other. All these years, you've been coming to see me, and I kept waiting for you to bring it up. Hell, between you and Hannah, I thought for sure one of you would give in and tell me eventually. You didn't and I told myself to be patient, but after all this, I've gotta know. What the hell is going on between the two of you?"

"Honestly, Mr. Scott, I wish I knew," I tell him, still trying to figure out what to say.

"I wish you did too, because I've gotta say, I've never seen either of you as happy as you were that summer. And I don't mean to be dramatic, but I'm an old man and she's all I've got left. I just want to know that when I'm gone she's gonna have someone to look after her. I don't know what happened, and honestly, I know it's none of my business. But I also know that if anyone in this world deserves happiness, it's the two of you. And I hate the idea of the both of you throwing that away," he says, and I just stare at him in shock for a minute.

"Yeah, I know you're right," I admit, trying to gather my thoughts. "But I don't know how the hell we got here, and I don't know how to fix it either."

Mr. Scott nods, and I can tell he's deep in thought. "Just don't give up on her. My Hannah Banana is a lot of things—smart, hardworking, caring. But she's also scared to get hurt again—the way she did when her parents left. She needs someone to love her that she can't push away."

I nod, knowing he's right. "I promise," I agree, turning back to the board in front of us and making a move. "Your move, old man."

CHAPTER 44
WILL

SEVEN SUMMERS AGO

I look down at my watch, feeling a slight wave of frustration hitting me as I realize I never heard back from Hannah after her appointment. But we'd agreed to meet tonight earlier in the week, so I push those thoughts aside, figuring she may have just gotten busy working around the farm.

Plus, I haven't had an extra moment to check in with her the way I normally would. Between the shitshow of a conversation with my dad earlier today, the summer coming to an end this week, and the knowledge that my dad managed to break my mom's heart all over again when I told her about everything that happened, my mood is already shit.

I pull into the driveway and fire off a text to her, letting her know I'm here, dimming the headlights and running my hand over my face.

The last thing I want to do is let my fucking dad ruin our last few days together, the way he tends to ruin everything else. I attempt to push him and his bullshit out of my mind so I can focus on Hannah. It's taking her longer than normal to make her way to me, but I figure she may not have seen my text right away. After a couple more minutes, I finally catch a flash of movement in the darkness ahead of me, and Hannah emerges, pulling up the door slowly.

I can immediately tell that something isn't right with her. Even in the dark cab of the truck, I can see that the usual fire in her eyes is gone, and she makes no move to kiss me like she normally does when she crawls up beside me, sitting as far away from me as the truck will allow.

I feel an alarm of unease go off in my head, but I shake it off, telling myself she's probably just as sad as I am at the prospect of going back to college this weekend.

"Hey, Han," I tell her, pasting on the best smile I can muster and leaning over to drop a kiss on her forehead. She doesn't reply, just gives me a tight smile that looks more like a grimace, and I turn back to restart my truck.

Just as I turn the key, she reaches out and places her hand on my arm. "Just stay here."

My face twists in confusion as I look over at her. "I thought we were going to our creek. You don't want to tonight?"

Hannah refuses to look at me, crossing her arms over her chest and holding herself tightly before whispering, "Will, we need to talk."

I feel like ice floods my veins at those words, and I just stare at her, waiting for her to say whatever's on her mind. After a moment, she continues. "This summer has been incredible, but we've got to be realistic. We can't go on like this."

"Like what?" I ask her, trying to figure out where this is coming from. "I told you we just have to make the distance work for a year, Han. Really just a couple months while school's in session. Then, I'll be done with school and I'll do whatever it takes to make this work. If next summer you want me to move to Tuscaloosa for your senior year and work odd jobs until we're both ready to move home, I'll do it. But I can't let you walk away because you're scared."

"Fuck you, Will," she snarls, and I'm taken aback by the

anger in her voice. "I know you think you're Superman, but you can't fix everything. You don't just get to decide that we're gonna be together!"

"What the hell, Han? Are you serious? We literally just talked about this the other day and you told me that this was what you wanted! And now you're acting like what? I made it all up?"

"I don't know what to tell you, Will. We've been acting like a bunch of fucking idiots, and I can't do it. I'm sorry, but I'm done."

I reach for her, refusing to accept the bullshit she's spewing right now. "I'm sorry, Hannah, but I'm not okay with that."

As soon as my hand brushes her arm, she pulls back, finally looking at me long enough to notice the tears streaming down her face. "Han, please talk to me. If this is really what you want, then why the hell are you crying?"

I try to pull her to me again, but she yanks back, and I see a determination in her eyes that wasn't there before. Straightening her back, she glares at me with an anger that I don't understand. "God, Will, what do I have to do to get it through your fucking head that I don't want you anymore. The summer was fun, but I'm over it, okay? The sex was nice, but you were just a distraction from the fact that none of my friends are here. So just move on and forget about me, okay?" she says, glaring at me again.

"Oh, and here. You can have this back. I don't need it anymore," she says, reaching up and undoing the clasp of the necklace I gave her for her birthday a few weeks ago before holding it out to me.

My breath catches in my throat, and I try to argue. "Han, that was a gift. I don't need it back. You keep it."

"Will, just take the damned thing so I can get the hell out of here," she says, frustration evident in her voice.

Feeling like I don't have any other choice, I reach out and take the necklace from her, tucking it in the pocket of my jeans. "Please don't do this, Han," I mutter, unable to help myself.

"Will, I've told you, nothing you say is gonna change my

mind, so you need to accept that this is over," she argues, folding her arms across her chest.

I open my mouth a few times to respond, but no matter what I do, I can't force any words to come out. I sit in stunned silence, coming to terms with the fact that she basically just ripped my heart out and stomped all over it.

"I need to go," she says, leaning over and opening her door. "Lose my number and don't contact me again because there's no future for us, m'kay?"

And with that, she's gone, slamming the door and running back to her house.

I watch her go, trying to piece together what the fuck the last twenty minutes just were. My chest fucking hurts at the thought of losing her, but what the hell call I do about it? After watching the way my parent's marriage ended, I should have known better.

There's no such thing as a happily ever after, and the people who claim to love us the most always fucking leave.

I sit in the silence of my truck for a few minutes, willing away the sadness I feel at losing what Hannah and I should have been and trying to convince myself to replace it with anger at the way she ended us. And as hard as I try, I know I'll never be able to convince myself that that's the truth.

CHAPTER 45
HANNAH

"Let's go, Springside," we chant just as the Williams County kicker lines up to attempt the extra point. We're in overtime, and the Saints just managed to score prior to this drive. We thought that might be the end of it, but on the next drive, Williams County retaliated, and now if they score this, we'll be starting the whole process over again.

"God, Will and the boys sure know how to keep us on our toes, huh?" Margaret asks from beside me, causing Caroline and I to laugh in agreement.

"You're definitely right about that," I mutter, shaking my pom-pom and joining the crowd in making as much noise as possible.

As soon as I see the angle the football leaves his foot at, I can tell it's no good. I can't tell if it was a problem with the snap or if the nerves got to him, but either way, I hold my breath to make sure I'm right.

The ball hits the outside of the field goalpost and bounces off, and the Springside crowd goes wild, cheering and screaming."

"Oh my God!" Caroline yells! "We're going to state!"

We cheer and yell along with the rest of the crowd, before grabbing our things and stepping down to the field to help the girls make sure all of our stuff is ready to go back to the bus. As soon as we walk over to the girls, several of the football players run over, grabbing their girlfriends and pulling them into a tight hug. I turn to say something smart to Caroline, but she's already moving toward Theo, jumping in his arms with a squeal.

I stand there, trying to figure out why I feel so uncomfortable all of a sudden until I make eye contact with Will. He's not standing that far away, and we both just pause, neither of us seeming to know what to do. Suddenly it hits me that all I want to do is throw myself into his arms and tell him how proud I am of him and the team, but I can't. He's not mine, and even if he was, this probably wouldn't be the best place to spill our little secret. But even with the reminder, I feel a pang in my chest at the fact that this is just another thing that I can't have.

Unable to help myself, I mouth "Congratulations" in his direction, and he smiles and nods back at me. I'm close to just saying screw it and running to him despite the consequences, but Caroline and Theo walk over before I can continue that thought.

"Hannah, what are you doing? I was yelling for you over there," Caroline says, gesturing to where she was just standing with her fiancé.

"Oh, sorry. You know me, always in my own little world," I apologize, hoping she'll leave it at that. "What'd you need?"

"I asked if you'd mind snapping our picture? I promised Heather I'd send her one tonight," she says, referring to Theo's foster mom, before holding out her phone to me.

As I'm handing it back to her, Huey comes over and slaps Theo on the shoulder. "Hey, Coach. One heck of a game! State champs, here we come," he says, and Theo smiles.

"Yeah, I hope you're right," Theo says just as Will walks over and shakes Huey's hand.

"Will! Incredible job this season! You ready for your first championship game?" he asks, and Will nods.

"Yeah, I'm excited. We've got a lot of work to do this next

week, but I'm just proud of everything we've already accomplished."

I lock eyes with Will again, and I'm pretty sure this is the worst form of torture. I know that the old me would have made some smart-ass comment right about now, but I don't want to fight like that with him anymore. As he and the guys continue to talk, it sinks in that all I want is him. Not just the sex. Not just the stolen moments we manage to sneak in together at the farm. No, I want every single piece of him, and it's the one thing I know I'll never have.

CHAPTER 46
HANNAH

FOUR SUMMERS AGO

*C*ome on, Hannah. You're a big girl, you can do this, I tell myself as I see Will across the room of Maracas. Caroline suggested a night out to celebrate us both landing teaching jobs at Springside High earlier this week, and I agreed, not realizing she also invited a few of the other teachers. Since Will took an assistant coaching job two years ago, I shouldn't be surprised he's here, but I thought I'd have a few more days to prepare myself before seeing him again.

I've thought about it a lot over the last few years, and I know I owe him an apology. It wasn't fair for me to take out my fear and frustration on him, and while I know we'll probably never go back to how we were, I still think we could be friends.

Blowing out a breath and giving myself a mental pep talk, I straighten and start to make my way over to where Will is standing, talking to Seth, another guy we went to school with. I know he works at the school too, and I'm pretty sure he helps with the baseball team. Their backs are to me, and as I get closer, I start to hear them talking as they take sips of their beer.

"Yeah, it'll be nice to have Caroline at Springside. All the kids are gonna be fucking obsessed with her," Will says, and Seth nods in agreement.

"Hell, I'm just glad we'll finally have some other young people around campus. I'm tired of everyone acting like you have to be ready to draw Social Security to be good with the kids," Seth says with a laugh. "And you forgot about Hannah. I think she's cool too."

"Ugh, whatever," Will scoffs, taking another sip of his beer. "She gets on my damn nerves. I don't know what on earth Principal Hale was thinking when hiring her.'"

I briefly register Seth trying to defend me, but the rushing in my ears makes it impossible to figure out exactly what he's saying. I've stopped dead in my tracks at their conversation, and I know I need to move, but I can't. My heart sinks at the way Will's talking about me. I know we didn't leave off on great terms, but the hatred I hear in his voice makes me want to cry.

I force myself to change directions, heading to the bathroom, not wanting Will and Seth to know I overheard them. Locking myself in the small bathroom, I take in my reflection in the mirror, shaking my head in frustration over the hurt I feel.

I haven't talked to Will in years, and I certainly don't have to grovel for his approval now. Yes, I wanted to apologize, but he didn't even try to come after me when I left. The man had made all these promises and just like everyone else in my life, he didn't intend to stay when things got hard.

I wipe my eyes where the two lone tears managed to fall and promise myself that these are the last tears I will ever cry over Will Thompson. He wants to hate me? That's fine. I can match that same energy right back, and I'll pretend that he isn't still holding a few pieces of my heart that I'll never get back.

CHAPTER 47
HANNAH

"Hey, sweet boy," I say, nuzzling the nose of my old American Quarter horse, Merle. I know I'm already running late to meet the girls for Margarita Monday, but I've got to finish checking on Falling Oaks first.

"I know. I haven't been spending as much time out here since Ruby was born. But she was so little and I needed to make sure she was okay," I tell him, trying to push aside my guilt at not being as present as I'd like for all the other animals over the last few months.

Merle blows a warm breath into my hand and I hold out a carrot for him. He snatches the treat from me, and I run my hands through his mane as he chomps away at it, clearly forgiven.

"Such a sweet boy," I tell him, giving him one last pat before turning and heading back to the house. After making sure that Leroy and Ruby are taken care of, I jump in the car and race to Maracas to meet Caroline and Margaret.

I smile as I see my friends sitting in the corner under the *"save water, drink tequila"* neon sign when I make my way inside, both of them waving frantically as if I wouldn't notice them in the tiny restaurant.

"Hey, Han! You okay? We were starting to get worried?" Caroline says, holding out a margarita for me to take as I slide into the booth.

"God, I'm sorry. I didn't mean to hold everyone up. I was trying to make sure all the animals were taken care of before I came over, and it's definitely gotten better since the boys finished fixing the fence. But I still feel like I don't spend enough time with all of them," I tell them, taking a long sip of the drink Caroline offered me.

Margaret and Caroline both just nod, before Margaret says, "No worries. I was actually running a little late too. I got carried away baking this afternoon and lost track of time. Each day we're getting more and more visitors at Deer Valley, and I can barely keep up. I'm definitely gonna have to hire more help if this keeps up once I open the bakery."

"Oh my gosh, it definitely will. I think you're gonna have more business than you know what to do with," Caroline tells her, and Margaret smiles at that.

"I sure hope so. I'm so excited to really get to work in a few weeks while y'all are out for school. I've been saving some ideas, and I think it's gonna be so cute," she says, pulling out her phone and turning it to show us some pictures of what she has planned.

"It's gonna be adorable. Once Seth and the other boys get all the construction stuff done, we'll be happy to help you paint or whatever else you need," I offer, and Caroline nods in agreement. "Now that the farm isn't falling apart quite as much as it was and I'm not drowning in all the bills like I was a few months ago, I for sure owe you both a couple hundred favors for all the chaos I've caused you."

"Oh my gosh, would you stop? You don't owe us anything. That's what we're here for," Margaret argues with an eye roll. "But I will take the help if you're offering."

We all laugh at that, taking a sip of our drinks before Caroline asks, "So, Han, that payment plan we worked out still helping? If not, you can tell us, and we'll come up with something else."

"Nope, it's still great. Honestly not having to worry about Gramp's expenses has been a lifesaver. I don't know how they managed it at the nursing home, but I'm so grateful."

Both my friends nod at that, before Margaret adds, "You know, I never expected to have people I could call for help, especially this soon after moving to Springside. I'm just really grateful for the both of you."

"Same," I say with a smile, holding up my glass to bump it with theirs before taking another tequila-filled sip.

Caroline opens her mouth to say something, but as she does, I feel my phone vibrate with a message. I pull it out while she and Margaret talk, seeing Will's name on the screen.

> WILL: I know you're out with the girls right now but please tell me I can see you tonight.

> WILL: This week's gonna be wild with the championship, and I'm not gonna last if I don't get inside you at least once before the weekend.

I feel my face flush at his words before Caroline gives me a questioning glare. "You good, Han? Who is that?"

"Oh, I'm fine," I say quickly, clicking my screen off before looking up at her.

I can see the suspicion on her face, but I ignore it until Margaret asks, "So, I know it's been a few months, but did anything ever happen with Kent? Like, do the two of you still talk?"

Her words catch me off guard, having not thought about Will's assistant coach in weeks, but I just shake my head. "Nah, he's a really nice guy, but I don't think he's my type."

Margaret nods in understanding, just as our waitress brings our food to the table. With Margaret and Caroline distracted, I pull out my phone and send a quick text before turning back to my friends.

HANNAH: Sure, come over around 9. See you then. :)

AFTER ALMOST TWO hours of chatting with my friends, we finally start to make our way to the parking lot, and I try to hide my excitement at the fact that I'm about to get to see Will. *It's just sex. Nothing more,* I remind myself. *You're just excited to see him, but it can't be more than just sex. Feelings or no feelings, this is all you get.*

"Does my brother not get tired of sitting out here in his truck every week?" Margaret asks, shaking her head as Caroline smiles, bringing me back to the present as we walk up to Theo's truck where he's waiting to take Caroline home.

"I've told him I never drink enough to not be able to drive, and even if I did, I could just walk to your apartment and stay with you, but you know how he is," she says with a laugh. "We all know he's a bit of a caveman when he thinks my safety might be in danger," she adds, rolling her eyes at her fiancé's overprotective nature.

"I think it's sweet. I mean I'm perfectly capable of driving home, don't get me wrong, but I think it'd be nice to have someone who cares that much about me," I admit, before noticing Caroline and Margaret's shocked expression.

"What?" I ask, caught off guard by their reactions.

"I just don't think I've ever heard you say anything that made me think you wanted a man," Caroline says hesitantly, and Margaret nods in agreement.

I open my mouth to tell her she's being ridiculous before thinking about what she's saying and realizing she's right.

Feeling uncomfortable, I shrug them off, before saying, "Anyway, I'll see you both later this week I'm sure?"

"Yep, I'll be at the game Friday if I don't see you before," Margaret says, pulling me into a hug.

"And I'll see you tomorrow," Caroline says, still looking at me with suspicion as if she's waiting for me to say something else.

"Sounds good. Good night, girlies," I say, turning to get into my car and closing my door. Before I pull out of the parking lot, I reach into my pocket for my phone to send off a quick text to Will.

> HANNAH: I'm leaving town now if you still want to come over.

I switch over to Spotify, clicking on my favorite 90s country playlist and setting it to random when my phone pings with his response.

> WILL: Give me about fifteen minutes or so and I'll head that way. Are you good to drive or do you need me to pick you up and bring you back to your car before school tomorrow?

I feel a wave of emotion roll through me at his text, but I try to tamp it down. I know he's just being nice, but God, sometimes it feels like the man can read my mind. But there's no reason for me to take him up on his offer, and leaving my car up here overnight raises the possibility of someone seeing us together when he drops me off. I type out a quick reply, singing along to the music as I remind myself about the rules of Will and I's agreement.

HANNAH: I just had the one drink, and that was a couple hours ago now. I'm·good. I'll see you in a few.

As soon as I press send, I throw my phone down and make the drive home. The closer I get to Falling Oaks, the more the butterflies in my stomach multiply at the knowledge that Will's on his way. As I pull in the driveway, I try to push the thoughts from my brain, smiling as Leroy and Ruby both run to greet me.

"You two are so silly," I tease, leaning down to pat them both on the head. "I guess we're just done with the whole pen idea, huh?"

They both wag their tails at me excitedly, and I just shrug, making my way up the steps and opening the door to let them follow me inside. They immediately run over to their new favorite spot in front of the fireplace. Cozying up together, they both collapse, and before I can take my thick coat off, I can hear the sounds of them snoring softly.

Shaking my head at them, I make my way into the kitchen, filling a glass of water before heading into my bedroom. Stripping down, I throw my head into a knot on top of my head and jump in the shower before Will gets here. Once I'm done, I dry off and grab my favorite oversized sleep shirt and some panties to throw on just as I hear the sound of Will's truck pulling up the driveway.

I make my way to the front door to greet him, smiling as he opens the door and immediately pulling me into his arms and kissing me hard.

"Hey, Han. God, I missed you," he whispers in between kisses, pushing me against the wall and caging me in with his body.

"I missed you too," I admit, threading my fingers through his hair and pulling his mouth back to mine.

After a few more minutes of frantic kissing, Will pushes my back so that I'm leaning against the wall, before reaching down and pulling my shirt off over my head. Since I didn't bother with a bra after the shower, I'm left standing in front of him in nothing but my panties.

"God, you're so freaking perfect," he groans, running his hands over my body in a slow caress.

I'm still caged in between the wall and his body, and I'm about to pull him closer so that I can wrap myself around him like we did in the shower, but before I can Will leans down and picks me up, carrying me to my bedroom.

As soon as we reach my plush, white bed, he throws me down gently, leaving me to sprawl across the comforter as I wait for him to join me. Deciding he needs a little encouragement, I rise from my position on the bed, reaching out and starting to pull off his clothes until he's standing naked in front of me.

"Somebody ready to get to the good stuff tonight, huh?" he teases, and I reach out and trace my fingers lightly down his already hard cock in response.

He hisses a breath through his teeth, pushing his hips toward the direction of my hand. I can tell he's about to tell me to stop, knowing he usually won't come until I've finished at least once. Deciding to push his resolve a little bit, I lean forward, sinking to my knees on the floor in front of him and running my tongue across the head of his dick before teasing my tongue down his shaft.

"Holy shit, Hannah. You have no idea how incredible you feel. But we need to stop if you're gonna come on my cock," he insists.

Looking up at him, I pretend to consider what he's saying before whispering, "Maybe later," and taking his cock down my throat.

He lets out a moan of surprise, shifting his hips to give me better access. "God," he mutters, as I find a rhythm and start to take him deeper each time.

"So pretty when you're on your knees for me," he praises, running his fingers through my hair and rocking his hips to lightly fuck my face. I look up at him from my position on the floor while he slides in and out of my mouth, and as soon as we make eye contact he lets out a curse, before pulling back and reaching down to pull me up off the floor.

I debate arguing with him, but before I can get a word out, he reaches around, lying me face down on the bed with my ass up in the air in front of him. "You look so fucking perfect sucking my dick, but I told you I need to be inside you," he explains, lining himself up and sliding inside my pussy.

I moan at the feeling of him starting to fuck me, immediately starting to writhe under him, desperate for him to find the spot inside me that drives me wild. After a few gentler strokes to make sure he's not hurting me, he starts to build a rhythm, kneading my ass with his hands as his thrusts get harder.

I'm lost in the sensation, bucking my hips against him and chasing my release when his fingers reach around, pulling my back to his chest. He wraps one hand around my neck, not hard enough to hurt, but more in a show of dominance that has my pussy clenching around him.

Using the other hand, he reaches down and flicks my clit over and over, mixing up the intensity and frequency until I'm a babbling mess. "That's right, baby. Come for me and squeeze my cock with that perfect pussy," he praises.

The combination of his words, the possessive way he's holding me, and the hand teasing my clit as he fucks me hard pushes me over the edge, and my orgasm slams into me, causing me to scream at how good he feels. As my climax starts to fade, Will's fingers press into my hips, his motions becoming more and more frantic until I feel his cum filling me.

"So damn perfect," he mutters, reaching down and twisting us so that we're both lying across my bed. After a moment, he slides out of me and wraps his arms around my shoulders, letting me rest my head on his chest.

I cuddle next to him for a minute before he brushes his fingers through my hair. "God, I don't think I'll ever get tired of this. Pretty sure I could hold you every night for the rest of my life with no complaint," he mutters, dropping a kiss on the top of my head and pulling me closer.

I nod in agreement without thinking, before I realize what he just said. Alarm bells start going off in my head. This was not a part of the casual, just sex relationship we agreed to. I tell myself to calm down, but instead, I feel my heart start to race and I start to panic.

I realize with a start that, despite my best efforts, there's nothing casual about the relationship Will and I have. I've sworn up and down that he means nothing to me, but that couldn't be further from the truth.

God, I already walked away the first time when we let ourselves believe in a future we'd never have, and it damn near broke me. My heart breaks at the realization that I'll have to do it again, despite the fact that a future with him is all I've ever wanted.

I feel my eyes well with tears as Will lays beside me with his eyes closed and his arms wrapped around me. Knowing I can't let this go any further without losing even more of my heart, I push the tears down and steel myself to get this over with.

"Okay, so this has been fun and all, but I think it's time you leave. We can't keep doing this, Will."

CHAPTER 48
WILL

I freeze at her words, half expecting her to laugh and tell me she's joking. Opening my eyes from where I was savoring the feeling of having her in my arms, I look around for the source of her words, confused when I come up empty.

"Hannah, what's wrong?" I ask, recognizing the look of panic that's suddenly on her face, but she appears like she's lost in her own world. "Hannah, I swear to God, just talk to me."

I can feel my panic rising the longer she's silent, and I try to block out the fear that I'm losing her again.

After a minute, Hannah blinks, and I can tell she's about to try to feed me a load of shit. Before she can start, I interrupt her, fighting to keep my cool. "Hannah, if you even think about telling me that nothing's wrong, I won't be held accountable for my actions."

"You just need to go," she says, already getting up and grabbing for her clothes that I'd thrown across the room when I undressed her.

"What? No. I need to stay, and you need to tell me what the hell just happened," I growl, feeling my frustration rise at the thought of her leaving like this after what we just shared.

"Why do you care, Will? Just please go," she says, grabbing

her panties and throwing them on, already heading for the door. "Get dressed," she demands, but instead I stand and grab her arm, trying to keep her from leaving.

"Would you please just stop for a second? I don't want leave like this," I tell her honestly.

"Will, I swear to God, if you don't get out of my way... We're just fucking, right? Well, we've already checked that off the list for the day, and I don't feel like doing this shit right now. So let go of my arm, and get dressed so you can go home," she snaps, and I blink at her harsh words.

"What the hell, Han? I don't understand what's going on. And I don't care what we are, but you don't get to walk out like this again. And you sure don't get to force me to walk away without an explanation," I argue, feeling both my fear of losing her and the anger at the way she's talking to me come to a head.

"Oh, that's fucking rich coming from you. Sure, act like I'm the only one who walked away from us," she snarls. "Where the hell is my damn shirt?"

"Um, yeah, you were. You walked in that day and it didn't matter what the hell I said. You decided you were done—right when I needed you. I was trying to hold my family together and planning on forever with you, and out of nowhere you're gone. Just like you're doing now. And then for the last seven years, I've wondered what the hell I did that was so bad that you would run and act like I'm the worst man in the world. What is it, Hannah? Please tell me because I'm getting fucking whiplash. You scared that someone might realize you aren't the cold-hearted brat that you pretend to be?"

"Fuck you, Will," she screams, still looking for her shirt. "What the hell were we thinking? This shit isn't ever gonna work. I just need my damn shirt, and if you won't leave then I'm getting the hell out of here."

"Hannah, listen." I breathe, desperate to keep her in the room.

Okay, yelling probably wasn't the best way to keep her here, dick-

head, my subconscious reminds me, and I growl, knowing that I need to calm down. If I've learned anything over the last few years, it's that Hannah will put her defenses up and block me out when she feels too much, and I can't let her leave until she talks to me.

I reach out and pull her into my arms. She fights and claws at my arms, but I ignore her tantrum and hold her to me, wrestling my own temper under control. "We're not doing this shit again. We're gonna sit right here until you decide to stop throwing whatever the hell that tantrum was. And then we're gonna talk through whatever the fuck it is because we're both adults. Do you understand?"

She continues thrashing in my arms for a few minutes before the fight leaves her, and she collapses against me. I wait for her to say something before I realize that she's sobbing silently to herself.

The sight catches me off guard because I've never seen her look this upset or vulnerable. "Whoa, whoa, Hannah, please, tell me what the hell's going on."

"Just please let me go, Will," she sobs.

"Don't think I can do that, sweetheart," I tell her, all of my previous anger deflating out of me as quickly as it came. "I'll give you a few minutes but then I need to know how we went from having what I thought was a pretty perfect night, to whatever the hell that just was."

"I—I—I can't," she cries, and I hold her as she shakes with the sobs still tearing out of her throat. "I can't do this with you, Will. It's too much. This whole damn thing is messing with my head, and I can't think straight."

"I need a little more of an explanation," I say, reminding myself to keep my voice even.

"I just..." she starts, but she trails off after a few seconds, crying to herself until she whispers, "damn it. I'm getting too deep in this, Will. And I need to go and remind myself what the fuck this is. Okay? Are you happy?"

"Okay," I say slowly. "But why is that such a bad thing, Han? What's so wrong with wanting to be with me? What was so wrong with it then? I'm sorry, Han, but I'm just really damn confused."

"Because there's no future with me," she cries. "And I can't do that to you, Will. I know we've been horrible to each other the last few years, but that's what I needed to remind myself that I don't get to love you. And for the most part, it's worked. But then we started this, and now I don't know what's what anymore. So I need you to go home so I can pull myself together, and maybe we can try this again later. But until then, I need for you to get out of here."

"Hannah, what the hell are you talking about? Why would you say you don't get to love me? I was desperate for you that summer. What aren't you telling me?" I ask, continuing to hold her while she cries.

"I can't give you what you want, Will, okay? I'm broken, and you deserve somebody who can give you the life you deserve," she continues, and I feel like she punched me in the gut.

"Han, please, stop talking like that. This isn't like you. What am I missing?" I ask, desperate for her to make me understand.

"Do you remember what you told me that summer? That night I snuck out, and we spent most of the night talking beside the creek. You told me about the future you wanted. Do you remember what you said?" she asks, and the heartbreak on her face catches me off guard.

"Umm, there's nothing about that summer that I don't remember, to be honest. I remember we talked about the future and how we wanted to take over the farm, raise a house full of kids, and spend the rest of our lives together right here. But what does that have to do with this?" I question, pulling her closer to me.

"Do you remember the day we broke up?" she asks quietly.

"Yeah. Like I said, I remember all of it. What about it?" I say, hoping the pieces of this puzzle will start to click soon because I hate seeing her like this.

"Do you remember where I went before I came to see you?"

I think back to that day, remembering she'd mentioned some sort of an appointment, but I don't remember the specifics. "Didn't you have a doctor's appointment or something?"

She smiles sadly at me and nods. "Yeah, I went in for what was supposed to be a simple checkup and a prescription for birth control. But they found something when I was there, and not to mention the doctor was the biggest asshole I've ever met."

"But you're healthy. What did they find? This doesn't make any sense to me, Han," I tell her, brushing her hair out of her face.

"I look healthy," she whispers. "But I went to that appointment that day, and the doctor told me that I have something called Polycystic Ovary Syndrome or PCOS. Which, honestly, probably would have been okay if he sat down and explained it to me. But he didn't. Instead, he told me I was the worst case he'd ever seen. And then he told me I'd never be a momma, Will. He even laughed like the idea was so freaking ridiculous. I left and cried in my car because as soon as he told me that, I knew the future you had for us was broken. That I was broken."

Her body is shaking with sobs as she chokes out her last few words, and I feel my heart break at the realization that she's carried all this by herself the last few years.

"Come here, baby, it's okay. You're not broken. I can't believe you never told me this. You didn't need that asshole doctor anyway. You can get a second opinion, and—" I start, but she interrupts me.

"I did. I got a second opinion—and a third actually—when I went back to college. I did some research and I do have PCOS, but since the doctor didn't explain anything, I didn't realize how common PCOS was or any of the possible treatments that were out there. Eventually, I found a doctor I liked, and I realized I probably overreacted, but it was just too much at the time you know?"

I nod at her, and before I can say anything, she continues. "I took some time to myself, and I convinced myself that we needed to talk. That I needed to lay everything out for you and give you the chance to make a decision for yourself. Honestly, I was just starting to have hope again. But that's not the end of the story."

My heart sinks at the thought that there's more she kept from me. "Go on," I tell her, holding her closer to me and preparing for whatever's next.

"Do you remember the surgery I had a couple years ago?" she says miserably.

"The appendectomy?" I ask, vaguely remembering Caroline telling me that she was in the hospital for a day or two a few years ago. It was a summer or two after I graduated, and since Hannah and I weren't talking at that point, I didn't get many details.

"Yeah, I guess you could call it that. But they didn't just take my appendix. On top of the PCOS, I have something called endometriosis. Basically, these cells grow where they aren't supposed to—usually on the ovaries. Anyway, they can't identify it without surgery, so the doctor went in for the appendectomy and had no idea I had some rare case of endometriosis on my appendix. The bad tissue was everywhere. From what they told me, it was a mess. The endometriosis had fused several of my organs together, and it had basically killed my ovaries too. They had to perform an emergency hysterectomy when I was twenty-three," she explains through her tears, and I fight to keep up with what she's telling me. I feel like I've been punched in the damn chest just listening to her talk.

"Oh my God, Hannah. And no one else knows about this?" I ask, my brain still struggling to catch up.

"No. I was in Tuscaloosa for the week finishing up my Master's finals, and Caroline was already done, so we weren't together. I didn't even list my gramps on my emergency contacts because I thought it would be a routine surgery and I didn't want him to worry."

"Hannah," I whisper, pulling her to my chest. "Why in the world didn't you tell me? Or hell, forget me—you didn't tell Caroline? You've walked around shouldering this by yourself for years. Did you honestly think that none of us would want to be there for you?"

She doesn't reply for a while, continuing to cry in my arms, before sobbing out, "I couldn't do it, Will. I'm sorry. And plus, I overheard you telling Seth how much you couldn't stand me, So I didn't figure you wanted anything to do with me."

"What? When?" I ask, the confusion clear in my voice as I try to remember what she's talking about.

"At Maracas. I'd just gotten hired at the school, and I heard you telling him that I got on your nerves. You sounded like you hated me, so I just told myself I'd give you the same energy," she says sadly.

I vaguely remember making an off-handed comment about not wanting her to work at the school, and I feel swarmed with regret. "Hannah, I'm so sorry. I didn't mean it. All I could think about was seeing you every day, and never being able to have you, and I just snapped. But I still shouldn't have said it."

"It's okay. I wasn't exactly open with you about any of this," she says, nuzzling closer to me as she cries.

I hold her, and I realize I've never felt so helpless in my entire life. After a while she pulls back, wiping her tear-stained face, as she whispers, "Listen, Will, I'm so sorry. I shouldn't have said yes to starting anything with you again. I spent some time in therapy right after it happened, and I've done what I can to come to terms with all of this on my end. But I can't force you to shoulder this too. I'm never gonna be able to give you the future we both wanted. And I can't be the reason you look back in twenty years and wish everything was different. I'm broken, and there's no fixing me."

I kiss the top of her head and open my mouth to argue with her, but before I can get a word out, she holds up her hand. "Will, I'm serious. We can't do this. Please just let me go," she sobs, trying to pull out of my arms. Instead of letting her go, I pull her closer, refusing to let her walk away this time.

"Baby, you're not going anywhere. Just stop so we can talk about this. And while we're at it, let's get one thing straight right now. You're not broken. There's a difference between breaking down and being broken. You've held it together for everyone in the damn world over the last few years, all the while you were letting this shit eat away at you from the inside out. But, Hannah, you don't have to hold it together all the damn time. Breaking down and letting other people in doesn't mean we're weak; it means we're human. Sometimes life is just too fucking much, and that's okay. But pretending to not need anybody doesn't get us anywhere," I continue, holding her close to me and trying to force her to listen to me.

"Maybe you're right," she mutters, reaching up to dry her eyes again. "I should have told you sooner. And I should have given you a choice."

"Yeah, maybe, but I understand why you didn't. That was so much for you to take in, and I was so distracted with trying to hold my own family's shit together, I didn't fight for you the way I should have. I was so scared of admitting that I'd completely fallen for you, and I fucked it all up. But I love you, Hannah. And I'm not letting you go again."

She freezes at my words, and I see the mix of panic and hope in her words at my confession. *Fuck, that's not how I planned to do this but whatever.*

"Damn, that probably wasn't the right time for all that, but it's true. I gave you my heart seven years ago, Hannah, and I don't want it back. As much as I've tried to convince myself I didn't need you, I was wrong. I loved you then, and I love you now." She opens her mouth to say something, but I hold up my hand, stopping her. "You don't have to say anything tonight.

WHY WE BREAK   257

This has already been a whole lot, and I don't want you to say something you regret later."

She just nods, nuzzling closer to me in my arms, and I wipe one of the stray tears from her eyes. "Just let me hold you tonight, okay? We'll figure all this shit out later, but right now I just need to know you want to be mine."

"More than anything," she whispers. "But I'm terrified of what that'll look like, Will. What if you wake up tomorrow and decide this is all too much?"

"I can promise you that'll never happen, Han. You're all I want. But I do think you need to talk to Caroline and Margaret before we take this any further. I know why you've kept it from everyone, but they'd want to be there for you, baby. I'm not going to pressure you, but just think about it. Once you've told them, then we can figure out how we want to handle the rest of the town."

"But what about our jobs?" she asks, looking nervous. "What if they tell us we have to break up? You know there's a rule about staff members dating, and we both really love those kids."

"Hannah, I've already told you, none of that matters. Yes, I love my job, but I'm done living without you—if this is what you want," I tell her, my tone leaving no room for argument as I pull her body closer to mine.

"Okay, fine," she mutters, and I lean down to press a light kiss to her mouth. "I'll talk to the girls, and we'll figure out the rest of this shit later. But I want it to go on record that I tried to change your mind."

"Whatever, Han. One day you'll realize that there's nothing that could keep me away from you this time. I don't know how, but we're gonna get everything we want. Now, go to sleep. We'll figure the rest out later."

CHAPTER 49
HANNAH

"Okay, girls, those signs look great!" Caroline says, smiling at the large run-through signs the girls spent the last hour of practice working on today. "Just leave them here for now, and y'all can go. We'll let them dry tonight, and then tomorrow we'll fold them all up and pack them with everything for the game. Just remember to practice that new dance for the pep rally Thursday night, and we'll run it hard at practice tomorrow."

The girls nod, grabbing their stuff and making their way out of the small cheer room off the side of the gym.

Before we leave, Maggie runs over, holding out her phone for us to see. "I wanted to wait until everyone else was gone because I'm terrified of jinxing it, but I got this email today from the coach at Smith's Valley University. She saw our state routine and she wants me to come to their clinics this spring. She said she thinks I would be a great addition to the Wildcats!"

"Oh my gosh, Maggie, that's incredible!" I tell her, hugging her quickly before Caroline does the same.

"Thank you. I know I've gotta keep working, but I think this might really work. And it wouldn't have been possible without the both of you spending so much time helping me these last few months. I know it's not been the most convenient, but I'm really grateful for everything the two of you have done for me," Maggie says with a smile.

"Of course. We're so glad we could help. Now, we gotta get you on that team so we can come watch you on that sideline next year!" Caroline exclaims, and I nod in agreement.

After another minute of chatting, Maggie heads out, leaving me alone with my best friend. Caroline and I both stand and spend a few minutes straightening up, before getting ready to leave. I'm throwing on my oversized jacket to get ready to make my way to my car when Caroline says, "So, no pressure, but do you want to talk about it yet?"

"Talk about what?" I ask, turning and looking at her in confusion.

"Whatever it is that's had you acting so weird the last few weeks. I mean, obviously you don't have to tell me, but I just want you to know I'm here for you, no matter what," she tells me, and I don't miss the look of concern on her face.

I blink at her before feeling my shoulders sink under the weight of everything I've been keeping from her, but after everything Will said last night, I know it's time to come clean to her.

"I—I—I'm sorry Caroline, but I've been keeping something from you and Margaret. I've honestly been keeping this secret for a long time. I think I'm ready to tell you, but God, it's so hard," I tell her, feeling my eyes already filling with tears.

Caroline's eyes widen, and she comes over, wrapping her arm around me and pulling me into her arms. "Hannah, you know you can tell me anything. I've been waiting, and Theo told me you'd come to me when you were ready, but I hate seeing you like this. Why don't we text Margaret to meet us at your house? We'll eat pizza and junk food, and you can tell us whatever you're ready to share."

I nod, allowing her to lead me out of the gym and to her car while I continue to cry quietly to myself. "I'm not letting you drive like this. Either I'll stay with you tonight, or I'll give you a ride back in the morning."

I don't say anything, just allowing her to take control while I sit in the passenger seat and try to figure out how I'm going to explain everything that I've been keeping from her. Before I know it, Caroline's turning down the driveway of the farmhouse, and I look up to see Leroy running toward the car in excitement.

"He really just does whatever he wants, doesn't he?" Caroline teases, and I feel my mouth lift in a smile at the sight.

"Yeah, I've given up at this point," I mutter, getting out of the car and heading into the house. Caroline follows with Leroy right on her heels. After a moment, Ruby comes running to the door from her pen, not wanting to be left out. Caroline just steps back, letting them in before shaking her head at my chaos.

"Margaret will be here in less than five. She stopped to grab pizza," she announces, throwing herself on the couch while I head to the fridge to grab a bottle of wine. "Leroy, I don't think you're supposed to get on the couch, buddy!"

I roll my eyes at his antics, pouring three glasses of wine just as Margaret bursts through the front door. "I got the 911 text, and I came bearing junk food. Is something wrong on the farm? Is your gramps okay? And wait, why is Leroy on the couch? And did you know there's a cow in your house?" She points to where Ruby's curled up on the floor, and I just shrug.

"No, nothing like that. And ignore him. Hannah just needs to talk to us," Caroline explains, holding out her hand to take the glass from my hand.

Settling onto the couch beside her, I curl up next to her and grab a piece of pizza while Caroline and Margaret wait for me to begin. Taking a deep breath, I finally say, "I'm really sorry, but I've been keeping something from the both of you. And I know what I'm about to say is a lot, so I'm sorry."

Both of my friends' eyes widen at that, but I know if I stop I'll lose my nerve so I continue, looking at Caroline. "You know the summer before junior year in Tuscaloosa? You stayed back to work and I came home to help Gramps on the farm?"

She nods in acknowledgement, before saying, "Yeah, I do. I remember you seemed so sad when you came back in the fall, but you never wanted to talk about it."

"Yeah, you're right. There were so many times I wanted to tell you, but I could never figure out what to say. But here we go. That summer, Will had a job working for my gramps. We spent the whole summer together, and we fell head over heels for each other."

Both Margaret and Caroline's mouths are open in shock, but I continue. "I don't really know how it happened, but I gave him my entire heart that summer. We promised each other forever and made plans to move back here when we were both done with school. All we wanted was to start a family together."

I pause to take a sip of my wine, and Margaret interrupts, "Wait. What? I know I'm still new here, but this doesn't make any sense. I thought y'all hated each other. What the hell happened?"

"I'm getting to it," I say, looking over at Caroline who still hasn't said anything. "Just let me finish before you decide you hate me, okay?"

"I could never hate you, Han," she says, wrapping her arm around me. "I'm just shocked. I mean, I've always thought y'all would be great together if you ever stopped wanting to rip each other's heads off. And don't get me wrong, there've been times that I definitely was a little suspicious. I just never thought you'd ever really go for it."

"Totally understandable. But as for what happened, here's where it kinda gets ugly."

"I swear to God if he broke your heart and you've just let me live in oblivion…" Caroline mutters, leaning back on the couch and crossing her arms over her chest.

I smile sadly at that before responding. "Not quite. Actually, I was the one who called it off."

Pausing and tipping back my wine, I drain my glass before deciding to go for it. "Right before the summer ended, I went to the doctor to get on birth control, and it didn't go well. He was the biggest ass I've ever met, and I was diagnosed with PCOS. But instead of explaining it and talking me through it, he told me that I'd never be able to have children. I knew that the life that Will and I had planned was never gonna happen so I ended it."

"And he let you walk away because some doctor said you might not be able to have children. What a fucking pig!" Caroline blurts, and Margaret nods along with her.

"I didn't tell him why," I mutter, and both of my friends freeze at that.

"Oh, Han," Caroline mutters. "What did you say then?"

"I told him that there was no future with me, and I didn't want to be together. That it had just been a silly summer fling, and I hadn't meant a word when I said I wanted us to stay together. I didn't know all the details at the time, but apparently, he was also dealing with some stuff with his dad. Honestly, I don't think either of us were in the right headspace that day to have any sort of real healthy communication."

"Well that does make sense, but, Hannah, it's been years. Why didn't you talk to him after everything settled?"

I smile sadly, nodding in agreement. "I should have. I'd actually hyped myself up to do it. But life kind of struck again, and by the time I got it together it felt like too late."

"What else happened?" Caroline asks, her eyes wide.

"You're gonna be mad," I mutter, feeling the guilt tightening in my chest as I brace myself to drop the rest of the truth on them.

My best friend leans over and hugs me again, before responding, "I promise I won't, Han. I just want to understand."

"Well, I promised myself that I'd talk through everything with him as soon as we both moved home. I got a second and third opinion, and I was feeling pretty good about what the future might look like. But then, I had my appendectomy."

"I remember that. I was already home, and you insisted I didn't have to come back," Caroline adds. "But I guess there was more to it?"

I nod. "Yeah. It turns out that my appendix wasn't all they had to take. In addition to the PCOS, I had something called endometriosis. It doesn't show up on scans or anything, so they had no idea. Most people just have it on their ovaries and stuff, but mine had spread. It fused a lot of my organs together, and it basically killed off everything. There wasn't anything they could do, so they had to do an emergency hysterectomy."

My voice shakes at that, and I wipe a lone tear as it streams down my face. Caroline and Margaret stare at me for a moment in shock, before Caroline throws herself at me, knocking me over with the force of her hug. "Oh my God, Hannah. I'm so fucking sorry. I can't believe you've been dealing with all this on your own. I'm not mad, but why didn't you tell me?"

I hug her back, as I try to figure out how to make her understand. "Honestly, I don't really know. I'm sorry, Caro. I just felt like if I talked about it, it was real you know? I thought that if I could just pretend none of it had happened, then it'd be okay. And by the time that happened there was just so much, and I didn't know where to start.

Margaret leans over and squeezes my hand. "I get it. I know I'm still kinda new here, and this was a little before my time but this was so much for you to process. There's no way to deal with grief, Hannah."

Caroline nods. "She's right. None of this is about me. I just hope you knew that I would have been there for you, and you didn't have to take this all on by yourself."

"I know. And I'm sorry. I shouldn't have kept this from you," I tell her, as we both wipe the tears that have started streaming down our faces.

"But wait. What about you and Will? Does he still not know? And why act like you both hated each other all this time?" Margaret asks.

I blush at that, thinking back to all the silly arguments Will and I have had over the last few years. "Well, I overheard him telling Seth how much he couldn't stand me a few years ago, so I decided to act like I hated him as much as I thought he hated me. It turns out we were both wrong—we were just both sexually frustrated."

The girls laugh at that before I continue. "Will does know. I actually fessed up to him last night, and he encouraged me to talk to y'all."

"Last night?" Caroline asks, raising her eyebrows. "But you were with us last night…"

"He came over after I got home. We've been acting like idiots, and we thought we could be just sex. But, I guess you could say we failed at that."

"Oh my God, Hannah!" Caroline exclaims, her eyes wide. "I knew you were hiding something, and I was suspicious at the state cheer thing, but I just told myself there was no way. How long has this been happening?"

"Umm, the night we went to Boot Scooters," I say sheepishly, while Margaret and Caroline shriek.

"I knew it! Headache, my ass. You weren't looking for Tylenol!" Caroline accuses and I shrug in acceptance.

"You caught us," I tease, reaching forward to refill my wine glass before taking another long sip.

"But wait, that was months ago. So, are y'all together, together? What's the plan?" Margaret asks curiously before leaning over to rub Leroy's belly where he's spread out on the sofa beside her.

"I guess you could say we're figuring it out. We've been sneaking around, and it was supposed to be just for fun, but it's definitely more. I didn't tell him anything until last night, and it was obviously a lot to take in. He's been hinting at wanting a relationship for weeks, but I said no because I thought he'd run in the other direction once I told him why I ended everything. Plus, we haven't talked about how to handle the school thing."

"Okay, well, from everything you've said, it sounds like he's not going anywhere. So what do you want?" Caroline asks, and I take a minute to think over my response.

"I mean, in a perfect world, I'd want to be together. I gave my heart to him that summer, and I've never really gotten it back, you know? But I also can't help but feel like I'm being selfish because I know he wants a life I can't give him."

"Hannah Marie Scott, I know that you're not thinking about giving up a life you want just because you're scared!" Caroline exclaims, sitting up straight and looking like she's ready to fight with me if she hears an answer she doesn't like.

"No, no. Not anymore. Not really, at least. I mean, a small part of me is probably always gonna worry about that, but I'm working on reminding myself that it's not the truth. We just decided we'd figure it out after I talked to y'all, plus we all have just a little bit going on this week with the championship coming up in two days," I tell them, and they nod at my answer.

"Yeah, that makes sense. But wait, can the two of you date since you both work at the school? I thought I've heard you talk about that before," Margaret interjects.

"That's been my argument," I admit before adding, "but apparently Will isn't really worried about it."

"You know, I've always heard people talk about that, but I've never actually seen any proof that a rule exists," Caroline says, and I shrug.

"You may be right. I just figured that we'd figure it out after Friday."

"That makes sense," Margaret agrees as Caroline reaches over and grabs my hand.

"I know this has been a lot, and I'm so sorry you've been dealing with all this on your own for so long. But I hope you know we're always here for you, Han. We love you, and you're never getting rid of us."

I feel my eyes well with unshed tears at the sincerity in her voice. "I know, Caroline, I'm sorry. And I love you both too."

Margaret and Caroline both lean in to hug me, and I soak in the feeling of being surrounded by my best friends. After a minute, Leroy looks over from his perch on the couch and scoots closer, not wanting to feel left out.

"You know when I moved to Springside, I didn't really see myself cuddling on a couch with my girlfriends and her pet pig, but here we are," Margaret says, and we all burst into a fit of giggles.

"Yeah, it wasn't exactly on my bingo card, but I wouldn't change a thing," Caroline teases, causing me to smile.

"Me either," I admit, as Caroline looks up expectantly.

"So, now that the cat's outta the bag, I gotta know... You said the two of you tried doing the whole just sex thing, but you didn't mention how the sex was?"

"Yeah, no offense to Caroline, but I'd love to hear a story that didn't involve my brother," Margaret adds, causing us to chuckle again.

"Oh my God, y'all would not believe," I tease, taking another sip of wine and patting Leroy who's pushed Margaret out of the way to cuddle in closer to me. And as my friends settle in to gossip, I finally feel like everything might work out.

CHAPTER 50
WILL

"You ready for this?" Theo asks as we get ready to run out on the field for the state finals on Friday night.

"Ready as I'll ever be, I guess," I tell him, grabbing my headset and putting it around my neck for later.

"You're right about that. Well, I gotta say, this whole coaching thing definitely wasn't something I expected when I moved to Springside, but I'm really proud to be a part of all this," he admits, and I fight the urge to laugh.

"Damn, man. What happened to the grumpy asshole who moved to town? If I didn't know any better, I'd say you've actually liked spending the season with us," I tease.

Theo rolls his eyes at me before responding, "Yeah, yeah, whatever. I guess this town's turned me into a big old softie or whatever. But I mean it, this team is something special."

I look out into the locker room where the boys are waiting for us to start the pregame speeches, and I nod. "You're right. And as much shit as I may give you, you're great with these guys. We've done all we can do though, so it's kinda up to them."

"Yeah. So, you ready to get this thing started?" he asks.

"May as well." I shrug, blowing out a breath and taking a

step toward the players in front of me. I raise my hand to get their attention and the locker room goes silent as they wait for me to say something.

"I know I'm supposed to come up here tonight and tell you how big of an opportunity this is. I'm supposed to remind you how hard you've worked this season and tell you that you probably won't ever get a chance like this again in your lifetime so you'd better take advantage of it.

"That's what I think I'm supposed to say, and honestly, it's all true. But you already know all of that. So instead, I'm just gonna tell you that I'm proud of you. There weren't a lot of people who were betting on us at the beginning of the season, and week after week, this team has shown up, put in the work, and won ballgames. And as much as I hope there's a trophy and some state championship rings in our future, I'm not all that worried about the outcome. I know y'all have given me a hundred and ten percent of everything you've had over the last six months, and I couldn't ask for anything else."

The boys in front of me nod as I continue. "Before we run out on that field tonight, I want you to take a minute and soak this in. The other coaches and I have given you everything you need to come out of tonight a champion. So you've gotta decide right now how you want to feel at the end of these four quarters. What are you gonna do to make sure you don't come out of tonight with any regrets?"

I pause, letting my words sink in before gesturing to the other coaches. "In just a minute, I'm gonna shut up and Coach Marcus is gonna get you all hyped up before we go out there. But before that, I just wanted to remind you that you can do this. Now, what do you say we win one more?"

The room erupts in cheers, and I nod at Marcus to take over. Theo, Kent, Jason, and I laugh at his usual antics, while he hollers encouragement at the boys, jumping up and down while he hypes them up. After a few minutes, we motion for the boys to line up to run out of the locker room, and I take in a deep breath when I see the huge college stadium where the state championship is being held.

"All right, let's get it one more time boys," I yell as we hear the band start to play the fight song. "Let's go!"

With that, the team runs out of the locker room and through the run-through sign that the cheerleaders are holding up, leaving the coaches and me to jog behind them over to the sidelines. We clearly traveled well, despite the game being played in Crestview over an hour from home because the noise our fans are making is deafening.

"Damn, I wasn't expecting this many people," Theo admits, taking in the crowd.

"Yeah, me either," I admit, looking over at the sidelines and immediately see Hannah. She's standing with Caroline as they wait for the cheerleaders to run back to the sideline, and I have to shake myself to keep from staring.

After our emotional talk on Monday, all I've wanted was to spend some more time with her, but this week has been way busier than I thought. Between meetings, practice, and the community pep rally last night, we haven't had time to do much more than send a text here or there. But seeing the way her face lights up when she sees me, I know I won't be able to stop myself much longer from showing everyone that she's mine.

She mouths "Good luck, Coach" at me, and I smile and wave in acknowledgement before turning my attention back to the field where the captains are lining up.

"That was cute," Theo teases, and I shake my head in his direction. "It's about damn time y'all admitted you want to fuck instead of fight."

"I don't know what the hell's gotten into you, but I'm not sure I like it," I answer. "When did you become so observant?"

He just shrugs in response, and we both let out a whoop of excitement when the speaker crackles with the announcement that we won the coin toss and will defer to the second half.

The other coaches walk over as the team gets set for kickoff, and I pull on my headset. After making sure it's ready to go, I blow out a breath. "Let's do this thing, boys."

"COME ON GUYS! We're better than that," I yell when the defense jumps offsides for the second time tonight. It's early in the fourth quarter, and while we're up by a touchdown, I'm not impressed by the careless errors we're starting to make.

Looking over, seeing the other coaches have similar looks of frustration when Jason walks up, motioning out to the field before asking, "What the hell do you think's gotten into 'em? We haven't looked like this all season."

"Yeah, I think it's nerves and they're psyching themselves out. Not to mention it's the coldest weather we've played in all year. But we need to get it the hell together."

Jason nods in agreement as the defense moves closer to the end zone after the penalty and lines up, waiting for the Bakersville Tigers to snap the ball.

As soon as it's snapped, their quarterback dashes through our line and sprints down the field heading straight for a touchdown, leaving all of our players behind. "Damn it," Kent curses under his breath, before running a hand over his face. "I don't know how many times we ran that exact scenario at practice this week, and they were all over it. But now they look like they've never seen a football before, never mind practiced the play."

I watch as the kicker from Bakersville gets ready to attempt the field goal and fight the urge to groan when it's good.

We're down to the last three minutes and we're tied. Blowing out a breath, I motion to the referee to signal for a timeout and wait for the team to make their way over to me.

"All right, bring it on in," I tell them, gesturing for them to pack in so they can all hear me. "Okay, we have three minutes, guys. Three minutes that decides if we win or lose. If we go home as champions or not. Now, I told y'all before that I'm proud either way—and that's still true. But I just gotta tell you that team out there is not better than you. So let's do what we can to score and keep this thing out of overtime, okay?"

The boys all chime in with a chorus of "Yes, sir" and "Okay, coach" before Marcus calls out the play we're about to run. I remind myself to breathe as the team lines up for kickoff and then groan when the return is marked down at the fifteen-yard line.

"Damn, that's a whole lot of field to cover," Theo mutters, and I nod in agreement. After they set, the center snaps the ball into Blake's hands. He catches the snap and executes a beautiful pass to one of his receivers on the forty-yard line before he's tackled.

"First down, Springside Saints," the announcer calls out over the loudspeaker and the crowd behind me cheers.

"We're gonna be cutting this one close," I say, mostly talking to myself, before turning back to the field.

"We need to get to at least another twenty yards before we can even consider a field goal," Jason adds.

Just as the words come out of his mouth, the center snaps the ball again, and all of a sudden Blake is running straight toward the end zone. "Come on, come on," I chant under my breath as a Bakersfield player tackles him.

I look up at the clock, noting that there are less than thirty seconds before the end of the game. I look over at the coaches beside me before pointing out, "So, we can go for the touchdown, but if we don't get it, we risk losing in overtime. Or we go for the field goal, but if he misses it, they could run it back and score."

"Yeah, pretty much," the other coaches agree before Marcus says, "What you wanna do, Coach?"

"Hmm, let's go for the field goal. If we make it they won't have time to score after, and if we miss it we aren't risking a turnover as long as he doesn't kick it too short. He's been pretty consistent in practice too," I decide, and Marcus motions for the kicker to head out.

"God, this might be the most stressful game I've ever seen," Theo mutters, and I nod, waiting to see what's about to happen.

CHAPTER 51
HANNAH

"Oh my God, I don't think I can watch," Caroline whispers, covering her face with her hand as the Springside kicker lines up for the field goal. There are less than thirty seconds left on the clock, and I don't remember the last time I was this nervous about a football game.

"I don't know that I can either," I admit, looking down at where several of the girls from the squad have similar expressions. They start chanting "Make that kick!" over and over as the center snaps the football. It seems like the entire stadium holds its breath as the Saints player kicks the ball and it soars through the field goalposts. The Saints sideline erupts in loud cheers and screams as I reach out grabbing Caroline while we lose our shit with the rest of the fans.

The clock reaches zero, and Caroline whispers, "Oh my God, they actually did it, Han."

"Hell yeah, they did," I say, watching as the boys try to dump the Gatorade cooler on Will, but he jumps out of the way just in time, causing Theo to take the brunt of the cold liquid. He stands there in shock for a moment as Will, Caroline, Margaret, and I, along with several of the fans in the stadium, cackle at his expression.

"Oh my God, that literally couldn't have played out any better," Caroline says, already moving toward the field. I trail behind her, keeping my eye on Will as we go. One part of my brain says to wait, knowing if I run to him, our secret will be out, but he turns, searching through the crowd of people as the team celebrates around him, and suddenly I don't give a shit about any of that.

I run to him, flinging myself into his arms as soon as I'm close. He catches me and twirls me around before dropping his mouth to mine and kissing me hard.

I hear several shocked gasps behind us, but I tune them out, pulling back and smiling at him, "Congrats, Coach! I'm so proud of you!" I squeal, before whispering, "And I'm not sure, but I think they may be onto us now. We're totally gonna be the newest headline in the STS tomorrow."

Will leans in and kisses me again before shrugging. "Oh well. I told you I was through pretending like I'm not in love with you."

My heart stops again at his words, and before I can think too hard about it, I whisper, "I love you too, Will Thompson."

We both freeze at my admission before his mouth breaks into a smile, and he pulls me in, kissing me hard. I hadn't planned on telling him like this, but as I talked to Caroline and Margaret earlier this week, I knew it was just a matter of time before I told him how I feel.

"I swear to God, I'm never letting you go again, Hannah Scott," he murmurs.

I cling to the front of his shirt, and I'm about to kiss him again when I hear a loud cheer behind us. We turn to see our friends making their way over, smiling and glancing at us knowingly.

"It's about damn time," Theo says, rolling his eyes at us.

"Yeah, I don't know what all's been going on between you two for the last few months, but I was starting to think you two wouldn't ever figure your shit out," Seth adds.

Margaret and Caroline both run to me and pull me away from Will, hugging me hard.

"Please tell me you're done pushing him away," Caroline whispers, and I just nod before squeezing them both hard and going back to stand next to Will.

As soon as I'm close enough, he wraps his arm around me and pulls me close to him, as a wave of coaches and fans start making their way over to congratulate him on the win.

Huey reaches us first, smiling and waving his shaker in his hand frantically. "What a game, Will. I knew you had it in you. I'm so proud," he says, wrapping Will in a hug and patting his back hard. "And it looks like that's not all we have to celebrate." He gestures to where Will still has his arm around me and gives us both a smirk. "I may be old but I've sworn for years there was something between you two."

"Yeah, yeah. You and your old man intuition," Mayor Brian teases with a laugh as he makes his way over to shake Will's hand. "Great game, Coach. It's been a long time since Springside had a state championship. You should be proud."

"Thanks, Brian." Will nods just as Principal Hale runs over. I tense, wanting to bask in the happiness we're feeling right now before making any decisions about work, but bracing myself for whatever's about to happen.

"Coach Will, that was incredible! Great job!" he exclaims with a wild smile.

"Thanks, Principal Hale. We've worked hard, and I'm really proud of the team. But, I do need to let you know that Hannah and I are together, obviously. And if that's a problem, I'll have my resignation on your desk first thing Monday morning," Will declares, his tone leaving no room for argument.

My mouth drops open in shock and I'm about to argue when Principal Hale beats me to it. "Resign? Why in the heck would you do that?"

"The policy," I interject. "You know the one that says staff members can't date?"

Principal Hale furrows his brow in confusion before he mutters, "This darn town and their rumors. I think there's been some confusion. There's no policy against staff members dating, Miss Scott. We used to even have married couples that both worked for the school. There was an incident years ago when a principal tried to date a teacher, and she was uncomfortable with it. He tried to threaten her job, and the board fired him. But it was because he was trying to use his position to pressure her, not because they were both staff members."

I freeze. "So there's nothing that says that Will and I can't date?"

"Nope, not a thing," Principal Hale says. "And I do hope you'll both stay. We don't want to lose either of you at Springside High."

"Thank you," Will states while I just stare into space, trying to wrap my brain around the fact that there's nothing keeping us apart any longer.

As soon as Principal Hale walks away, Kent runs over, clapping Will on the shoulder before looking at the two of us. "Can you believe we did it, man?" he asks excitedly.

"I think it may take a few days to sink in," Will admits before adding, "we couldn't have done it without you and the other coaches though."

"Well, I've enjoyed learning from you. And I'm already thinking about how we can build on this for next season," Kent exclaims, before looking down and finally noticing Will and my linked hands.

I brace myself for an awkward encounter, but instead, his face splits into a wide smile. "Oh my God, I can't believe it. Y'all are finally together?"

"Yeah. Listen, man, I know you talked about wanting to ask her out, but—" Will starts, but before he can finish Kent brushes him off.

"Will, we're good. It was actually a bit of a test between me and the other coaches. We noticed how into her you seemed, despite the fact that the two of you fought like crazy. So Theo told me to mention asking her out to see how you'd react."

"He what?" Will asks, his eyes wide as he turns to where Theo is standing, still dripping in Gatorade talking to Caroline.

"I'd say I'm sorry, but I'm not," Theo says with a shrug, while Caroline shoves him playfully.

"Wait, you did all that without telling me?" she declares, crossing her arms over her chest and poking out her lip in a pout.

"Sorry, Sunshine, but you and I both know you wouldn't have been able to keep it a secret from Hannah. We just wanted to see how Will would react. But he's so damn stubborn. So we just decided to keep pushing. By the time we got to the bonfire, I kept expecting smoke to start coming out of Will's ears," Theo tells her, dropping a kiss on her forehead. She leans into him, obviously deciding to forgive him.

Will shakes his head at Theo's confession while Kent turns to me. "Sorry, Hannah. I wasn't trying to lead you on. But we could all tell it wasn't me you were interested in, and we were trying to get you both to get your head out of your ass and just be together."

We all laugh at that, and I wave him off. "No hard feelings, Kent. You're a nice guy, but I was obviously already spoken for, even if I didn't want to admit it."

Will smiles at that before whispering, "Hell yeah, you were." He pulls me in for another kiss, and I hear a bunch of the kids coming up behind us, yelling and cheering.

"Oh my gosh, they're actually together," one of them yells, causing us to pull back with a laugh.

"Coach Will, can you believe it? We're state champs!" Blake yells over the noise of the crowd.

"Heck yeah, we are." Marcus whoops beside us before asking, "You about ready to go claim that trophy?"

Will nods. "Yeah, head on out to the middle of the field. I'll be right behind you."

The coaches and players start to move, as Will pulls me in close again. He drops his mouth back down, kissing my forehead before whispering, "I told you we'd get everything we wanted."

CHAPTER 52
WILL

"D amn, what a day," I mutter to the other coaches as the bus pulls into the parking lot of Springside High around midnight after the Championship.

"Yeah, I'm freaking beat," Theo agrees. The bus comes to a stop, and the boys rise from their seats, eager to move around after sitting still for the last few hours.

"All right, guys. Grab all your stuff and you're free to head out. But listen, I know it's late and y'all want to celebrate tonight, but let me just say, please be safe. Just make good choices, okay?" I say, and all the players chorus back with "Yes, sir."

I nod before motioning for them to get off. Looking out at the parking lot, it looks like pretty much all of the parents whose children aren't able to drive are already here, and I breathe out a sigh of relief that I should get to leave shortly.

My phone vibrates and I turn it over to see Hannah's name on my screen.

> HANNAH: Just made it home. Are you coming over tonight? I know it's late so no pressure if you'd rather go home and come over tomorrow that's fine.

> WILL: Do you really think I'm gonna be sleeping without you after everything that happened tonight? I'll be there in twenty.

> HANNAH: Sounds good. I'm about to ride out to the barn and double check the horses are good, but I should be back home by the time you get here.

> WILL: Okay, be safe. If you want to wait until I get there, I'll go with you.

> HANNAH: Thank you, but the sooner this gets done the sooner we can go to bed... See you soon.

I slide my phone in my pocket and turn back to my assistant coaches. "All right, guys. You can all go on home. I'll double check everything gets locked up, and I'll text you in a day or two. I'm sure the school will do some ceremonies to celebrate the win, but I'll do something for just y'all once everything gets settled down. Thank again for everything."

They all nod in agreement, clapping me on the back and saying good night before heading to their cars and leaving me alone.

After grabbing the trophy and locking it in my office, I double-check that all the players were picked up before jumping in my truck and heading to Falling Oaks.

I make the drive pretty quickly, smiling as I pull up to the house when I see her pull up on the ATV from checking on the horses with Leroy sitting in the passenger seat. Making my way over, I drop a kiss on her lips before leaning over and patting Leroy on the head.

"I swear, this damn pig," I tease, shaking my head before wrapping my arm around her shoulder and leading her inside. Leroy scampers off the vehicle, and Ruby runs over from where she was frolicking beside her pen to join us inside. "What are you gonna do when she's not a little calf anymore?" I ask, and Hannah just shrugs.

"I don't know, but I guess we'll figure something out. Leroy over here taught her all his tricks, didn't ya, buddy?" she coos, opening the front door to let them in before leaning down and sitting her boots on the porch.

Straightening to her full height, she smiles before asking, "So, Mr. State Champion, how are ya feeling? Has it set in yet? You know you're probably gonna get all sorts of job offers and opportunities after this right?"

I reach out, pulling her body to mine and threading my fingers through her hair. I drop a gentle kiss to her lips before I admit, "Yeah, maybe. But you know I don't give a shit about any of that. The title's cool and all, but the best part of tonight wasn't the game. It was hearing you finally admit that you're in love with me."

"Did I say that? I don't remember," she teases, and I growl, scooping her up and throwing her over my shoulder and I lead us to her bedroom.

She giggles, bumping my back with her fists as she tries to get me to put her down. "I'll put you down as soon as you admit that you love me," I tell her. "And get ready, because I've waited seven years to hear you say those words, and now that I have I don't think I'll ever get tired of them.

The room goes silent as I hold her up above the bed, and she pulls back in my arms to look at me. "I love you, Will Thompson. I loved you seven years ago when I was too scared to admit it even to myself. I'm pretty sure I've loved you every day since, but I'm definitely in love with you now. I know there'll be days when I'm a pain in your ass and you get on my damn nerves, but I don't want to spend another day without you."

My heart races at the words, and I sit her on the bed, dropping my mouth to hers as I kiss her, feeling like I'll never get enough.

"I love you too, Hannah. This life with you is everything I've ever wanted, and I hope you mean it when you say you're in this for the long haul because I'm never letting you go again," I tell her, kissing her again and running my hands under her sweater to feel her bare skin. After a moment, I pull it off as she reaches for my coach's pullover.

We become a flurry of hands, both of us desperate to feel the other until we're both stripped bare, and she's reaching out her legs to wrap them around my hips.

I move to help her, leaning down and lining up with her entrance and slowly pushing inside her. "I'm never gonna get enough of you, you know," I murmur, kissing her lips before rocking my hips into her gently.

All of the other times we've had sex, it's been wild and passionate, but tonight, I want to take this slow and savor every minute with her naked in front of me.

She groans, reaching up to pull me down for another kiss and wrapping her legs around me tighter. "You're so damn tight, baby," I murmur, pushing in and out of her slowly.

"Faster, please," she begs, but I ignore her, reaching down to tease her clit in the way that I've learned drives her wild.

"Come on, baby. You're gonna come for me, and then when we're done, we're gonna go to bed because we have the rest of our lives for this right here," I tell her, feeling her pussy starting to spasm around my cock as she comes.

"Yes, you feel so good. Don't stop," she begs. I pump my hip harder, feeling myself follow her over the edge and filling her with my cum.

We both lie still for a moment, basking in the feeling of having the other close. After a few minutes, I pull back, smiling at the sight of her pussy leaking with my cum. "You know, I don't think that'll ever get old."

She rolls my eyes at my statement, before murmuring, "Okay, as wonderful as that was, I need a shower."

I thread my arms under her legs and carry her bridal style into the bathroom, sitting her on the counter while I get the shower ready. As we wait for the water to heat up, I walk over to her, pulling her into my arms and kissing her again.

"I'm pretty sure this has been the most perfect day ever," she whispers, and I tighten my grip around her.

"Yeah, you're right. But now we can spend the rest of our lives trying to beat it," I say, kissing her forehead.

"You're on," she agrees, before pulling back. "I love you, Will."

"I love you too, Han. Now, let's get this shower over with so we can go to bed. I have a feeling tomorrow will be a busy one. And you know, we've gotta go by and drop the news on your grandfather. I'm sure the STS will probably beat us to it, but still."

She laughs at that. "You're right. I also need to take Merle for a ride tomorrow afternoon, and I need some help getting the tractor to start after the last cold front so we can set some hay out for the cows. Oh, and the latch on the barn still needs fixing from where you busted in there last week."

I shake my head at her with a smile. "Don't tell me you just want me around for the farm help."

"You know, it is a perk," she teases. "But the sex is pretty good too."

She stands, scurrying away from me and laughing at her joke. I chase after her, swatting her ass playfully before pulling her to me and planting a kiss on her lips.

"Life with you won't ever be boring, will it?" I ask, causing her to giggle.

"Not even a little bit."

"KNOCK, KNOCK," Hannah calls out the next morning as we stand in front of her gramps room at the nursing home.

She enters ahead of me, yelling, "Hey, Gramps. How ya feeling today?"

"Oh, I can't complain. I just..." he starts, pausing when he sees me entering the door behind her. "Well, I'll be damned. The two of you actually worked it out."

We both pause, trying not to laugh as he looks between us over and over again, like any second we're gonna come up for some reason why I'm here that doesn't have to do with a relationship.

"We did," I tell him, grabbing Hannah and pulling her to me.

The old man throws up his hands and lets out a whoop of excitement, causing us both to laugh. "It's about damn time," Hannah's gramps says. "Gladis showed me the blast about y'all in the STS last night after the game, but I've told her I don't believe a damn thing those old ladies say. Looks like Miss Mabel might have gotten it right for once though, huh?"

"Yeah, I guess so," I say with a laugh. Hannah and I chuckled when Huey sent me a screenshot of the gossip this morning as all the older ladies tried to figure out how we kept our relationship a secret from them.

"You know, I thought I was gonna have to resort to threatening to kick both of your asses if you didn't stop acting so damn stubborn," Mr. Scott says, winking at me.

"Gramps, you're on a walker. Did you really think we'd be scared of you?" Hannah teases.

"Hush up, girl. We both know I wouldn't have done it even if I could, but I felt like I had to do something. You need each other too dang much to let whatever it was keep you apart," he says defensively.

"You're right," I tell him as we walk over to sit around the table beside him. We spend the next several minutes making small talk with him before one of the girls from the office knocks on the door.

"Oh, hey, Mia," Hannah says with a wide smile. "How are you today?"

"Hey, Hannah," the girl replies before turning to Mr. Scott. "Hey, Mr. Scott. We're working on plans for the Christmas party this week, and I wanted to make sure you and Miss Gladis will be joining us?"

Hannah's gramps nods. "We wouldn't miss it. I've got my dirty Santa present ready to go too." He thinks for a moment, before turning to Hannah. "You think Margaret could make us some desserts?"

"I'm sure she can. I'll text her when I leave," Hannah responds before turning to Mia. "I haven't gotten a chance to thank you, but I just wanted to say thank you so much for all your help. I don't know what magic you managed to work with the Medicaid gods, but I'm really grateful. I know you said you'd do what you could, but I never expected you to get my gramp's care covered in full. It was a real lifesaver though."

Mia's eyes widen as she looks around awkwardly. Mr. Scott and I make eye contact, and he nods at me, indicating that it's time for me to come clean.

"I'll take this one," I murmur to Mia, and I feel the immediate relief when she realizes she won't have to try to explain. As she leaves, I turn to Hannah and decide to get this over with.

"Actually, Han, that was me. I didn't want to tell you because I knew you'd freak out, so I asked for them to keep it vague for me. They couldn't actually lie to you, but I figured if they just told you it had been taken care of, you'd assume it was his insurance or whatever."

"Will Thompson, what in the hell were you thinking? That's thousands of dollars!" she cries, her eyes widening in panic.

"Baby, don't do this. I've saved up a lot of money by sharing that apartment with Seth these last few years, and I found the bills at your house one night while I was working on the fence. I knew you'd never ask for help, but we could all tell that you were stressed. So I took care of it and a few of the smaller miscellaneous ones I didn't think you'd notice. And I'm sorry I kept it from you, but honestly, I'd do it again. I'm never gonna let you struggle with something if I have the power to fix it."

Her eyes fill with tears at my declaration, and I worry I've said something wrong before she flings herself into my arms. "I don't know what to say. I can't believe you did that! I still think it's too much."

I just shrug, running my hand down her back, before turning back to her gramps. "So, are you and Gladis gonna have a wild time at this Christmas party?"

"Oh, you know we will," he responds with a laugh. "I told Melvin I was coming for him again if there were games involved."

"Gramps, you've gotta leave that poor man alone," Hannah scolds before turning to me. "Melvin is the guy across the hall and he has a leg cast up to his thigh. For some reason, Gramps has a vendetta against the poor man."

"Hey now, just because he had surgery doesn't make him innocent," Mr. Scott argues. "I caught him trying to cheat at bingo last week, and he tried to flirt with Gladis at breakfast yesterday when I was in physical therapy!"

"Okay, okay, my bad. I didn't know about that," Hannah says, holding up her hands in surrender, causing both of us to laugh.

"But enough about the nursing home drama. I know y'all have better things to do than listening to me running my mouth all damn day. But feel free to bring my granddaughter with you on your weekly visits, Will."

Hannah's eyes widen in surprise again. "What the hell? You two are just full of secrets. You visit him every week?"

"Yeah," I tell her honestly. "Is that okay?"

"I'm absolutely in love with you," she murmurs, and I feel another rush at her words.

"I don't think I'll ever get tired of hearing that," I tell her honestly. "And I love you too."

She leans in for me to press a kiss to her forehead, while her grandfather looks on with a smile.

"Okay, okay, you two have spent enough time in here today. Y'all go on so I can watch the *NCIS* marathon this morning. But I'm happy for you both," he says truthfully before pulling Hannah into a long hug. He whispers something in her ear and she laughs before moving to stand.

I stand to shake his hand, but he grabs my arm and pulls me into a hug. "Just make her happy, okay, son?"

"I intend to," I tell him honestly, before moving to the door and taking Hannah's hand.

"Bye, Gramps. I love you," she says, turning back to look at where he's reaching for the remote.

"I love you too, my Hannah Banana," he says with a wink before we make our way into the hall.

"You ready to go home? I'm pretty sure there's a pig who could use a bath," she says, causing me to groan at the prospect. But after a beat, I realize she's referring to Falling Oaks as home for the both of us, and I smile, deciding it's worth all the chaos that will definitely ensue from trying to give her wiggly pig a bath.

"Yep, let's head home, Han," I say, pulling her close and kissing her forehead. "But if he squeals the same way he did when you clipped his hooves, we're gonna have to invest in some really good headphones because the little fucker is loud as hell."

CHAPTER 53
HANNAH

"So, Hannah, we're gonna need all the details on how this weekend went," Caroline says, a minute after I slide into our booth at Maracas on Monday.

"Yeah, please, tell me y'all spent the weekend naked after everything the two of you have been through," Margaret teases, causing Caroline and I to laugh.

"Well, in case you both have forgotten, I still have a farm to manage, so we did have to tend to the animals, but I will say it was still a pretty great weekend."

"I bet," Margaret teases before adding, "I also heard you and Will were the main topic in both of the STS blasts this weekend."

"Welcome to my world," Caroline teases. "If I had a dollar for every time Miss Sally and Miss Ethel included something about the fire chief, I'd be able to retire."

We all laugh at that before I respond, "Yeah, I heard, but there's no real surprise there. I just can't believe this is really working out after all this time."

"Believe it, Han," Caroline says, leaning over to grab my hand. "You know we've always said 'brighter days ahead.' It looks like you finally found yours."

I smile at the mention of our phrase, and nod in agreement.

"I'm happy for you both." Margaret sighs. "But it looks like I'll be the only one not getting any around here from now on."

"Oh, Marg, we both know you're gonna find someone," Caroline encourages. "You're hot, funny, and you can cook. I mean, clearly some guy is gonna be lucky as hell to snag you one day."

"Yeah, yeah. Whatever you say. I guess it's for the best. Once Seth wraps up the finishing touches of the bakery over the next few weeks, I'll be working like crazy."

"Okay, that may be true, but I still think that you and Seth could be something," I say, as Caroline nods in agreement.

"I'm pretty sure you just want to know if the rumors about those piercings are true," Margaret teases, referring to the triple dick piercings Seth got after he lost a bet last year.

"You know, I may've read a few books about that, and I can't say I'm not curious. I mean don't get me wrong, I'm completely in love with your brother, and I'm not looking to try out anyone else's cock, but you should totally try it out and report back."

We all laugh at that and pause to take sips of our drink. I feel my phone vibrate in my pocket, and I smile when I see a text from Will.

> WILL: Leroy and I miss you. How long until you're home?

> HANNAH: I guess I miss my boys too. I'm not sure. At least an hour or two.

I tuck my phone away and reach out to snag a chip as Caroline asks, "So, Marg, how's the pop-up at Deer Valley going? Still a success?"

Margaret's eyes light up at the mention of her business. "It's been so incredible. I can't believe how busy I've been. I didn't have a ton of expectations when Brian mentioned it, but it's made me even more excited to get my storefront open."

"That's awesome! Pretty sure Gramps is counting down the days too," I tease, feeling my phone vibrate again.

WILL: Turns out I couldn't wait that long.

I read his text twice, feeling the confusion on my face at his words. I'm about to type out a response when I hear a familiar voice behind me.

"So, you ladies come here often?"

All three of us turn to see Seth, Will, and Theo making their way over to our table.

"Oh my gosh, you three are not allowed to crash our girls' night!" Caroline says with an eye roll, before reaching out to grab Theo's hand to pull him down for a kiss.

"Just this once I think y'all can make an exception," Will says, sliding into the booth and wrapping his arm around me.

I lean over and kiss him before asking, "So did you boys finally create a group chat without us to plan this."

Seth smiles from where he's sitting across from us. "We sure did. We decided we're done letting y'all have all the fun."

We all laugh at that as the waitress comes over and places another round of margaritas in front of us. The boys reach for them, but Margaret, Caroline, and I make eye contact before we all snatch them for ourselves at the same time.

"Sorry, boys, but you crashed our night. The least you can do is be our designated drivers," Caroline says, taking a long sip of her peach-flavored drink.

"Fine," Theo says, ordering water for him and the other boys.

"Since you boys wanted to join girls' night, you also have to listen to our gossip," Margaret declares before saying. "But, I was about to tell you before we were interrupted—I'm pretty sure Mayor Brian and the new event planner are dating. Her name's Millie. I met her last week in the coffee corner and she's really sweet. But as you'd expect, Deer Valley's going crazy with rumors."

"I've heard something about that," I tell them, leaning in to rest on Will's arm. "But isn't she leaving next week after the holidays?"

"No one knows," Margaret says with a shrug. "I guess we'll have to see."

The six of us spend the next hour making small talk, sipping on our margaritas, and snacking on the appetizers we ordered for the table. Finally, Seth points out that it's nearly nine o'clock and we groan at the reminder that we all have to be at work in the morning.

We all stand as Margaret says, "You know, it's gonna be kinda weird not having a football game to go to this week? I'm pretty sure there's been one every week since we moved into town."

"You're right," Theo says, pulling Caroline into his arms. "It seems like we've been here a lot longer than six months. But I can think of several things we can do to fill our free time, can't you, Sunshine?"

We all laugh as Margaret pretends to gag at his statement. "That's my cue to leave. Seth, you mind driving me back to the apartments? I can't listen to this any longer."

"Sure, ready when you are," Seth tells her.

We all walk to the parking lot, saying our goodbyes before Will and I make our way over to his truck. He helps me in, and I smile as he leans in to kiss me before closing the door and coming around the truck to sit in the driver's seat.

"You okay?" he asks, reaching over to grab my hand as he pulls out on the county road that leads to Falling Oaks. "You look like you have a lot on your mind."

"Oh, no. I'm okay. I'm just thinking about how this all feels too good to be true," I admit. "I mean, this is basically everything I've ever wanted, and I can't help but feel like I'm waiting for the other shoe to drop."

"I get it," Will says reassuringly. "But, Han, we've fought like hell for this, and we deserve to be happy. Everything was broken for so long between us, and it's hard to accept that everything's suddenly all okay again. But I've thought about it, and I think this is why we break. We needed time apart to realize exactly what we meant to each other so we never take what we have for granted. But I spent the last seven years missing you, and I don't plan to ever spend another day without you by my side."

I take in his words, feeling some of the tightness in my chest immediately lift. "God, I love you."

"I love you too, Han," he says, squeezing my hand before adding. "Now, let's get home because we still have seven years to make up for, and I don't think I'm ever gonna have enough of you. Not to mention, we have the neediest little cow and piggy that are gonna want some cuddles when I'm done fucking you."

I smile at that, before whispering, "You know, I can't think of a better way to end the night."

EPILOGUE

HANNAH

SEVEN MONTHS LATER

"Han, you've gotta keep your eyes closed. I swear if I find out you're peeking…" Will growls, grabbing my arm and helping me out of the car before leading me in the direction of wherever this surprise is.

"I swear I'm not," I promise, running a hand down my blue and white sundress and letting him steer me wherever he wants. "God, it's hot as hell."

"Well, babe. It's the middle of July in South Alabama, I'm not sure what you were expecting," Will teases, and I stick out my tongue at him, despite the fact that I know he probably can't see it from his position behind me.

"Yeah, you're right, but still. So are you gonna tell me where the heck we're going?" I ask, not really caring what the answer is but knowing the question will get him riled up.

"I swear to God, woman. Have you never heard of the word

surprise?" he asks, and I can't help the laugh that spills out of me at the exasperation in his voice.

"Oh, real funny, Han," he adds, and I can practically feel him rolling his eyes, even with the blindfold he put on me to cover my eyes. "Come on. We're almost there."

I continue walking wherever he's leading me. I have no idea where the heck we are, and I'm both excited and anxious to find out what he has planned.

The last several months with Will have been incredible. A few weeks after the state championship he moved in with me, and every day I fall a little more in love with him. As an added bonus, he's also taken on some of the farm chores, and I've finally stopped feeling like I'm waiting for the rug to be pulled out from under me.

It's still hard work keeping everything afloat, but I spend a lot less time panicking and a lot more time getting lost in my own world with Will.

"Okay, we're here. Give me just a second and let me make sure everything's set up," he calls out, moving away and leaving me standing alone.

I wait for a few moments and hear the sound of Will struggling with something. "Wait, what's going on? Are you okay?" I ask, reaching up to pull off my blindfold.

"Damn it, Leroy, this is not what we practiced," Will groans, and I look up to see the creek where we spent so many hours that summer, hiding out and making promises to each other. But this time, the bank is full of freshly cut wildflowers, some of them looking a little crumpled. Across from me, Ruby and Leroy are standing on the bank where Will's trying to hold them back. They wiggle in his arms, clearly wanting to run in my direction, and not appreciating the way Will's gently restraining them.

"Babe, I know you're strong and all, but I don't think you're a match for the two of them," I point out with a laugh. And it's true. Leroy's always been pretty impossible to restrain, and now that Ruby's about half grown, she's also a force to be reckoned with.

"Fine. Go on then," he says, throwing his arms up in defeat as both of my animals scamper my way. "Hey, babies," I coo, leaning down and patting them both.

After giving them some attention, I stand, gesturing to the flowers and the farm animals around us. "I feel like I'm missing something. What's going on?"

"This is not how this was supposed to go," he growls, running a hand over his face in frustration. "The flowers were no match for the wind and these feral farm animals, and Leroy was supposed to let me attach this little collar on him so he could bring you this note."

I raise my eyebrows in surprise, holding out my hand to take the paper from him. Unfolding it, I smile at the sight of Will's handwriting before starting to read.

Hannah,

The last few months with you have been some of the happiest of my life. I don't know what I did to deserve another shot at a life with you, but I'll never take it for granted.

You always know how to make even the worst days feel magical, and I've never met someone who works or loves as hard as you do. I can't promise you a perfect life, but I can promise you will never find anyone else who loves you as much as I do.

I've already told you there's no getting rid of me this time, but I decided it's time to make it official. Will you spend the rest of your life with me?

Will you marry me?

I freeze as I realize what he's asking, before looking up and seeing him down on one knee. "Will, what?" I murmur, trying to catch up. "You want to marry me?"

"Of course I do, Hannah," he confirms, and I feel a tear run down my face. "I told you a long time ago that all I wanted was a life with you, and I meant it."

I smile at that, taking in the sight before Will clears his throat. "So, uh, do you need to think about it, or…"

"Oh my gosh, of course I will!" I say, "I didn't mean to leave you hanging. I just can't believe this is actually happening."

He smiles, holding out a ring box before he opens it. I feel a fresh wave of tears at the sight of my Mimi's ring nestled against the velvet of the box.

"How in the world did you get that?" I sob, rubbing my eyes and trying to convince myself that I'm not imagining this moment.

"Your gramps gave it to me when I told him I wanted to ask you to marry me. He said it was about time we both pulled our heads out of our asses and made it official," he says, and we both laugh at that.

"Yeah, I guess he's right," I say, laughing as he slips the beautiful vintage square cut diamond onto my finger. Standing to kiss me, I sink into him for a moment before pulling back and furrowing my brow. "Wait, so where the heck did you ride me around for the last twenty minutes if we never left the property?"

"Up and down the driveway," he replies sheepishly. I was trying to give our friends time to set this up and get Leroy and Ruby in position, but you can see how well that went."

"Wait, then where the heck are they?" I ask, expecting Margaret and Caroline to pop up from behind a tree any minute.

"They had plans," he answers dismissively, and I look at him in confusion.

"My two best friends were just up here setting up for my proposal, and they didn't stay because they had plans?" I repeat skeptically, and Will nods.

"But anyway, I'm sorry the flowers were a bit of a mess, but they originally spelled out 'Will you marry me?' Caroline and Hannah spent all day collecting what they could find from the field over there, so if they ask, don't tell them that Leroy ruined it," Will begs, and I laugh.

"We'll keep it our little secret," I agree, starting to walk back toward the clearing to head home before Will grabs my hand.

"Wait, before you go I have another surprise," he murmurs, and I feel my eyes widen at that.

"What on earth?" I ask, as he reaches down into his pocket and pulls out a long black box. I take it from him, and my mouth drops open in shock. Inside the box is the ruby necklace he gave me years ago, and I blink back a fresh wave of tears.

"Oh my God, Will. I can't believe you still have this," I cry, lifting the jewel out and smiling as it sparkles in the sunlight.

"Yeah, after you left I told myself I needed to throw it away or get rid of it. But I couldn't do it. I found a little jewelry bag in my sister's stuff when I got home and I tucked it in my truck. I told myself if I kept it, you'd find a way back to me. And it looks like I was right."

I don't know what to say, so instead I just pull his mouth to mine, kissing him hard before whispering, "You know I really do love you, Will Thompson."

"And I really do love you, Hannah Scott," he replies, fastening the necklace around my neck before grabbing my hand and pulling me to the truck. "Now come on, I want to show you something."

"I think I'm surprised out," I tease, sitting in the truck while he loads up Leroy and Ruby.

After he has them safely in the little trailer Caroline and Margaret left up here for us, he slides into the driver's seat and heads in the direction of the house.

"So I was thinking about asking Dr. Ava if she thinks—" I start, before noticing the driveway full of cars. "Wait, what the heck are all these people doing here?"

Will just smiles, continuing down the drive until I see a huge white tent full of all our friends and people from around town. He barely has time to stop the truck, before Caroline and Margaret are running in our direction, tearing open the passenger side door and pulling me into a hug.

"Oh my God! You're engaged!" they scream, and I hold out my left hand to let them see the ring.

"It's so gorgeous. Caroline told me it belonged to your MiMi, and I think that's so special. Did you cry when he asked you?" Margaret babbles excitedly, pulling my hand closer to her face to get a better view.

I smile at her excitement before nodding. "There may have been a few tears. It is really special. But what the heck is everyone doing here?"

"Come on, Han. You know we couldn't have an engagement in Springside without an engagement party," Caroline says with a laugh. "Your grandfather was talking about it with Gladis at the nursing home earlier this week, and obviously it hit the STS within an hour. Thank God you don't usually look at that stuff."

I let out a laugh, shaking my head. "This damn town," I say with a laugh. "I can't believe y'all pulled all of this off so quick."

"We had a little help," Caroline smirks, pointing over to where Miss Ethel, Brian, and Millie—Brian's fiancée and the infamous new event planner from Deer Valley—are overseeing the DJ set up. Across the tent, Huey, Seth, Theo, and Kent attempt to set up a row of lawn games. And nearby, Gramps and Gladis direct a group of caterers, carrying trays of food. I blink in surprise when I realize it's the owners of Maracas.

"I'll say. Wait, how on earth did you get Maracas to do the food? They don't offer catering!"

"No, not usually. But they agreed to offer margarita flights and taco platters for us since we're some of their most loyal customers," Caroline answers, and we all laugh.

"You all really thought of everything. I just can't believe this. Pretty sure the entire population of Springside is here," I admit as Gramps sees me and makes his way over as fast as his walker will allow.

"Gramps, I love the ring," I say, hugging him hard as soon as he's close enough. "But are you sure you want me to have it?"

"I'm certain, Hannah Banana. The kind of love that your MiMi and I had doesn't come around that often, but I have no doubt that it's the same kind of love that you and Will share. Just promise me you won't ever give up on each other," he murmurs.

"I promise," I say, continuing to hug him as Will walks over.

"Are you ready to start a new life together?" he asks, taking my hand and leading me into the tent.

"Let's do it," I tell him, kissing him quickly before muttering, "you know, sometimes it still doesn't feel real that we could be this happy. I mean some days I feel like I'm waiting for things to go back to the way they were."

"I know what you mean, but that's never happening, Han. And I can't wait to spend the rest of my life proving it to you," he says, dropping his mouth to mine.

As I look around the tent filled with our friends, I can't help but wish I could go back and hug the girl that fell in love with Will eight summers ago. I've thought about her a lot over the last few months, and I wouldn't change our story for anything. But I do wish I could tell her we were wrong. The people who really love us don't always leave, and there really are brighter days ahead.

ACKNOWLEDGMENTS

Wow! What a journey this book has been! These characters challenged me, pushed me, and made me cry more than I'd like to admit. There were so many times I didn't know if this story would ever make it out of my head, but I'm so incredibly excited that it's currently in your hands. Hannah and Will were tough to write, but they'll always have an extra special place in my heart.

I've talked about this before, but 2024 was a really hard year. Between work, my health issues, and other things going on in my personal life, there were so many times writing was put on hold. But like they always do, my incredible support system encouraged me and pushed me make this became a reality, and I'm so grateful!

First of all, none of this would be possible without the love and support of my incredible husband. C, I love you more than anything. You always push me to go after the things I want, and I fall a little more in love with you every day. Thank you for keeping everything running while I hide away in the writing cave and never being frustrated when I zone out thinking about my fictional characters. Forever and always, babe.

Mom and Dad, thank you for always being my biggest cheer-leaders. Your encouragement and advice is invaluable to me, and I'm so grateful that you've always pushed me to forge my own path. Nonnie and Dah, you two believed in me before I believed in myself. I'm pretty sure you've promoted my books more than I have at this point. You're so incredibly special to me, and I feel so lucky to know I have such unconditional love and support. I love the four of you so much, and there's no way any of this would have been possible without you.

Brittni, I still don't know what I'd do without you! I'm so grateful for your ability to work through my chaos. Thank you for always reading my mind and helping my words be the best they can be.

Erica and Caroline, y'all are the best! Thank you for always making sense of my silly grammar mistakes and answering my comma questions. I adore working with both of you!

Ali, you never fail to make all my cover dreams come true, and I can't thank you enough. I adore working with you!

Cassie, I truly don't know how I published a book without you! Knowing you're handling all the graphics and PR stuff has been the biggest blessing! Thank you for letting me focus on writing and being the best hype woman!

To my betas— Emma, Hunter, Rose, Brianna, Lillian, Katie, Morgan, Emily— thank you so much for your incredible feedback and your unhinged reactions. I looked forward to opening the doc each time I saw a new comment, and I can't thank you enough for loving my characters the same way I do.

To Alexis, Ambar, Jenn, and Erin, thank you so much for always encouraging me to keep writing and answering all my author questions.

Tabitha, thank you so much for your help with the medical terminology. I adore you!

Rae, thank you so much for helping me behind the scenes! Your advice and organization was so helpful and I'm so grateful!

To my ARC readers and the rest of the Bookstagram community, thank you so much for continuing to share about these books. Every DM, tag, comment, and share means so much to indie authors like me, and I'll never be able to say thank you enough.

And finally, dear reader, thank you so much for taking a chance to read Hannah and Will's story! None of this is possible without you, and I can't thank you enough for your support.

A NOTE ON THE MEDICAL SCENES

As someone who has personally struggled with Endometriosis and PCOS, it was incredibly important to approach these topics with the care they deserve. The scene where Hannah is diagnosed is nearly identical to the way I received my diagnosis, but it was also important to me to consult several nurses and people who have been diagnosed with PCOS.

I realize that the way Hannah and I were treated is not representative of the millions of incredible health care professionals out there, but unfortunately it is still my story.

It is also important to note that other doctors would have probably handled the situation differently, like waiting until the ultrasound was over to discuss the results and helping Hannah better understand her diagnosis. This is ultimately a work of fiction and is not meant to represent the way every health care professional would have responded.

According to the World Health Organization, PCOS affects between six and twelve million women, and endometriosis affects over six million women both in the United States alone. They are often debilitating conditions, and they are incredibly under-researched and misunderstood, even by many in the medical community.

If you are one of those people, I hope you know that your worth isn't determined by the state of your ovaries or your ability to have children. You are seen, you are heard, and there are always brighter days ahead.

FULL LIST OF CONTENT WARNINGS

Explicit Language
Explicit Sexual Content
Infertility
PCOS and Endometriosis
Diagnosis by an insensitive medical professional
Parental Abandonment
Parental Custody Battle
Livestock death (natural causes)

BE THE FIRST TO KNOW

Want to stay up to date on all the things? Join my newsletter, sign up for alerts on upcoming signings, and follow my reader group here!

ABOUT THE AUTHOR

Hollie Luckie is a small town girl that wholeheartedly believes in happily ever afters. Between teaching English and writing romance, she is always getting lost in a fictional world. She resides in south Alabama with her high school sweetheart, her dog Memphis, and her own farm of quirky farm animals. You can find Hollie on Instagram at @authorhollieluckie or on Goodreads.

ALSO BY HOLLIE LUCKIE